The Collector of Tales

By
David Payne

www.dwarftales.co.uk

Independently Published in Great Britain by Oakleigh & Garden 2016. Oakleigh & Garden is a trading style of Mortgagecomply.com Limited.

ISBN 978-1792864698

For my friend Jane, of course.

Forty years and nine children is not enough.

Exordium

How did I first come to know of the Fire Dancers? Sadly, it wasn't through the maternal whisperings or the fireside tales that I would like to have laid claim to. Nor, for the avoidance of doubt, was it something so detached or so clinical as to be read from some obscure book.

I met a man on a road as I was heading for home one day and we talked to pass the time. He was traveling south as I recall: a scholar from one of the cities down that way. I was returning home from one of my sorties into the western lands. I had a little more coin than I had started out with some months before: enough to get the family through the next winter before I too headed off to the south.

I was cautious of bandits and so understandably was a little apprehensive when first he called out to me from the shade of an old tree by the side of the road. It hadn't helped that he was hidden as I approached and my heart leapt a little when this other human voice called out in what I had taken for solitude.

I must have looked a little fearful as I turned to the sound because he laughed and repeated his greeting. I don't recall his name as I am hopeless at remembering these things. Up close (for at a distance everyone looks the same blur to me) I could see that he had very blue eyes that sparkled with mischief and I guess he was in his late twenties. I only had my staff for walking and a small knife which I used for eating with. It could hardly be called a weapon unless I wanted to gut a small fish. He was younger, larger and fitter. For all I knew he was hiding all sorts of exotic items about his person. I couldn't run and so I saw no other choice: with all the voices in my head shouting caution, I walked towards him and returned the greeting.

It was hot and the sun was high in the sky. He told me that he was resting for a while as was the custom in his country and that he would not take the road again until later in the afternoon. He wondered at me risking the heat and the sun (and I heard the unspoken words that whispered afterwards, "at your age"). I was a little annoyed, I and my fifty-two years of treading this sweet earth.

"My boy," I replied with as much authority as I could muster. I then proceeded to tell him that in these lands, I thought it better to keep walking until I found somewhere safe to rest. He smiled and cut a piece of cured meat with a knife that he retrieved from a sheath on his back. The knife was long and sharp looking with a slight curve to it. I could understand his argument quite clearly but it was testament to his lack of maturity that he would use a fine weapon for such a purpose. Of course, it was for show and he continued with an elaborate gesture in cleaning and re-sheathing the blade. Although he had made his point, it hardly seemed worth the effort.

I don't actively seek out the company of others but I do not avoid it when it presents itself to me. So it was on this occasion and we shared a light meal and some company under that tree. I had some cheese and a little bread. I offered some wine and produced two battered leather tumblers from my pack. He took the wine in the southern style with seven parts water which he poured from a large skin that lay on the ground beside him. I did the same with my own though it did seem a bit of a crime. The red was particularly good but I guess that it was still early in the day and I had a fair way to walk before nightfall.

As we talked over our impromptu meal, he opened out a tale of his travels and of his journey to a northern town known as Trellsheim. He didn't expand on the reason for his journey but he told me a fair bit about the place and whilst the sun hung above us in an azure sky he seemed happy to talk endlessly.

I listened to the words as they washed over me, nodding now and then and responding at various points. I try not to interrupt a tale when it is in progress but often my own innate desire to talk makes this a bit of a challenge. All in all, I managed to keep relatively quiet.

After some while he stopped and then began to ask me a series of questions. What I was doing here on the road? Where I had been? Where I was going? It being my turn, so to speak, I also unrolled a tale of my travels and mentioned a little of my purpose.

"Ah," he said at one point, "so you are a bard and a story teller?"

"No," I replied, "I am a Collector of Tales."

A pause slipped gently between us with the indelicacy of a child and then a moment later, as the flies buzzed and darted around the cured meat beside him, he spoke once more.

"They are not the same?"

"No, they are not the same."

This had more or less killed that part of the conversation and we moved on to other matters. We talked of the weather past and to come; of the nearest towns and villages; of boots and blisters and the nature of burdens: all those many things that travellers might discuss when they have been alone for a long while. In this manner the afternoon passed by and at last he started to prepare himself for moving on. He invited me to walk with him and, having decided that there had been plenty of time to slit my throat had he so wished, I agreed. Two men walking together in an empty landscape are more of a threat and less of a target than one. Particularly if one of them is getting on in years.

He set a cracking pace and so we walked for a while in silence, partly because I struggled to keep up with him and, I guess, because we had said enough for now. Then as we came to the top of a gradual incline, he turned and asked me more about my 'work' as he called it.

Yes, I suppose it might be called work or perhaps even a vocation but to me it is just what I do. I am a hunter of sorts. I seek out tales or stories or legends, call them what you will. In the older days, yes, I might have been called a bard but to those who have met me, I am simply The Collector of Tales.

I told him how I had traveled far to the south where the sun scorches the sky and where the great desert stretches out into the lights of oblivion. I shared with him my crossing of the great sea to the east where I had seen the nations of people who are not people. As I was speaking, I could see him looking at me now and then and I could tell that he didn't believe all that I was saying. To be honest I don't blame him but there was a general truth to it.

I wanted to tell him how, in all these lands, I had captured tales both in the language of their tellers and in my own. That I now had stored these in my mind: all of them ready for the telling; ready for the passing on. It wasn't always easy and I confessed a level of pride in my work that may more than occasionally have bordered on arrogance.

You see, it isn't just the remembering and recall of the words, in languages that may often be strange to the tongue and to the palate or uncouth to the ear. It isn't the learning of the sounds or seeking out the translation of words and ideas and understanding of cultures that may be unusual or indeed, in some cases, offensive to my own background and beliefs. It is the thrill of the collection and the fact of the collection and I guess that is what does it most for me. The finding, the acquiring, the understanding, the cataloging and the taking away with me: those are the things that do it. Yes of course it would be nice to think that there was some higher purpose in all this but if there is, it is an unconscious one and I will unwittingly deliver it for I am a simple man: a hunter and collector. No more or less.

Yet that is not what I said. Instead I rattled on about nothing as the miles passed beneath our dusty feet. He listened and when I had finished he thought for a while and then with a little hesitation, offered me a tale that he had heard. He apologized in advance for the quality of the telling but in the event he spoke well and clearly.

He told me of a group of people who traveled the lands. They were a secretive and cautious folk, often avoiding the towns and other centres of habitation unless need drove them. He referred to them as the unhoused and they were regarded with suspicion by many; held in contempt by others. The authorities in many lands saw them as vagabonds and thieves. To some they were also called the Illuvaqu'e, the Fire Dancers. They were from a culture older than most, steeped in traditions held close and secret over the countless years. For some considerable while he spoke of them, talking at times in an animated manner and at other times in hushed tones that gave me to believe that he held them in awe or respect, perhaps even in fear. He told me of their rituals. How they walked into fires and how they communed with the dead. I looked at him in much the same way that he had looked at me earlier: I didn't believe him.

Though it was brief, the tale that he told on that day struck a note in me and I decided that the subject would warrant investigation when I had the next opportunity.

That was to come a few months later.

PART ONE
THE INFERNAL VILLAGE

I
A Tale of Two Choices

On a cold winter's day beyond the middle years of my life, I find myself in a darkening wood on a road that now divides before me. One way is broad and well-trodden with the wheel marks and grooves of vehicles showing that it is the main roadway. The other is darker and less inviting: narrow and straight and disappearing off into the growing gloom in a line as straight as an arrow. Frozen along the path from this bifurcation, snow-covered dung marks this lesser path like a secret message.

At this time of day there is little choice. I'm too old to be thinking about sleeping outside in this weather. I'll do it at need but it is not something that I would choose. Besides, it is that time when the world starts to take on a dark and sinister feeling about it. A time when you know deep down that you want to get home, wherever home is. A moment when you know that you need to be safe again, whatever safe is.

That is why I choose now to walk what will probably be three miles or so along a rutted and frozen road covered in snow. It will lead eventually to a settlement that I have never seen before and which could, in all possibility, be a nest of thieves, bandits and assassins. The alternative is to walk a short way along a narrow path until I find a suitable spot to build a makeshift shelter and light a fire for warmth. Here to sleep until morning wakes me or death collects me. So I ask myself one more time: am I seeking safety or is it the comfort of humanity?

The road fulfilled its promise and was every bit as difficult to travel as I anticipated. I struggled for what turned out to be about five miles to the next village. My reward at the end of a slippery trudge to the top of a low ridge was the sight of a small number of grey houses before me. They were fading now into the gloom of the low-lying land below and partially smothered lights shone dully. Curling wisps of smoke rose heavily and reluctantly from unseen home fires, up through the murky blanket of mist that was hugging close to the ground, before they twisted away in the clear moon-lit sky that sat above it all.

At the edge of the village was a small inn and stable yard. A weary and faded sign swung from the main building and a few painfully drawn letters were scrawled on the wall below it. I think it said 'hostel' but it could have read 'brothel' from the poor spelling and from what I knew of the dialect of the area, it could equally have sounded as 'stable'.

I kicked what snow and frozen mud and any other filth that I could from my boots on the lowest of the steps leading up to the main entrance. The door was low and solid looking, studded with brass and with a small view port which was now firmly shut. Though made of wood, the door felt as solid and cold as iron and when I turned the large boss of a door handle, I could feel the ice mashing inside the latch.

Three things came out as the door opened. First there was the noise of many voices within. Then came the warmth (although perhaps it was the relative warmth compared to the cold night air outside). Then came the smell which was nothing if not pungent. It was a heady mixture of wood smoke and tobacco, vinegar and over roasted meat, farmyard and the overwhelming smell of dog – if you know what I mean. It all but took my breath away and pretty nearly removed the contents of my stomach as well. Still, nothing else to be done about it. I wasn't enthusiastic, I admit, but at least I wasn't as committed as the pig that was roasting in the large hearth opposite.

I stepped into the reek.

Although I understood the language quite well, the dialect was a bit of a challenge and I have to say that a lot of the noise that I heard was pretty unintelligible at first. Fighting off the desire to walk back out into the snow and find that remote camp fire up in the woods regardless of wolves, bears or bandits I made my way as carefully as I could through the crowd.

I headed towards the bar where a fierce looking creature in possession of a face that would curdle blood was engaged in a brutal dialogue with what looked to be a couple of badly stained, if animated, blankets. I presumed that this creature was female. Even to my feeble vision she appeared to be wearing a shawl and some kind of strange bonnet. She had to be the proprietor or, at the very least, the proprietor's wife but she looked like Grendel's mother.

Squeezing my way through the steaming and noisome crowd I could not help but notice that I was being studied. In particular, one individual was watching me with serious intent from his seat at one of the tables to my right.

Whether it was a random act or whether it was at a signal or maybe because I had crossed some unseen line, something in a large trench coat lurched to its feet knocking a filthy looking tankard of slops that was before it on the table. A good quantity of the dirty tan coloured brew splashed onto the tabletop and slipped sinuously over the side.

"Ere, can'tcha watch'at wot'ya doin' ya gert tusspot," shouted a toothless old guy sitting on the other side of the sticky and shiny table.

The speech that spilled from his collapsed mouth degenerated further as he looked down to brush away the greenish brown liquid that pooled briefly in his lap before soaking in.

8

"Nar lookat wot'ya dun te'ma kegs ya leetl basdad!"

I had no time to hear more of the exchange as I was brought to a halt by a large hand that was placed on my shoulder. It belonged to the individual in the huge trench coat which was badly stained with something brown that I didn't want to guess at.

He was a big man and in the few seconds afforded me for assessment I determined number of things. I didn't like him. He was filthy. There was movement amongst the thick black beard that covered much of his face. He also had absolutely no sense of personal space as he leaned right into my field of vision.

"You's a leetl su'thun basdad in'tcha!"

The words proceeded from his mouth with the same incontinence as the beer and spit also issuing from that orifice. His eyes, which were brown and cow like, had an obvious vacancy that wasn't necessarily associated with his intellect. Of course, I had to respond. Failure to do so would invariably result in the repeating stubby finger jab to the shoulder followed by a series of accusations dotted with expletives. The fact that he was a lot bigger than me may also have influenced my desire to co-operate.

"Aye mayt, ye've been down tha'ways a waheel."

I hoped that he understood my slightly purer form of the language and to reinforce it I added.

"Yes'm! ye'ma jevellin' abaht a'bit."

I have to say that I was quite pleased with myself and thought for a few seconds that this response would do the job. The hand came back off from my shoulder and, as I took a step back to remove myself from the serious halitosis that was making me feel nauseous, its owner did not move with me.

Then I looked into his eyes. There was absolutely no sign that he had understood or indeed even heard me. The same brown-eyed vacancy looked out from them towards me (I do not say that he was actually looking at me). I noticed how big his pupils were: far too large to accommodate the dim-lit smokiness of this place. I noticed also that his teeth were stained red and that the saliva in his beard was also reddish or at least might have passed off for red in better light. I thought perhaps it might be betel although I didn't think that it was grown this far to the north.

"Ah say'd," he slurred as he drew himself up to his full height.

He was alarmingly bigger even than I first thought and in my head I could hear a strange little voice making frightened, strangled noises.

"You's a leetl su'thun basdad in'tcha, ya horsun!"

Even with the additional distance now between us, I felt his spit hitting my face. It stung like a mild acid. I wondered what it was he was drinking, or perhaps chewing, that would do that. Then I considered whether it might have been something about his metabolism. It also didn't escape a thought that I hoped he hadn't got any infectious diseases.

I decided to go for the obvious.

"Yer raht, ye'ma."

A look of smug satisfaction split out across his hairy features.

"Faw shor mayt, ah nowse it," the giant said grinning at me, "ish*'ta smell, yu'see."*

He paused for an effect that was lost on me and then continued beaming with an obvious sense of pride. That was also lost on me.

"Yu is smell good!"

He tapped the ugly protuberance that seemed to have been squashed hurriedly into his features as an afterthought at some time between his conception and his birth. Once again, there was that sense of pride radiating from him. Once again I remained oblivious to the cause.

"Ish'ta nose, yu'see."

He paused just long enough to thump his barrel of a chest with his huge right hand.

"Ye'ma tracka!" he said.

More radiated pride glowed from him, seeming to add further to the oppressive partial warmth of the room.

He offered me what I took in context to be a smile, although had I been female I might have been more concerned. I noticed also that far from being merely a figure of speech, the left hand was in fact quite a bit smaller than the right. Nature or nurture, I wondered. Perhaps it was a standard configuration around these parts.

"Yu lookin' tracka?"

My heart sank. Here was another question and it also had a hint of menace in it. I went for the obvious again.

"No mon."

I refrained from adding 'sorry' as I knew that it would antagonize him and that the usual forms of politeness were culturally unacceptable in these parts. He looked at me and I would have said that it was an appraising look had I not doubted the level of processing going on inside his head. After a pause and without another word, he simply sighed and turned back to the group of people that he had risen from. The last thing that I heard from him was a plaintive exhalation.

"Nebin wantin' no tracka!"

Although his tone sounded quite sad, I suspect that he didn't give me another thought. Once he was seated amongst the other worthies, he took a noisy gulp from the huge and filthy leather tankard on the table in front of him. I noticed then that there was only one drink on the table and, as I watched for a few morbidly curious moments, it became apparent that this was being shared by all those sitting around it with him. That would explain the size, I guess, for it looked more like a quart than a pint.

I watched for just enough time to see the tracker launch into what I could only take to be an obscure variation on animated conversation with his fellow tankard sharers. After a while, the sight of a number of dirty looking men sharing an even dirtier looking tankard began to take its toll on my sense of propriety, not to mention my stomach. I moved away leaving them to it and trying, unsuccessfully as it happens, not to think too much about the nature or quality of the various liquids that had been sprayed over me a matter of moments ago.

I made it the last few steps to the bar and to the creature that I took to be in authority. It is a simple observation that whilst I was watched with hawk-like intensity by this woman from the time that I opened the door to the moment when I stepped within a few feet of the bar, I became invisible as soon as I actually got there. I was a part of the scenery as it were.

I looked meaningfully in her direction but she had started to swill a tankard in some brownish liquid from a basin behind the bar. She appeared totally engrossed in that task as well as in an animated conversation taking place on the far side of the room. With all the noise around, I was pretty sure that she couldn't possibly hear anything of what was being said.

I tried coughing and clearing my throat but even I knew that was pointless in the din and besides it prompted a series of hackings and spitting from a couple of men at the bar that made me sound like a girl. I waved: not a thing. I called out moderately loudly but in that room it was lost. I decided again on the obvious.

"Drank, ja'bas!" I yelled at the top of my voice.

A ripple of silence spread out through the room from where I was standing, passed out through the walls and was gone. It had worked though, for Grendel's Mother stirred from her labours and looked over at me. Actually, it was more like she looked through me. It was quite disturbing.

12

Again, there were those bovine eyes and again, the vacant look and the red saliva and, even more disconcerting, again the thick black beard.

"D'ya want?" she growled.

"D'ya got?" I barked.

"Horshp's!" she hissed.

"Ya'll 'ave it then," I grunted.

So far so good, I thought.

Then it was that I made the mistake. All those fifty-two years of good upbringing could not be held back. Much as I had tried, I simply could not help it and out it came uninvited from my hapless mouth.

"Thank'ee," I whinnied.

It had not been said loud. In fact, I had almost swallowed the words as they came out and yet the silence in the room was immediate and utter. I could hear my heart thumping. God's ear, I could hear a dozen hearts thumping! All eyes were on me. I could feel the hostility. Something quick was needed.

"Ye'll thank'ee t' gi'me sum o' that peg rosten 'er!" I said as loud as I dared, pointing with apparent enthusiasm (I hoped) to the pig roasting, for want of a better word, in the acrid smoke and sweaty warmth of the fire.

"Gi'me sum peg! Y'ah!"

I thumped my chest for emphasis with my clenched right hand.

"Ye'ma hangregish!"

I scarcely dared to look around in the unnerving silence that had enveloped the room so I kept my eyes on Grendel's Mother.

Her mouth twisted slightly and worked its way into what I think was a grin although it could have been pity. It could also possibly have been lust. Hopefully I would never know.

"Ye'll cut ye sum peg, lurv," she replied, softening ever so slightly.

I was relieved. It looked like I had pulled it off: one serious cultural faux pas into what was frankly an acceptably rude demand for food. I ignored the all too obvious mutterings of, "fawkin' far'ners," and a range of other similar obscenities and expletives from the others in the room as the volume went back up to full.

I then watched with detached interest as Grendel's Mother poured a rich, slightly greenish looking liquid from a large tin jug under the counter into the battered tankard that she had hitherto been immolating in the basin. The liquid had a thin, oily look about it as it was poured out and small, lumpy white things floated and bobbed about on the surface once it was placed on the bar before her. She gave it a vigorous stir with a stick that seemed to be lying about for the purpose and then passed the drink to me.

The detached interest gave way to mild concern as I watched the oily liquid whirl around in the tankard that was now sitting on the bar in front of me. There were far too many bubbles forming on the surface to be accounted for by the mild agitation of the stick. Something was clearly metabolizing in my drink. I noticed also that the lumpy white things had ceased to bob about. In fact, they seemed to have disappeared or should I perhaps have said 'dived' beneath the oily surface.

"Horshp's," she hissed once more at me.

There was neither pride nor threat in her voice. It was a take it or leave it kind of statement and from the look of the drink that was described, I was pretty sure now that I was going to leave it.

"Ye'll 'af a tab ye'll pay fer it now," she continued.

Then with a hard glint in her eye she threw the challenge at me.

"Fee trupps!"

To be honest, I had no idea what horshp's was but I presumed that it was now before me in all its greenness, floating a slightly thin and oily froth on a surface that looked vaguely off white. However, fee trupps demanded a response. This was a land of hagglers and I was expected to do the business.

As it was, I couldn't tell from the dialect whether she had said fee (five) or thee (three) and I was not going to pay five trupps for a drink I was basically afraid off.

"F-Fee trupps," I stammered, "nay, nay! Ye'm nev'a fawkin' far'ner here!"

That at least drew some interest from those nearby. For a start, it obviously wasn't true.

"Tu trupps and ne mur fur dese greyn puss!"

"Ya horsun far'ner is'ta shyte," she countered and followed it up with an emphatic hawk and spit, the like of which landed in all its redness at the base of my tankard just where it met the bar.

"Fur trupps – less halp fur coyn."

She added the latter part of this proposal in a slightly menacing tone, making what seemed to be involuntary stabbing gestures at the bar with a nasty looking knife that seemed to have materialized from somewhere within her voluminous skirts.

Three and a half trupps for cash was more than any reasonable man would pay but I threw down the coins in feigned disgust. At least that way I would keep all my remaining teeth, for now. I added for realism an obligatory, "Ja'bas," which, it seemed, she took more or less as a compliment because she flashed me one of her twitching, grimacing smiles.

"Ye'll get ye summat peg," she offered in a tone that inferred closure on the horshp's whilst at the same time opening up bids on the smoke-roasted pork.

"Oh crap," I thought.

More haggling and we haven't even got down to the main issue. Somehow I had to get myself a room in this place to sleep tonight. Best to go for it now I resolved.

There is something that I find fundamentally embarrassing about asking for a room for a night. To start with, I never really know what to say. Usually I'll try something like, 'Have you got any vacancies?' or, 'Do you have any accommodation?' or perhaps, 'Have you got a room?'

No matter how I try, though, it is never quite right. There is always that suggestion of embarrassment and invariably I'll swallow the words or mumble so that I will not be heard properly no matter what language I am speaking. Then I'll have to go through it all again. I guess we all create our own versions of purgatory one way or another.

That was more of less what happened when I tried to get a room sorted here. The only difference was that once we had got down to the issue, we haggled over the price. Well, that and the fact that I claimed that I was the mother of a smoking dog. Don't ask me how. All I know is that I swallowed a couple of syllables in my translation of the word 'overnight accommodation' and out it popped uninvited as it were. I have to say that this linguistic error was to my advantage though. It kind of caught her unawares and I think threw her out of focus on the price. Anyway five trupps was, I thought, a bargain even though there was the obligatory non-refundable deposit for fumigation, which the hairy witch told me was set at another five trupps in these parts.

"Fur dese calymeens," she had explained.

Then she had ducked behind the bar for a few seconds before emerging with a look of triumph and a rather unhappy and pale looking creature about the size of her rather meaty hand and vaguely resembling a trilobite. She dropped the creature onto the bar before her and then crushed it with a cudgel that she had expertly whipped out from under the bar before the poor beast could flee.

"Dese calymeens, hah," she said and then grinned a gap-toothed grin.

Personally, I think that she had kept that one there for the purpose. As the viscous juices of the hapless creature spread over sticky surface of the bar, I paid my ten trupps (and the shreeve tax – another trupp) and the key deposit (another two trupps but refundable if the key is presented on departure). Then with my bag, a huge key and my plate of smoke roasted and slightly warm pork on a dirty birch-bark platter I made my way through the crowded room to the dark narrow opening with the words, 'Slepish!' scrawled on the crumbling plaster above it in the hand of a large but moderately literate spider.

The tankard of horshp's remained on the bar untouched. The dead trilobite watched me through its lifeless calcite eyes.

II
The Lodger's Tale

As I left the main room and made my way carefully down the dimly lit passage I was reminded of just how cold it really was. Away from the animal warmth of the main part of the tavern the temperature dropped quickly. Soon my breath came in short sticky puffs of mist that I walked through as they hung in the gloom around me. I passed a couple of doors but the characters scratched on them did not resemble those on the dirty piece of fabric attached to the key that I held. I carried on and around a corner then up a narrow and unreasonably steep flight of stairs that my knees rebelled against as I struggled up against gravity.

A number or dirty tallow candles had been left burning in the passageway. I use the term burning here because they gave off very little light and substituted this inadequacy with copious amounts of black smoke. Lines of dark stain seemed to run up the walls beside them and it all added to make the darkness feel more pronounced. I passed two more doors but again there were no matching symbols. The third door on this upper passage was however mine and after a slight struggle with the lock, I managed to fumble my way into the room.

I expected it to be dark within but in fact some kindly person had left a small candle stump burning on the mantelpiece above the boarded up fireplace. This looked to be the real thing: beeswax. It is a sad testament to the nature of the world in which I live that I am a bit of a connoisseur when it comes to candles and I appreciated the gesture more than most persons might have thought normal.

In the room there was a bed, a table, some old carpet on the floor and a small window. In the candlelight, everything looked yellowish and dirty. The bed was un-made and the covers were thrown back with what seemed to have been the grim resolution of someone who had slept all night in all their clothes and who knew that it was still going to be colder when they got up. I abandoned the platter of pork to the table and placed my day sack on the floor.

From a pocket in my coat I took two small candles of my own. Nothing fancy, paraffin and white for the most part, a little rounded by wear in my pockets but a sensible amount of neatly trimmed wick. I am, I like to think, always prepared. I lit these with the candle that was already in place. That gave off a bit more light as well as offering a contingency in the event of any sudden drafts. It did not make the room look any better though. Still, it has to be said that despite the dragon-breath that issued from my mouth and which was bedewing my beard with oily droplets, it was still a lot warmer than sleeping out in the snow.

I retrieved the key from the other side of the door where I had left it initially and closed and locked it from the inside. The room might not be much but for tonight it was mine!

I didn't bother to make the bed and resorted to pulling up the covers to hide the bottom sheet. For one thing I wanted to keep the contents of the bed a mystery and for the other, I did not want to find out if the previous occupant had slept in his boots as well. From my bag, I took out my own sheet and a sleeping sack and laid these out. A spare jumper would have to double for a pillow.

On closer inspection, the pork smelled disgusting and was now stone cold so I left it on the table on the basis that hunger on this occasion was better than sickness. Then I tried to look out of the window but it was very small, pretty dirty and all that was visible was the dark wall of another building a few feet away.

So this was the extent of my environment tonight: pretty limited really. There was nothing else to do so it was either back downstairs and the company below or get to bed and wrap up against the cold. For tonight I opted for the latter and removed my boots and threw on a spare pair of socks against the bitter chill that was beginning to numb my extremities.

I passed what was truly an awful night trying to sleep on a mattress that seemed to be stuffed with logs as well as straw. On one occasion I was startled into sleep by a shape that vaguely resembled that of a rat and which seemed to be lying (or possibly sleeping) just below the small of my back. After I had leapt out of bed and beaten the wretched thing to death with my boot, I realised that it was probably nothing more than the shape of compressed straw that has been regularly slept upon by large primates over a frequent number of nights.

Of course, there was also the cold. Whenever I fell asleep I was snatched back into wakefulness the minute my casual movement brought another inrush of icy air into to the open side of my sleeping sack. After a while I began to realise that I was leaching warmth into the straw below me, no doubt to the great glee of any arthropods living therein.

Then there was the noise. I don't mean the noise from the bar below, nor for that matter the subliminal rumble of heavy snoring: my heavy snoring that is. The noise I refer to was the incessant scuttling back and forth in the darkness from a large number of creatures with a large number of stiffly jointed legs. The candles had burned out well before I fell asleep for the first time and no doubt this had given the little blighters the confidence to get up and move about once more. In my semi-conscious state, I kept picturing Grendel's Mother shouting, "These calymeens! Hah!" as she crushed an unfortunate trilobite time and time again on the bar before her.

I could picture a myriad malevolent little calcite eyes all looking up at me from the floor: all of them accusing me. I had never actually heard of anyone being bitten by a trilobite but I guess there's always a first time. From the noise and the obvious number of creatures, it was clear that the room had not been fumigated for some time. Clearly my non-refundable deposit of five trupps was being put to other uses.

I was still mulling this last thought over when I realized that there was light starting to come in through the tiny window. I hadn't heard any bird song but then it occurred to me that it would be a foolish bird to start singing at daylight this far north.

One of the less savory habits of these people was the eating of songbirds. They were roasted whole (and I mean whole, not gutted) with the feathers still on and were eaten with the unusual habit of covering their heads (the eaters that is not the victims) with a white cloth. I had once attended such a meal and it was amongst one of the most unusual ceremonies that I think I have ever participated in.

All the diners sat at table and the birds were plated and brought in under a cloth. Once all the plates were tabled, there was a brief pause as though someone should have said a grace. Then each diner picked the cloth from the plate and placed it over their head so that it draped down over the face. We then bent down towards the meal and got stuck in with fingers and teeth. The feathers had burned off of course but they gave the meat a slightly singed flavour. It was a very greasy affair. I never really got to find out why the white cloth, though. I always assumed that it was something to do with the look of the meal or the grimness of the attack.

Of course this short recollection was nothing more than an attempt to put off the inevitable. Now that it was light and, given the incredibly uncomfortable circumstances of the bed, there was nothing else to do but get up and face the day. It had seemed like an incredibly short night.

Although I could sense rather than see the trilobites lurking in the remaining areas of darkness in the room, there seemed nothing else for it. Pushing the various covers gingerly aside, I slid my legs out from the last vestiges of warmth (a relative term) and swung them around so that my stockinged feet landed heavily on the floor. Involuntarily I froze for a moment, awaiting the sensation of struggling Arthropods biting and snipping at me as they struggled to break free of their entrapment beneath my feet. It didn't happen however and so I stood up and felt the inevitable rush of pain to my knees and back.

I would just have to put up with the various discomforts however. There was no alternative place available to sleep and after an exchange with Grendel's Mother on the first morning, it became quite clear that - at least according to her - I had the best room that they could offer. This was one of those points of clarity and possibly of translation that went entirely wrong as I was to find out after I left the place to head for Trellsheim.

It was my intention to spend the next few days searching for and acquiring the tale of the Fire Dancers. Unfortunately, this meant that I would have to enjoy the services of this place for a few more nights. This was to be without a doubt a curate's egg.

The toilets and washing facilities that were available to me were less than rudimentary and were outside near the stable block. With facilities such as these, I could understand the general lack of hygiene in the population. After a brief attempt to wash and shave on the first morning, I gave up and convinced myself that I would get cleaned up once I left the place and had moved on to a larger and hopefully better hostel towards the end of the week.

Breakfast, on the other hand, was surprisingly good. It was served in the bar about an hour after sunrise. It was a pity that the people seemed to eat few other meats than pork but there were eggs also and some kind of bread that was crunchy on the outside and dry and sour within. The one particular pleasure was a type of blood pudding flavoured with herbs and spices and fried, of course, in pig fat. I had tasted similar fare in other parts of the northern world but I would have to admit, albeit reluctantly, that this was far superior in taste and texture to anything that I had yet met.

I could not establish how many people were actually staying at the inn. There was at least one other man, a short tidy looking creature who looked more out of place than I did. He was treated with a mix of grudging respect and caution by the staff and was avoided by everyone else. I later learned that he was a Shreeve Tax collector. Other than a terse, "morning," at breakfast each day I don't think we said a word to each other. After breakfast he would disappear (I mean figuratively and not literally) and would not reappear as far as I was concerned at least until breakfast on the following day.

The only other person that I saw regularly each morning was a rather large woman who seemed to have been staying in the place for some time. In fact, for all I knew, she may have lived there permanently. She was certainly well known by almost everyone and was greeted respectfully by the serving girl in the morning. Even the hairy tracker that I had the good fortune to meet when I first arrived and who I later named Grendel because I learned that he was indeed the son of the proprietress, showed a kind of respect for her. Well he didn't leer at her quite as much as he did at other women and he tended to keep out of her personal space more than he did for most other persons.

She had a small dog of indeterminate breed that she kept very close to her and seemed to spend a lot of time talking to. It was not much of a creature but it was even for its diminutive size, rather fat.

How a woman managed to stay in a place like this was a bit of a mystery to me. Having said that, exactly how anyone could stay in a place like this was probably fairly remarkable so we can most likely dispense with the woman part of this as being slightly misogynistic. That being said, on the one occasion I frequented the only wash room I did not see her there. Perhaps she rose slightly earlier to protect her modesty.

Still, she seemed to be personable enough. The obligatory, "morning," was offered and accepted at breakfast with some small talk about the weather, the quality of the breakfast or the dog's habits.

Personally I thought the animal was a nasty, snappy looking thing with a mean look. I didn't touch it: usually I take an instant dislike to dogs, especially the small kind and this occasion was no exception. However, I didn't want an enemy for the duration of my stay and so I made suitable noises and comments in its general direction. The only pleasure I could take was the look in the dog's eyes when it saw me. It clearly disliked me with the same enthusiasm that I disliked it.

"If I were bigger, and a bit fitter, I'd have his arm off," it seemed to say.

Other than the occasional wagoner or itinerant trader, I didn't see many other people staying at the inn. I never exactly established which room either the tax collector or this woman were actually staying in as I never saw them anywhere on the dark little corridor that went up to my room.

I didn't see the teacher (for that I learned was her former occupation) in the bar, though after the first night I spent each evening there. I came to be accepted quite quickly. From the second evening I seemed to be taken into the over extended family that was the population of the inn at any given time. When I was greeted with the crude but affable and almost affectionate, "Evenin' Fawkin!" This was a long walk from the, "fawkin' far'ner," mutterings of the first night.

The use of language here was quite interesting. A verb gets used as an adjective as a form of abuse towards a foreigner but then passes with familiarity and use into a noun that labels me affectionately as that very foreigner. Thus, after fifty-two years, I have been converted into an offensive word that describes the sexual act.

The communal area of the tavern was a particularly friendly place. On more than one occasion I was offered a drink and with appropriate reciprocity on more than several occasions I stood a number of large rounds: quite large, actually. However, this was the cost of doing business for this was my hunting ground and my library.

I established early on the second day, after a few carefully worded questions to Grendel's Mother and to a few of the more cogent inhabitants of the village, that my most likely source of material was from an old chap known as Markel the Tal'r.

Dialect and translation caused me some problems here. I managed to make a fool of myself in front of a small group of villagers on one occasion by asking where I could find the tailor. I had confused tal'r with a translation of tailor, rather than storyteller, which of course it was.

"Were yus'll always find 'im a curse. Nabin' were yus'ar," was one slightly quizzical reply that I got. Of course it was followed up with the almost obligatory, *"Ja'bas..."* thrown in for good measure.

The instrument of my discomfiture on this occasion was a wooden sign advertising the tailor's trade. It was nailed up slightly to my left on a relatively tidy looking building and painted clearly, black on white in a better than average spider scrawl that passed for writing in these parts.

"Clathes a' fix'd here, then."

Fighting off the half century of relative politeness and alleged good manners, I refrained from an apology.

"Ya, ya! I knows it a'curse. Y'em neyt a fawkin' far'ner here," I retorted using what was becoming my standard text for defense.

This brief tirade failed to restore my shaky credibility and I chose to make my escape before I came in for more abuse. I left behind me the motley crowd as they muttered and sniggered amongst themselves (yes, more renditions of "fawkin' far'ners") and headed off across the muddy road in search of somewhere to get some provisions for my next journey in a couple of days.

I had been told that there was, *"sum barn a sold stuffa aways durn thar,"* which I loosely translated as, "there was a general store on the main street". I had however forgotten to allow for dialect and that it should have been (obviously), "a barn where they sold stuff down there".

It took several peregrinations of the main street before I realized that there was no general store and that I would either have to broaden my search or at least lower my expectations. It wasn't long after that before I spotted the tatty note scribbled on some woodwork that read,

"Sayles a'bit. Goin' off to y'eat. See yu'se in a wheels."

Great! It was barely past breakfast and they were shut for lunch, brunch or whatever they chose to call the excuse for not being here right now where they could have sold me some provisions. This pre-supposes that they even have the things I want or, indeed that they have any provisions to sell at all. Not to mention whether they actually want to sell anything to a fawkin' far'ner.

As I had nothing else to do right now other than to vent my spleen to the empty air, I decided to hang about 'a wheels,' and wait for whoever it was that 'sold a bit' to come back.

I pulled a sketch pad and a couple of sticks of charcoal out of my day sack and perched on the tiny edge of one of the staddle stones to the barn. It wasn't particularly dry but it was drier than the ground and it gave me the chance to rest the pad on my knees.

The sight of me sitting there sketching drew absolutely no interest whatsoever from the few persons who passed me by. I should have found that a blessing because I really hate it when someone comes up behind me to study my work for a while before pronouncing some crushing comment on it. Something like,

"What's that smudge in the middle there?"

Or, if you are working in colour,

"What's that red patch? I can't see any red. I'll come back later and see what it turns into."

Yes, I hated those kinds of comments. Everyone is a critic. Obviously not here in this village, though. I might not have existed for all the people who went past me. No one even gave so much as a nod in my direction. I should have been grateful but I was not. It was very disquieting and in fact it put me off completely. Strange don't you think?

I gave up my sketching quite quickly and popped the charcoal back into my pocket, leaned back against the cold woodwork of the barn and closed my eyes.

III
The Merchant's Tale

I wasn't aware that I had I nodded off and so it came as a bit of a surprise when I suddenly heard a question being thrown at me out of nowhere. It was however obvious that something was amiss because I only heard the end of the sentence.

"...can ya hear me, ya fawkin' far'ner?"

"I'm sorry," I said automatically as I struggled to re-establish a link with the world, the surface of which I had temporarily slipped beneath.

It was fortunate that I had responded in my own language and so no offence was taken at the apology by the person who had put the question to me.

"Aben so," the voice declared with a triumphant edge to it, *"a fawkin' far'ner, sure."*

There was a large amount of smugness in the speaker's voice. I failed to appreciate why this should be the case. I was in a very small village and, at least to me, it was pretty obvious that I didn't belong here. By the time these thoughts had crystalised in my slow brain I was fully awake and feeling a little put upon. I decided to go on the offensive.

"Yes, yu' wuld 'a thawt a''was a fawkin' far'ner fur sure."

I paused in my stream of sarcasm to make sure that my accuser was keeping up and partly also to give effect to my next string of words which I added with just a hint of malice.,

"What ya sellin?"

This got his attention. It also demonstrated that I had guessed rightly. This was the owner of the barn back from his hunger break.

I watched his eyes carefully as he moved me quickly in his mind from itinerant and useless vagabond to possible meal ticket. His tone did not change though (nor I would have expected it to) but he did move into a different form of rudeness.

"Yu' expectin' to buy summat cheap 'ere, ja'bas?"

"Aye, a curse," I replied, "yu'se 'avin good stuffa 'ere or is it all shyte?"

That got him and now he went on the defensive. To give him all credit, he actually looked a bit offended.

"Ne, ne. E's all gud stuff 'ere wise. 'D ya want?"

"'D ya got?"

"Loads a' stuffa: ropes; pyks; vittals; drank. E's all gud stuffa."

"Wanna kerosene."

"Ne got it."

"'nd dried fesh?"

"Ne' got it naways!"

Oh great. He's got loads of things here but no kerosene and no dried fish. It was a one hundred percent failure so far and so I decided to try a few more obvious things to start off the transaction.

"Salt ne?"

"Aye"

"Reece?"

"Ne."

"Nowdles?"

"Aye, wheat, reece or fanguis?"

"Reece. Fee smorlll bags. Sawce?"

"Aye," he replied again before listing out the various sauces that he had.

I opted for *feshstynkas bru* which is a fermented fish sauce of uncertain ingredients something vaguely like garum from the classical world. This sauce however was thick and granular, not clear and aromatic. It stank so badly that one of its uses was as protection against the murderous swarms of northern midges that appeared in the spring and summer months in these parts. It also doubled as an antiseptic and mouthwash, I believe, although that was not something I would have readily accepted.

We worked our way through my list of requirements until we had either identified the item, found a substitute - he was a good salesman - or dismissed it. During the process he had unlocked the barn and heaved open one of the great oak doors. When we had finished he disappeared into the gloom, closing the door carefully behind him.

"Yu'as waitin' there, ja'bas," he shouted from the invisibility that was the other side of the door, *"I'sl just be a shawt wheel. E's all good stuffa 'ere."*

I had no choice but to wait. How he was going to remember that list and the quantities was beyond me and exactly whether a shawt wheel involved another food break was anyone's guess. I dreaded the re-match that I could see heading my way with the inevitability of an ox cart, once he finally came back put into the daylight with only half the half-remembered things on the agreed list.

In the event it was an unnecessary worry because after a lot of rustling and banging about inside, he finally emerged with all those items that we had agreed on. He brought out with him a rough homespun cloth which he dropped onto the ground between us before depositing the first batch of goods on it. He made several visits back into the barn before the task was completed and my order was assembled. Once he had brought out everything he stepped back with a look of almost sublime satisfaction, holding out his arms as though to signify that it was all there. He then looked at me with an almost predatory eagerness.

"Furty trupps!"

That was when the haggling began.

We agreed on twenty-nine which to my mind was a success as I would have paid thirty-five. As I paid him in the heavy coins of the region, I opted for some small talk and asked him what he knew about Markel the Tal'r.

"Ol Markel eh! Well ah reckon ah knows 'im summat."

He paused for some form of dramatic effect, I assumed, although it is just as possible that he was simply short of breath.

'Es ma bratfer," he said proudly.

His brother. That was a bit of luck and no mistake. I decided to press on.

"Ye'ma lookin' to pick up a tahl or too," I said, before continuing, *"and yema 'eren 'es a good'un."*

"Whe 'es a good'un alright and no mystake. But 'el no tell 'e no ways," he said without a hint of animosity about it.

"Werfor?" I asked.

"Why, yu'sa *fawkin' far'ner 'es werfor,"* was the merchant's rather petulant response.

Well that wasn't really a surprise as it was almost the standard response of any story teller. It wasn't actually that he didn't want to tell an outsider, he just wanted to be sure of the price. This was a universal form of currency amongst the various story tellers and bards as far as I could tell from my travels (and my journeys were extensive). In this particular case, the bartering was being introduced by proxy.

"Aye, aye," I found myself saying with feigned weariness, *"yu'sa alswyse told 'em a curse. Ye'ma fawkin' far'ner sur!"*

I left a brief pause for effect and then continued to press the point.

"'Appen 'e's a dranhk then?"

"Dranhk ne? Dranhk ne? Abben 'es a fesh."

"Oh ah," I said, *"abben 'es a drinkin' a' Champ'nys affen?"*

I should have already explained that Champneys was the name of the inn that I was staying at but in all the excitement since I had arrived, I had more or less forgotten to mention it. I should also point out that this was the name by which it seemed to be known, for there was no name visible on the faded sign that swung pointlessly over the door.

This valuable bit of information had been gleaned earlier in the day by accident in a short conversation with Grendel. It had been an interesting exchange, punctuated by a number of expletives and some almost lyrical descriptions of what he would like to be doing with the serving girl. I assume that this had been inspired at the time by the sight of her washing tankards behind the bar and leaning forward provocatively, offering us the enticing sight of her large but matted woolen tunic.

Well to be more accurate, when I use the term serving girl I am actually referring to a woman in her early middle age with a fairly ample physique. When I refer to a conversation, what I really mean is that we had exchanged a few words, grunts and gestures at breakfast and this name slipped out unannounced. I don't think it was meant to be a secret though.

"Aye 'e's always there, alla's naht."

"Alla's naht eh," I repeated, before adding as an afterthought, *"Abben e'sa in 'un laste naht?"*

"Abben a fesh 'a skals," replied the merchant with an affable grin. It wasn't a question.

If the story teller was in the inn every night, he had probably been there when I had first arrived yesterday. Now I didn't spend very long in the bar so I probably hadn't seen him. I hadn't really noticed anyone other than the hairy witch behind the bar and Grendel along with the toothless old man whose trousers were mired by the communal drinking brew.

zxxHe wasn't likely to be an y of those characters, I was fairly certain and I was also sure that he wouldn't have his name tattooed on his forearm or forehead.

Obviously I needed to know something about him, preferably a bit about what he looked like if I was going to locate him in that crowded place. It seemed that an approach most likely of success was to find him by sight and offer to buy him a drink. Alternatively, I could always walk into the room and yell at the top of my voice, *"Markel the Tal'r, ja'bas!"*

He would be the one who didn't look up.

If the merchant was his brother, then there would no doubt be some similarity so I had something to start with but I thought I had better get further clarification. After all he could be a half-brother and these people, I understood from other northern visits, had an unusual interpretation of the term, family.

"Appen Ol' Markel's your older brother?"

I asked this as carefully as I could, not knowing if I was moving into a sensitive area, but in truth there was no easy way to ask it. At least not for me.

"Aye, a bit," he replied thoughtfully, *"abaht an hour in fact. Abben e's ma tu-bratfer."*

He grinned at me as if it was some kind of joke. I didn't get it.

"Ye was!" he whooped at me.

It was unintelligible and it let it pass me by, the words swishing quietly around in an empty corner of my mind before heading off into oblivion. However, as it happened, it was a bit of good fortune. They were twins. I thought I should stop whilst ahead. Being a twin was close enough: I didn't need to know if he was identical.

"Ah so 'es 'em to-bratfer eh?" I repeated stupidly, offering a bit of my best faux familiar colloquial, *"Ye was. 'Appen yu'sa a Tal'r, mayhap?"*

It was important to keep the familiarity going because I hadn't yet acquired all the information that I needed. I carried on a little further.

"Abben es en'a fumly, so to say?"

"Ne, nebut," he replied, *"Ye'ma saels abit:'em a Tal'r. Ye'ma lurned aways. E'sa dranhk ne'bas."*

He looked quizzically at me and winked.

"Abben 'es a strange ways, ne bas?"

"You're telling me," I thought.

The merchant waved his right arm over the goods in front of us – technically my goods now – and assumed that look of sublime contentment on his face once more

"Aye, 'es gud stuffa 'ere," he offered a small sigh.

This brought me back to my collection of newly acquired possessions which were still spread out on the ground before us on the merchant's square of homespun.

We had just about come around the full circle. It was a good thing because I now had more or less all the information that I was likely to get about Markel. My feet were also beginning to feel a little numb and I now realized that I had started to shiver with the cold. The only thing left for me now was to gather my acquisitions and get back to my room.

Of course I needed a bigger bag than my day sack and of course I couldn't borrow one from the merchant and of course we had to haggle over the price and the quality of the sack that he was prepared to sell me. And of course I felt that I was ripped off as another trupp went into his purse.

To be fair, he packed the bag for me and although I watched him in case anything got forgotten or otherwise overlooked, he was careful and thorough so that not even the spare lace-wick for my lamp got damaged on the walk back. This even after the woven nettle handles of the bag had separated from the bag itself almost the minute I picked it up.

"Ye was, 'en nebbut gud luck ne was," I complained angrily to Markel's twin as I attempted to stuff items back into the carefully packed sack with stiff, irritated little gestures more appropriate to an automaton than to a human being.

"Nebbut gud luck, eh? New as sure as then," he added, *"aber 'es as gud stuffa!"*

As if the quality of my purchases made any difference to my good fortune or rather the lack of it.

I thought that this was the last parting comment from the merchant as he stepped back into his barn and closed the door behind him chuckling to himself but I was wrong. I had turned and was walking back to Champneys when I heard him yell out behind me.

"O ah! Abben 'esa skegs dranhk na!!"

Oh crap. He drinks skegs. That'll cost a few trupps. Not to mention the unusual and sometimes unpredictable side effects of the stuff. I had only planned on a stay of three nights at the maximum and to be honest I didn't think that I could handle any more than that in the dreadful room that I failed to sleep in. If we were going to be drinking skegs then it was pretty much certain that at least one of us would be out cold at least each night and the only true variable was the time it took to get to that position.

I spent the walk back to the inn totting up the cost of a few more nights both in trupps, personal hygiene and state of mind. In the end I decided to play it a bit by ear. After two nights I would pretty much know how long it would take to get the story in full and I was fairly sure that there wouldn't be a lot of demand for the miserable room that I was staying in. The only real problem as far as I could see would be price that Grendel's Mother would charge for those extra nights. I could already see the lustful look in her eye at the thought of another thirteen trupps at least heading their way towards her chubby outstretched hand.

When I finally got to my room, I realized an error in my calculations. In fact, the error was asleep in my bed, snoring and farting alternately. My pack had been pushed recklessly to one corner where somehow (for such a small space) it had managed to fall onto its side and spill out half the contents. Two tins of fish had somehow managed to land near the bed where, it appeared, they had burst open and the contents had mostly made their escape: pepper oil as well.

I didn't really think that this was the work of the trilobites that were peering out at me from the darkness under the groaning bed. To be honest, the biggest clue was the ring pull and attached tin lid that was clearly wedged on the smallest finger of my bed's occupant. I say 'my' bed but of course my lack of understanding was clearly set out before me. About twenty-two stone of it at a guess.

I swore under my breath as I didn't really want to wake the occupant of *the* bed: he was a pretty big creature. Then, taking my provisions with me, I made my way downstairs to search out and remonstrate with Grendel's Mother.

I found her behind the bar immolating a collection of leather tankards with a skill honed by custom in a basin of greasy looking water. She didn't look up as I walked into the room but my presence was noted with a simple word.

"Fawkin'."

"Abben's a troll a'sleppin ma bed," I said as forcefully as I could without seeming unduly rude. (I thought perhaps that I actually sounded a little petulant.)

She looked up at that point and with more sarcasm than I would have thought possible of her, replied simply.

"Yu'as slepish a naht ne was?"

Then she added, *"and yu'sa payin a bed a naht e naht?"*

She looked at me as if expecting me to make some acknowledgment or assent. I refused to comply and after a hiatus that was only uncomfortable to my presence of mind, she continued.

"We'll 'Es a pay in' a daylart time. Abben esa wurm beddin' ne was."

It was disgusting, that's what it was and I wasn't going to have any more of it. Internally, I hit the roof. Externally, I began to shake with anger. This was wholly ridiculous. Who had ever heard of paying for the same bed night time and day time like that? And the whole thought was seriously unhygienic. I was pretty glad that I had packed away my sleeping sack when I left the room that morning.

"Ne, neggit," I thumped the bar to make my point. I noticed, as an aside, that my assault on the bar was not approved of by the hairy witch who scowled menacingly at me from her basin but frankly I didn't give a damn.

"Newas, neggit. Ne' ma ne wyse a hear'd en at," I proclaimed in what I intended to be righteous indignation but which probably came across once more as petulance.

"Humuch d'ya want?" I asked.

I had decided to go straight for the money argument as I could see no point in making a stand on other principles.

"Ne, ne. Es nebbut es trupp," said Grendel's Mother, *"Es'a naht wotchmon en as furty dalart a trupps paid."*

She looked at me and, presumably failing to see any recognition or understanding, yelled.

"En a mas stecki!"

She offered up her palm, spat on it and smacked it down to indicate that she had made an agreement with the troll. Well who was going to argue with that. Not I, that was for sure. He had paid forty days upfront and I was there for three nights. What is more, I don't have any other option tonight or for that matter any other night in this place. I tried one last hope.

"D'you enas rum?"

"Nebbut."

Of course I knew the answer before I asked the question but it was worth a try. Trying to rationalize the situation I chose to convince myself that getting into that bed tonight would be no different to getting into it last night. The only difference is that I now know the occupant – at least indirectly. In theory that was a kind of improvement. However, there was absolutely no comfort in this knowledge.

Grendel's Mother must have seen the struggle going on in my head for she added a few words of her own, in a rather kindly manner, I thought.

"Newas feckit ne mur. Es enas few nahts enas wurm enas yu'as naht tame."

I didn't find this too much comfort but I wasn't going to split hairs about warmth, possession and relativity in this backwater of backwaters. Besides, Grendel's Mother wasn't finished yet.

"Es'a gud crowd ere enas naht. Abben yu'sa spekin a Markel ne was."

She paused and looked at me in a manner that, had she been prettier or I more desperate, might have been taken as an invitation.

Then she added slyly, *"Enas gud skegs er was,"* and tapped the bar gently just to the left of her bucket of filthy water.

I hoped that this was simply a convenience and not juxtaposition but chose to leave it there. Then she offered me one of those weird smiles that I had come to recognize, although I still didn't understand.

Those were possibly the most sympathetic words that I had yet heard come from the woman. To be fair, they seemed pretty genuine too. Of course it also occurred to me that I had only a little while ago managed to establish that Markel would be drinking here tonight and that I had, albeit indirectly, determined to meet him here.

News obviously travels fast in this place although it could just as well have been a pretty obvious guess. Either way, I decided to make my excuses and go out. First I left my provisions in *the* room (I felt that I could no longer call it *my* room). I hid the new bag behind my pack although I did this with little confidence about ever seeing the items again. Then I wandered out once more into the cold of what was now the afternoon.

IV
A Tale of Lust And Onions

I spent a long afternoon wandering first around the village (which did not take long) and then off towards the woods up on the surrounding hills. These were the outlying trees of what was once the ancient forest of Sumah which had spread from the River Awata to the south of the village and then north until the ground became permanently frozen and would no longer support trees. Here, the great ice bears reportedly still roamed.

The snow was still lying quite thick on the ground, making the whole scene look bright and glowing. The sky above was a beautiful clear blue and there wasn't a cloud visible. The trees dangled great frozen beards of rassa moss from their boughs and now and then these would twitch with the movement of the tree mice that would invariably be overwintering in them.

A couple of times that afternoon I heard the mournful, eerie call of a *cormoran* as it wheeled in the chill air high above me. I couldn't see it even though the sky was perfectly clear, then my eyes aren't what they used to be so it was hardly surprising. I should perhaps make it clear that I am referring to a large predatory bird, the *cormoran*, a native of the edges of this cold wilderness. I am not talking of the *Cor'moran*, the great winged creature of legend that, it was believed, could fold time and speak the languages of all men. Perhaps more of that tale another time.

I took out a dry cloth that I carried in my day sack for such occasions and settled myself on the bough of a gnarled and stumpy holly tree that had gone over in a storm some time past and still managed to cling to life through the remains of its root system. From here I could look out over the village and beyond it towards the river. I could see for miles and followed the tiny strip of the Great North Road as it ran straight, away from the village, up into the icy foothills of the Trellsgut Mountains. That was to be my next road in a few days. For now, it was just geography.

I removed the last remaining tin of fish from my day sack, opened this and ate the contents, pepper oil as well, with a piece of oat bread that had probably seen a few more days than it should. Still it was pleasant, although a tomato and some salt would have made it perfect. As I ate, I watched the little droplets of oil fall to the snow and gather there staining it with small spots of red. I gave some thought to the beauty (and perhaps the profundity) of contrast: dark on light; vermillion on white.

Once I had finished both meal and contemplation, I took out my sketch pad and charcoals and started drawing in the sure and certain knowledge that there was no one around to ignore me and no one about to ask those facile questions about which bit of the picture was which bit of scene.

I stayed there until it was starting to get dark and my fingers could no longer hold the charcoal. Then I packed up and headed back to Champneys.

It is always traumatic for me when I move from utter solitude, such as I had experienced up on the hillside, back into human company. As I approached the inn in what was now darkness, I saw once again the sign that was hanging loosely from its broken hinges. Now in the faint and flickering yellow light of a burning torch I could just about make out some of the letters of the word "Champneys" but I still couldn't tell whether the scribbling on the wall below spelled, "inn" or, "brothel" although now I was pretty sure, from the general state of the place and its clientele, that it probably didn't claim to be the latter.

There was nothing for it. Once more I stamped the snow and frozen mud from my boots, turned the boss handle and felt the ice grind in the lock. Then I went in.

I was expecting much of what hit me as I opened the door: the relative warmth; the noise; and, the smell. What I wasn't expecting was the nearly full leather tankard that hit me square on the forehead. I went down like a stone.

Somewhere in a mass of unpleasant and angry thoughts I could vaguely hear people shouting. It was muffled as though they were under blankets or in another room. I couldn't work out what they were shouting though or even if they were shouting at me. After a while I opened my eyes and looked up into the brown cow-like eyes of Grendel's Mother. I also took in the stench of some kind of ale (or something passing itself off as ale) and, curiously, the smell of onions.

Grendel's Mother was really close to me, peering down with a look of concern; it could have been hunger; it could have been lust. I hung on to the thought that would hopefully never know.

"Fawkin'! Is yu'sa raht, lurv," she cooed,*"Fawkin', speak t'me ja'bas."*

I was now back on the planet, as it were, and was at last beginning to tune in.

"Wha's 'at shmell?" I asked.

"Wha's 'at, Fawkin'. Wha's 'at ya sayin'?", she sung back at me.

Then in her more customary voice she yelled to no-one in particular.

"Gi yim summat rume, ya maggots!"

This was followed up with a short bark.

"You!"

This was to Grendel, the unfortunate tracker and in this world of curiosities, her son.

"Gimme skegs 'ere!"

Then when the hapless wretch started looking aimlessly about in the approximate vicinity of the bar she almost screeched at him.

"Ne, nebbut in tha bar!"

Then she snarled to another body standing nearby.

"Stand 'ere ja'bas! Es'll be doin it masef!"

She stood up quickly and my head dropped back to the hard floor like a small sack of potatoes. This further injury both to my person and my pride was not noticed by the hairy witch as she stomped off towards the bar and reached under it with her left hand.

"Yes," I managed to think, "it is right next to the slops bucket."

The hand emerged with a heavy looking jug and at the same time and almost in the same movement, her right hand lashed out and clipped the top of Grendel's head.

"'ere wha's 'at fur?" he whined, sounding genuinely offended.

"Wha's 'at schmell?" I persisted and, because I was being ignored, followed it up loudly with *"es'a scallions ne was?"*

As if in answer, Grendel's Mother (who had now returned and was leaning down over me, supporting my head between her legs in the rough fabric of her skirt) belched loudly, invading my nose with an answer that managed to offend my olfactory senses. The stench of onions from a distance of about six inches from my face – well inside my personal space – was far too close for my comfort. What was it with these people and proximity?

I had my answer though and I was now out of time. A large hand (it could only have been Grendel's) thrust itself under the back of my head (and, forgive me for saying so, between his mother's legs) and took hold of my thinning hair, forcing me up to a sitting position. Thus placed, a smaller hand forced the mouth of a small jug between my lips and stared pouring a fiery liquid into my reluctant and then rebellious mouth.

This was getting out of hand. Grendel's Mother was now rubbing my thigh with a meaty paw and an expression that, even in my dazed and confused state, I was now beginning to think was actually a form of lust. What with the burning liquid and the rubbing and all the proximity, possibly even the onions, I began to feel a relatively unfamiliar stirring in my nether regions.

Now that would really take the biscuit, if that little monster decided that now was the time to stir its ugly head. Having said that, with the baggy and thick trousers, not to mention the layers of underwear and my less than adequate physique, it seemed pretty likely and, it has to be said fortunate, that the matter would go both unnoticed and un-remarked.

"Ne. Ne, gi' me space wis'un," I spluttered, adding my own spit and the blood from the cut on my forehead that was running down to my mouth, to that of the skegs that had been forced into me. I managed to spray those close enough to receive it with this unpleasant cocktail of liquids. Although Grendel was not the closer of the beastly pair, he was in direct line of projection and took the main hit.

He appeared to take the blast in his stride. It was perhaps a common occurrence late at night in this place. I'm not sure if it was a credit to him or not but he didn't even flinch. I watched in a detached manner as the red gold droplets ran down his face and merged with the black matted hair of his huge beard.

"For God's sake gi' me space will you!"

I yelled in my own tongue, this time pushing Grendel and his mother away from me – or rather, back to the relative distance of arm's length. This being done, I felt for the wound on my forehead and groaned both with pain and misery when I felt a reasonable and irregular patch of wetness just above my left eyebrow.

"Crap," I shouted, without bothering to translate and then continued.

"Now look what you've done to me. I'll probably get septicemia! Here give me that!"

This last comment was to Grendel whose mental processing seemed to be struggling to keep up with the pace of events. Frankly I didn't care a bit that he was looking bemused and slightly wretched.

I snatched the jug of skegs from him and without warning flung the entire contents at the injury. Some of it missed. I heard a muffled squeal from behind me where, I assumed (but don't take it from that that I gave a damn) some unfortunate had caught a shot in the eye.

The drink in my cut hurt like nothing I can describe. I stifled without full success, a cry of pain and serious anguish as my head began to throb terribly and a stinging sense of utter injustice erupted on my forehead. The result was that I let out a noise closely resembling that of a squealing pig. I was beyond caring but held my breath as I attempted to gain control of the pain and also to re-establish what was left of any dignity that I could muster. At least the skegs would minimize the risk of infection.

"Who threw that?" I yelled, adding *"ja'bas!"* for good measure just because I felt like it.

It wasn't good grammar but I didn't care. I don't know whether it was the sudden assault or the skegs or the rush of testosterone around my system but my native timidity seemed to have deserted me, along with (if it has to be said) my common sense. I was furious and I was livid (I was pretty purple in the face as well I would imagine). I didn't give a damn who it was but I wanted blood. Someone else's blood, that is.

The room was silent. Then, as when the master of a class turns around and yells the same question to a pond of faces reflecting back at him, all expressions seemed (without actually looking) to point in one direction. I found my eyes drawn as though by some unseen power towards one individual in the corner of the room. He looked back at me through unusually bright eyes with a mischievous sparkle in them.

I glared at my alleged assailant for a while. He didn't even look remorseful. Actually, he looked positively gleeful. The response seemed to be so out of keeping with the moment that I felt the sails of my recent bellicosity unfurling, then collapsing and then eventually they were left flapping about a bit. Then they were still.

I took a breath.

"You'll be Markel, I guess," I said.

"Ay, that'll be me, lad," he said. "Did I catch your attention?"

"You's a..." I began but he interrupted me.

"Speak properly, boy. It's not often I get to try out another language," he paused before adding, "by the way, that's gotta hurt."

"Actually, it hurts like stink," I said as I tried unsuccessfully to stand.

It has to be said that the only genuine reason preventing me from getting up was that there were so many people crowding around me still that I could not find enough space to get myself back into an upright position.

"Gi' me space, ja'bas!" I shouted one more time, wondering at the same time what the plural was for ja'bas, and to be fair, this time they actually did so.

It took two more days in all collect the tale of the Fire Dancers and so I didn't have to stay any additional nights (although I had actually paid for an extra night just in case). This also meant that I didn't have to share any longer than was necessary with the night watchman who, I learned on the second night, was called Maucum. To be honest it should have been possible to complete the task sooner but Markel's strange sense of humour and the unpredictable influence of the skegs slowed things down even more than I expected.

Markel told the complete story of the Fire Dancers on that first night of meeting so that I only had to spend the remaining time with him consolidating it and checking out some of the more obscure points. When I stumbled up to my room in the darkness at the end of that first night however, there were two thoughts roiling around in my mind. Firstly, was I going to remember anything the next morning? Then, secondly and at that moment more importantly, would the dizzying effects of the skegs wear off when I lay down or would I just be sick?

By the time I got to the room and had wrestled with the key and the lock for a while, I just had to sit down. This I did, coming to an ungainly and poorly controlled landing on the unmade bed. On the floor somewhere distant by my feet I saw a scrap of paper and a couple of tins that seemed to move in and out of focus. The paper was a note from my cohabitee in this room and, oddly enough, it was written in my own language and not in the native dialect.

"I got you some soma fresh tins o' fesh from th' merchant and they're 'ere."

He had scrawled an arrow which I presumed had pointed to the tins when the paper was on the floor. The note continued.

"I hadn't meant to nick 'em the other night but I was hungry ...And they were pepper oil too!"

He had added this last observation as though it were both an afterthought and a justification. He had signed the note "Maucum".

This was the closest anyone in this part of the world was going to get to an apology and to be fair, it was pretty decent of him to replace the goods. It gave me a better feeling about the rest of my property in there and I noticed even in my skegs reduced vision that the pack and provisions bag had not been touched again by human hands. There were however unmistakable signs of attempted forced entry by a number of jointed legs. I knew this to be the case because those same jointed legs were still attached to the webbing on the pack and some of them were still twitching.

However, that was as much as I could take in. Dirty, unmade bed or not, I collapsed sideways onto it and slept soundly for about three hours, waking only when I was so cold that it was painful and in fact when the light had started to creep in again through the small dirty window. I was relieved to discover that I had not been sick in my sleep.

I hadn't got much to do the next day and had I the chance I would simply have spent most of it asleep recovering from the previous night. However, I didn't have that luxury as I had to give the bed up later in the morning. I guessed that Maucum got back around nine o'clock so I had a couple of hours before I had to vacate the place. I crawled under the covers for warmth and dosed in and out of a sleep punctuated with a weird assortment of dreams.

I couldn't face breakfast so instead as a form of penance for the overindulgence of the previous night, I went to the wash room and tried to clean myself up. That was no easy task with a bucket of cold water and a piece of rock hard soap that smelled of animal. (But which bit? That's what I didn't want to know). However, the water was cold and it certainly woke me up. Then I dried myself, using my own towel. I wasn't going to risk immolating myself with the filthy rag that was hanging on a peg looking and probably smelling like the remains of a corpse on a gibbet. I went back into the inn to sit in a corner of the bar. I had my note book with me and the intention was to make a few notes from last night and when the opportunity arose, to have a quiet sleep away from the rest of the passing world.

There were two barriers to this. Firstly, the fire was dead and the room was bitterly cold so that it was difficult to write for long and almost impossible to get any decent sleep. Secondly, Grendel's Mother seemed determined to perform what I took to be some form of cleaning operation on the room.

She spent a lot of time in the morning moving furniture and sweeping about in a fairly bizarre manner. Then after she had served the lunch time drinks to a very small number of people – two to be precise - she started on the great fireplace. She finished whatever it was she was doing just before the evening opening and had lit the fire just before she unlocked the door.

The result of all this activity was that much of the room (including myself) acquired a fine deposit of ash over it. It also meant that for the first three hours of the evening it was damned cold in that place. About an hour after the fire had burst into life and was finally throwing out some semblance of warmth, people started arriving. Prior to then, the only people in the place were myself, Grendel and his mother and a couple of wagoners who were stopping for the night. I thought that perhaps there was some kind of telepathy at work here or that it was generally known that the inn was being 'cleaned' today. However, if I had stepped outside the front door I would have seen written on the door in an untidy script the following:

"Nebbut com'in yin. Cleanin'.
Fawkin' cauld."

V
Old Markel's Tale

Just after nine by my old timepiece that evening, Markel arrived with his brother in the company of a small collection of folk. After the bitter cold of cleaning carried out by Grendel's Mother that afternoon, the place had finally returned to the nature and characteristics of the previous evening and it was, once more, pretty crowded. In spite of this Markel and his party somehow found a table, chairs and space to sit near to me in a corner of the room. It was pretty snug to say the least. The merchant was dispatched to the bar for the drinks and Markel leaned across to me.

"Evening Fawkin'," he said, *"you fit for another go tonight?"*

I replied that I was and he added.

"How's about I tell it in your speach and you translate for my friends here."

He had that mischievous look in his eyes as he said this and he winked at me.

"Then, if I forget any of it, you can fill in for me from what you learned last night."

He grinned at me. Of course, I knew that what he really meant was that if the skegs got the better of him, I should be able to pick it up myself and continue until he rejoined us, as it were.

Actually, this was a pretty good opportunity for me to consolidate a great deal of the tale as long as I stayed off the drink. That was going to be a challenge but I decided that the best tactic was to get a tankard of horshp's in front of me. That was a drink that I was never going to touch and if the tankard was full there was a good chance that I would be overlooked on any drinks round. It shouldn't cause any aggravation as long as I got in a round or three, myself at appropriate intervals during the night.

I also had to make it quite clear that I wasn't sharing a drink with any other person. Having noticed the unfortunate custom of the single tankard, I knew that I was going to have a problem explaining my issues. I had to try a number of different approaches including a claim that I had an illness of some sort. That only elicited enthusiastic interest about what I had, its symptoms and whether it was contagious although no one seemed particularly bothered about the fact. My response that it was incurable simply gained further interest and so I abandoned that route and told them that I was losing my teeth.

I thought that would have caused enough concern but my mistake was demonstrated when a number of the crowd grinned affably at ne and I could see that they were sporting barely a full set between them. Herpes didn't do much for it either and in fact when I looked closer at a few of them I could see why. In the end I capitulated and simple said, "Ok, I'll have horshp's." I got a number of odd looks at that and after a brief exchange around the table mostly through the language of the eyes, it was agreed that I would have a drink of my own. No one else, apparently, drank horshp's.

As it was I had only had a tankard of the "Old Ass" ale earlier in the evening and so was pretty fit to go. I just hoped that I could remember most of the tale from yesterday, given that certain parts of the evening seemed to have faded away in an alcoholic fog.

I had made a few notes during the cold day in the inn but there were a few areas where I was a little patchy and I was pretty sure from the lack of continuity, that there were an unknown number of places where the story was, well, unknown. However, whatever state Markel was in, he seemed to be a skilled story teller and I felt certain that he would spot any errors, omissions or deviations from the main line of the tale. All I had to do was to stay off the skegs.

"OK. You're on," I replied grinning at him, *"let's go for it!"*

We waited until his twin was back from the bar and the drinks had been distributed. Then, with the communal tankard and his own tumbler of skegs placed carefully in front of him, I with my Horshp's and everyone else watching with eagerly anticipated intent, Markel tapped loudly on the table with his pipe. In the relative quiet that followed, he introduced me to those who had not already had the pleasure. He then explained that he was going to tell the Fire Dancer's tale tonight in my language.

"Ol' Fawkin' 'ere 'll tell it in bruta speke."

He also warned those who knew the tale to show no mercy if I told it wrong or if I strayed from it in my solo performances if and when they occurred. These, it was tacitly understood by all, would occur when Markel had lost it in his skegs, as the saying goes in these parts.

All this being said, he began the story and, at a signal from him, I commenced my rendition.

"A long time ago in a time before our ancestors, in a time before people first came to settle in these lands, there lived a man, a hunter. He walked the path of solitude: a recluse who had forsaken the company of his kind and had travelled from the deep southern lands far into the north where the world was cold and the snow was thick.

As to why he had come to these lands, no tale is told. Perhaps he had fled some war or pestilence, perhaps some fearsome enemy or a blood feud. Perhaps he had fled the wrath of a wronged father or a vengeful husband. Of this no tale is told.

Yet he had travelled from where the stars are strange and where, it was said, the perfume of flowers on the summer's nights made the air seem heady and the senses light."

"A bit like old Fawkin' 'ere," chipped in the merchant.

There was some scattered laughter. It was a kind of clandestine, schoolboy laughter. I wasn't sure whether the reference was to my travelling or to the fact that, of the company present, I was possibly the least fragrant.

"Abben so," replied Markel with the hint of a scowl at his brother and the interruption.

He continued.

"Then one cold day, his journey ended when he came to a place deep in the forest of Sumah. Here the trees about him seemed to open out, giving space to breathe the cool air and high above his head he could see the dark snow clouds passing across the grey sky.

Here he cleared a place in the snow and built a fire, lighting it with great skill from the tinder and dried fungus that he carried with him in his fire sack. Then he built himself a shelter, cutting only as much live wood as was necessary and using what dead branches were visible on the snow covered ground about him.

He was a skilled woodsman and yet the task took him some while so that by the time he had finished the night had drawn in the snow had begun to fall once more in great soft white flakes.

Deep in the growing darkness of the forest he could hear the wolves howling. He had no fear of them, though he knew that they were close and that they would be aware of him and his smell. He had no fear of them, not through the false comfort in his fire or the vanity of the shelter. He had no fear."

At these words, Markel paused and, as I spoke out my last line of translation to the room.

"...nebbut fayr."

The old storyteller looked around at the faces of those who were listening – not just his immediate party but all those within earshot. The place was quieter than I had ever heard it before. It was even quieter than the previous night's telling.

Some of the story was different and the words, and the way that it was told, caught the attention of those now listening.

"*No fear,*" Markel repeated.

You could have heard a calymene cross the room on its spiky, scratchy legs, the quiet was so complete. Even Grendel's Mother stopped her customary immolation of tankards behind the bar. I would have sworn that even the fire, which seemed to have picked up at last was had been spitting and hissing in the hearth until a few moments before, stopped crackling for a while.

Clearly there was some significance in this "no fear" phrase but I did not fully grasp it and I wasn't going to speak up right now on a point of comprehension. For one thing, Markel's face held an expression that didn't countenance interruption. For another, I wasn't even sure that I was capable of saying anything right now.

Once he had them all, Markel continued, gesturing to me somewhat sharply where I sat with my metaphorical mouth open, reminding me to recommence my translation.

"The darkness of night had fallen quickly under the trees and as the sense of sight lessened with him, the man's hearing seemed to become more acute. He could hear other creatures moving about. He caught the tread of wolf paw on crunching snow: felt, rather than saw, the reflection of light in the eyes of the creatures that had drawn in around him attracted both by his scent and by the fearful fascination of his fire.

He took from his bag the last of his ration of dried meat and cut from it a shard of flesh with his great curved hunting knife. This food he chewed as he warmed himself before the fire and when it was gone, he spread his arms out in a curve over the flames like the embrace of a god. The yellow light painted his face and his skin glowed as if gold. His black beard glistened with the thawing snow and from his mouth his breath came like fire smoke in the chill night air.

There he remained, bent and motionless, neither moving nor responding to the sounds and the noises around him. The fire crackled and sparked as the wood dried and burned and the wetter wood hissed and spat smoke and steam and sparks into the air. The night moved on and the bright stars spun in an arc overhead. Still he remained motionless.

Around him in the dark, the wolves squatted down in the snow, their eyes on him: all of them waiting, all of them at rest and yet alert. Then the largest of them, a grey creature with a two-tone coat and a mane of russet fur over his head rose up from where he was resting at the edge of the clearing.

The pack, his pack, were suddenly alert, watching him. Away, a few paces to one side, one animal sat quietly apart. This was the sentinel.

In the darkness, a creature cried out: a cry of panic and of pain and of death."

I don't really know how he did it but Markel seemed to charge his words with such force that, for one moment, I thought that he had actually cried out. There was no time for analysis, though, because this master of storytelling had already moved on and I had no option but to follow.

"Perhaps it was the sound of death that caused the man to open his eyes at that moment or maybe it was nothing more than coincidence. He lowered his arms slowly, picking up a couple more logs to throw onto the fire as the grey wolf padded slowly and carefully further into the firelight.

Picking up the remains of the dried meat that he carried - his last rations - the man lobbed it towards the wolf. Winter was a lean time for all creatures. The animal bent to sniff the meat before picking it up and turning away."

Markel stopped to drink some of his ale, passing the tankard to the man sitting next to him and then downing the contents of the small tumbler of skegs. He looked around at those listening to him. In his eyes there was a feral look.

"There were worse things than wolves out there in the darkness deep in the forest of Sumah yet the wolves did not fear them. They did not fear this man either though, by sharing his meat, the man would acquire a tolerance of a sort.

That night, with the wolves lying nearby in the snow, the man slept without fear.

When he opened his eyes it was still dark and the snow was still falling. The wolves had gone and the fire had burned down low. The man stepped out from under the shelter where he had been resting and brushed the snow from some of the deadwood that he had collected earlier. This he then placed carefully on the fire together with some smaller pieces of drier wood that he had kept with him under the shelter. Blowing carefully on the embers he rekindled the flames and within a short while had a moderately lively fire crackling and spitting once more in the darkness.

Then he reached back under the shelter to take something from his pack. It was wrapped in oiled cloth that was stiff with the cold and he placed it inside his coat to warm it slightly so that he could un-wrap it easier once it had thawed a bit."

At this point Markel stopped, looked at me and winked. He then stood up and muttered something.

Ye'ma goin aht fur to pees so don't 'e make a mess on et whilst ye'ma ways."

He then stumbled off towards the main door, turning before he went out into the darkness and yelling.

"and yu'sa abbin et a gud tale else wyse these all be avin 'ee, ja'bas!"

He disappeared out into the darkness leaving me with a captivated but, I feared, uncompromising audience. I could feel a sudden sense of anxiety, not because I was afraid to speak in front of these people. That was my job, if you like. I was just concerned. I didn't want to get it wrong and more than that I didn't want to lose the atmosphere that Markel had built up.

Having said that, I guess it doesn't usually add to the tale if the story-teller gets up in the middle of the tale to go empty his bladder.

I looked around at my audience and saw a mass of brown cow like eyes all looking at me with that strange dilated pupil vacancy that they had. There was nothing for it. I just had to begin. Best not upset them, I thought.

I had absently picked up my tankard but it wasn't until a gulp of the foul brew was going down my throat that I realized that I had actually drunk some of the horshp's. I was horrified but I will say that it fulfilled all my expectations of it as a drink.

It was truly foul: bitter and sour and yet sweet and sickly at the same time. There were 'bits' in it too with the texture of cheese but I didn't want to dwell on those. Fortunately, I was neither vegetarian in diet nor Bhodlevict in my beliefs otherwise I might have added crisis of conscience to the general discomfiture of mind and rebellion of my guts.

It took a fair bit of willpower to suppress any thoughts about the creatures that I suspected that I had just unintentionally consumed. It took even more to keep the brew in my throat and finally to get it into a place where I could process it, pathogens et al.

Strangely, the drink left a warm sensation in the mouth and throat that was actually quite pleasant but enough of that. I took a couple of calming breaths and began what I truly hoped was a close approximation to Markel's version of the tale.

"After a while, perhaps when it had thawed a little, the man un-wrapped the package and removed a narrow piece of parchment. It was a dirty cream colour and about a foot in length. He sniffed it. It smelled of the earth and woodland with a hint of rotting ash-tree in it. He tore off a small piece and placed the package in his lap to keep it dry. He popped the smaller piece into his mouth and started to chew."

I was beginning to get a dry feeling in my mouth and it wasn't at the thought of chewing dried parchment. This wasn't flowing well enough. I was conscious of the almost staccato delivery of my words; aware of a sense of growing unrest amongst the audience. Nothing for it though, I carried on.

"The fungus, for that was what it was, seemed to dissolve on his tongue, diffusing a taste that was slightly acrid whilst at the same time being quite sweet. He chewed for a while and then spat out the remains of the pulpy flesh into the fire where it sizzled and burst into bright red, yellow and purple flames. He tore off another piece with his teeth and repeated this several times more, each time spitting the flesh into the fire where, each time, the fire burned with the tri-coloured flames.

By the time that he had disposed of the strip in this way and had put more wood on, the fire was ablaze with colour and heat and light. It had become so hot that the man had to move back from it to avoid burning his clothes. He piled on more wet logs which hissed and steamed and spat but soon burned and glowed with an intensity that you would not have expected from damp wood.

Around him it was still dark and now almost totally silent. The only sound was the crackling fire and the hiss of melting snow as the circle of heat from the fire spread outwards into the clearing.

Then the man took another item from his pack. It looked like a prayer mat such as the Farseems of the southern lands use. This he placed on the warm wet soil slightly away from the fire.

Next he removed his coat and knelt upon the mat, his knees together and his knuckles pressed to the ground a little in front of him on the cold earth. He remained in this position for a while, his body leaning slightly forward towards the fire feeling the warmth of the flames glowing in his face. Suddenly he bobbed his head and in an obvious gesture of subservience he bent to press his forehead to the cold earth, the heat of the fire now burning into the top of his head. He stayed in this position for a while. Around him it was still and still the fire spat and crackled and hissed. Yet there was a sense of quiet now that no other sounds seemed capable of disrupting.

And then it began..."

I stopped here partly, it has to be said for emphasis, but also if I am honest it was because I wanted to look at the faces of the people around me. As I had unrolled the tale I felt a growing sense of contact with them. Not, it has to be said, at the same level as Markel but at least, I felt, going in the right direction. I wanted to see that the look of naked doubt in all their faces had gone and that they were starting to hear me for real. I wanted recognition as a story teller in my own right. For all the gods' sake, I *was* a story teller in my own right!

It was during this pause, that Markel came back in from the cold. He stumbled towards us, slamming the door behind. His hair glistened from the snow that was obviously falling outside and soon started to melt. Soon his face and forehead would be streaked with wet. On the front of his trousers there was a large damp patch that nobody other than me seemed to notice. He slumped back down in his chair and scowled at me.

"Was aben a ma tahl, ja'bas," he growled.

Immediately I was worried that he had somehow been listening in to my performance and that he did not approve. I was, however, a little reassured when he put a further question to the dumb audience.

"Abben es ok?" he continued.

"*Well! Aye or ne?"* he demanded when no one seemed keen to speak up.

He was not impressed with the lack of response and looked around the room with a scowl fixed firmly on his face. Then at last, someone spoke. It was Grendel's Mother.

"Well, he's a good 'un, Markel," she said.

"Wha's 'a," he hissed, cutting her short.

"Aye, he's a good'un, Markel and no mistake. He's got the good stuffa, he has."

This latter comment was offered by the merchant, and it appeared either to register better with him or to carry more weight as an opinion. Markel relaxed ever so slightly but to my mind he still had a slightly feral look in his eyes. I began to wonder whether the skegs was taking its toll on him.

"For sure," he said, *"it's na'mur than ah knows."*

He rumbled these comments about me almost under his breath but then erupted enthusiastically about the bitter cold outside.

"Yeesh, it's fawkin' cauld out a th' ouse!"

Then he winked at me and continued.

"You go on a bit and I'll listen in. They seem to like you and no one has stabbed you yet, have they?"

He laughed as a frown of concern swept across my face and up over my head.

"Oh they do take it all pretty seriously around here. If you hadn't done the job, you would have known about it for sure."

He patted my hand in a slightly paternal manner (which was odd because I was pretty sure that I was older than him).

"One of those little details I didn't think you needed to know about. You know how it is."

Actually I didn't know how it was but then again I was pretty sure that I didn't want to ask either. Markel settled back in his chair and called for more ale and skegs, gesturing me to continue whilst Grendel's Mother got up and went to rattle and clatter about behind the bar to get Markel his drink.

I found it a little strange that the woman jumped to do the story-tellers bidding without so much as a murmur. Earlier, when Grendel had tried this himself, she had rounded on him with such a string of profanities that most of the audience had looked away in what I took to be embarrassment. I don't think I would have had any more success either, had I tried the same approach.

With the sound of tankards being clattered and immolated behind the bar, I picked up where I had left off.

"The first change was the fire. At its heart it seemed to glow brighter, going from red through golden and then to white. At the same time this glowing centre seemed to shrink as the colours changed in richness. Within a few heartbeats it had reached an intensity that hurt the eyes but then it winked out just like a candle gets snuffed out between finger and thumb.

The man had remained fixed in all this, looking into the flames, barely blinking: hardly moving. He had not looked away as the intensity grew and showed no reaction when the heart of darkness appeared before him. He remained still as in the black centre of the fire dark shapes began to form and move about. Then they seemed to solidify and coalesce into arms and hands.

These were the bodies of the lost that were reaching up out of that darkness, clawing their way out of a hole in the living world that was the fire. Arms reached up into the air like black smoke.

Then there came the noise: the chattering and the hissing sounds of many voices. A symphony of voices, some crying or laughing or shouting: anger; hatred; love; affection; happiness. So many emotions and sounds as all the while the smoky tendrils of arms flowed together to form bodies and heads and legs and feet. All were rising up into the air.

Now the writhing and dancing was in the air above the clearing. Above the fire the blackness of the shapes. Above the man, all the motion and commotion.

Then he looked up from the fire at the shapes above him and he lifted both of his arms up to them. In each hand he held something that was not there before: in the right, small brass cymbals; in the left a silver bell. He clicked the cymbals."

I looked around the room at the eager, expectant faces and held up my right arm. I clicked my thumb and index finger together. I could have sworn that I heard the sound of those brass cymbals.

"God I'm good," I thought.

"At that simple sound, from the darkness of the trees all around there erupted the low howling call of the wolves."

On a whim, I added a bit of my own and repeated the strap that Markel had given them earlier in the tale.

"There were worse things than wolves out there in the darkness deep in the forest of Sumah."

I paused to look around.

"Much worse, yet the wolves did not fear them."

Several pins could be heard hitting the floor.

"All the while the figures in the air above the fire swooped and dived, never touching the man nor the ground nor the trees overhead and around them. Blackness moved on greater blackness, dancing and weaving; heaving and breathing. It was the animation of a nightmare: claustrophobic and oppressive.

Other noises had started in the woods around. There were strange yelps and screeches, growling could be heard and the barking of foxes. Then a light was started in the east and with its appearance the first bird began to sing: the light of the sun adding first hints of vermillion and gold to the new day.

As the light grew, the returning wolves could be seen prowling around the outer edges of the clearing: cautious, alert and angry. The great black wolf raised up its muzzle to the sky and howled.

On the ground, the man was motionless again. Both arms held aloft. No dark shapes touched them, though many swooped near. The fire's heat scorched him whilst, from its cold black heart, more and more shapes continued to rise up into the air. Long he stayed there with the light creeping un-noticed into the clearing. The birds were now in full song. The fire still burned with its un-natural radiance.

He was standing when he rang the silver bell once.

The silence amongst the living was immediate and complete. The wolves as a pack dropped down into the snow. All birdsong stopped. No other sounds were heard but the crackling and spitting of the fire.

Kneeling once more, the hunter spoke for the first time. The language was strange and harsh and what he said has not been passed down through time. He spoke as though reciting a speech: formal and measured. His words had an effect on the shapes moving above him. At first they slowed but then began to move with visible direction as they flowed around and above him. By the time that he had finished, they were in a harmony of motion, watching over him and listening.

Then the hunter spoke a second time. The language was strange and harsh and these were words that have been passed down through the long ages. Thus he called to the multitude above him in a language that was ancient then and now is long since forgotten.

'I have travelled far from the south where the nights are warm and the stars in the night sky light up in wondrous constellations. Many days and many nights have I walked the lonely path to our ancestral home. Care have I taken in this wild world and care at need have I given. Know you also that I am a hunter and that there is blood on my hands yet I am no destroyer or despoiler. Though I have taken the lives of my brothers in life for food, yet I have graced their parting and have honoured their unwilling gift. The land is no longer strange to me and, though I am not one with it, I am still a part. I feel and I see and I hear when before I was senseless and deaf and blind. Thus I am able to know you. You who now are one with the land and have gone beyond our time and space.'

Then the man was silent and he cast down his eyes when before they had stared boldly up into the maelstrom. And he waited whilst above him the creatures moved and flowed, ever watching the man and never touching him. Long time was the man silent and long time was silence from the throng above him. There was no other sound in the forest: neither beast nor bird nor even the wind or creaking of the trees. The fire itself, no longer spitting or hissing, glowed silently as it pulsed gently with red and gold around the dense black inner heart.

Long it seemed, before they responded and it came to him like a memory; like a recollection of something told long past now and brought to mind by some trivial event. And thus it was that he remembered the words spoken long ago, in an age now passed, between a father and a son. In those words there was anger and betrayal and disbelief and great sorrow. Yet also there was great love and an overreaching sense of loss.

And it was that the voice in his mind spoke thus.

'Your ways are strange to me and your path is darkness to me: if I would walk that way with you I would be lost and also my kind. We do not go that way: we do not seek that way and I would that you would not. For you to do so, you would be lost to me for all time. Here we will remain, your father and mother, your brothers and sisters: our entire nation.

Would that you would rest here too with us as one and be at peace. Would that you should choose not to break your mother's heart and mine. Stay with us! Choose a mate and feed the fires of our ancestors as we have ever done. Why would you want more?'

Then the voice was quiet in his mind and the man now spoke out loud. Unwitting were his words and unwilling for they brought with them great sadness to him and in his eyes the tears welled and ran down his cold face.

'Father! Would that I could do as you wish or desire or command me but it is not to be. I cannot feed the fires of our forefathers whilst I remain here in indolence. And I speak to you thus. That there is a future for our kind out there away from here and it is not of ours. Never more will the fire dancers walk this sweet earth. I tell you with foresight, that the fires will diminish and darken here until there is none but a rumour remaining. And thus you will look to me from beyond the stone, always offering, always hoping for my return. And I for my part and my kind will ever look backwards to the stone: ever seeking you; ever looking to know where you have gone so that we may learn from your loss before it is too late for us.'

Thus spoke the man whilst above him now in the daylight, he heard the sounds and the sighing of great sorrow and misery and looking up once more he saw indeed the contorted and convulsed faces of the damned in the air above him as they moved ever closer but never touching. In the faces of a hundred generations he saw the wretchedness and the yearning. In the deepest parts of his mind he heard the words and recalled from memory yet more of the great sadness until he felt that his heart would burst.

'Then my son, alas you are lost to us and though we are brothers in life, you have no father here nor mother now, nor brothers nor sisters more. Our ancestral fires will not burn with the potency of your seed and for a mate you will choose the warm air and the bright stars that none can touch and none can hold close. Your being will be spent when your life ends and, child of oblivion, you will no longer be a fire dancer.'

Over the long years came the remembrance of those bitter words and the wounds that could not be healed. Unwitting and unwilling from the man's lips came a cry of pain and anguish that didn't seem to be his own. His knees gave way and he found himself on the ground sobbing, his hands at his head, tears falling without control. Through those tears and sobs and the gasping for breath he spoke now with new words. These were no longer memories but his own words now, in his time and place.

'It is you and your kin who have passed into oblivion. It is I and my kind that remain behind. The fires of your ancestors burned out long ago and the world around you is cold stone. All that I have of you is the ancestral memory that speaks to me for though we are no longer kind, yet once we were kin.

I have journeyed long and far to find you and to learn what became of you. When first I began my search I thought to find your tale in stone. Then as the rumour of your kind grew as I was drawn ever northwards I came to understand that though stone you had become, I would not find your tale written there. Thus I have sought the fire, ever our hope and our protector.

It seems to me that if my choices had been different I would be with you now, impotent and ethereal as you are in the air above me. Yet I know now that I am home: that I am neither a wanderer nor stranger any more. I have come back to the lands of my deep ancestors and here I now know that I wish to remain.'

Whilst he was speaking the man had remained on the ground but now he lifted himself up and looked about in the air above him where the damned swooped and soared still. He stood there a while arms outstretched and then as if prompted by a word he suddenly began removing his boots and the remainder of his clothes. Finally, he stood beneath the maelstrom naked. For a moment he was still again as he seemed to take a while to compose himself. He was home. He was a fire dancer once more.

Then without a sound he stepped into the dark heart of the fire. Both he and the maelstrom above blinked out of existence.

In the clearing, the light appeared to grow brighter. Of the fire, a few embers and smoldering bits of wood remained; circled by the grey ash and what remained of the snow. In a pile, still warm and giving off a little steam, the hunters discarded clothes remained where they would stay until they finally rotted away.

Over the seasons, the makeshift shelter would collapse and his pack, devoid now of all food and smelling only of man and man's things would remain untouched by the creatures of the forest until through the action of wind and rain the fabric and its contents would finally fade away.

In the wood the wolves stirred and rose up as a pack. They had watched it all: all the incomprehensible actions of the man with the man's fire and with the creatures of the night-that-lived-in-day. They had seen the man step into the fire so that he was not there and they had seen the creatures of the night-that-lived-in-day wink out.

They had seen it all and yet they had seen more as they and their kind had done a thousand times before: had seen the fangs and had heard the screams. There were worse things than wolves out there in the darkness deep in the forest of Sumah. Much worse, yet the wolves did not fear them."

VI
A Tale Of Two Breakfasts

You could have heard a pin drop for a heartbeat or two and the thought crossed my mind that just maybe I was going to get stabbed after all. Then I heard my name, or rather, the name that they had given me. The speaker was Grendel and he was speaking unusually quietly. I would have said thoughtfully but I think that that is pushing it a bit.

"Fawk'in..." he said and then added, *"Fawk'in monsters, they's a nabbin' 'im for sure. They's worse 'an wolves, ne'bas ne!"*

"Yu'sa shutten up yer face, ja'bas," hissed his mother as she made a curious gesture in front of her with her left hand. *"Yu'sa nebbut speak about dese things. Yu'sa knowin 'at!"*

Something had affected them all and not just these two. I looked around the room and saw fearful looks that I hadn't seen at the telling the night before. Then I caught Markel's eye. He was watching me with an appraising look and I couldn't tell if it was good or bad until he spoke.

"You've heard the tale before, it seems and not from my telling," he said.

It was not an accusation it was just a statement.

"No. I heard it for the first time last night," I replied.

"But I didn't tell it like that last night," he said, *"I have told it like that before though, when I have a mind to and the skegs doesn't stop me. That is the real tale. Last night was a tale for the children and for you strangers. The truth is a lot more sinister."*

He paused and was quiet for a while.

"So how did you know?"

I told him that I didn't know what he was talking about and that apart from a few additions of my own it was what I thought I recalled from his previous telling.

"It's the wolves. That's the real difference. Last night, not more than a passing reference or two and no wolf's eye view. So the true nature of the tale stays hidden. Without them, we end with a bit of a mystery but with them he is prey."

He was quiet for a while and then he went on.

"And that phrase about worse things than wolves. I used it once earlier without any particular emphasis but you seem to have picked up on its importance because you used it several times. It is a well known saying hereabouts and you must have heard it before."

"I heard it last night when you were telling..."

"You did not hear it from me, laddie, because I didn't use it last night. I wasn't so far in the skegs that I don't recall what I said or how I told it. How about you? How is your memory standing up?"

I had to admit that my recollection of the night before after a certain point was a little doubtful but then again, as far as I could see I had recalled the tale. Hell, it seemed as though I had remembered more than I had heard.

"Well I don't know," I said, "All I can say is that I have never heard the story before so frankly it's all a bit weird to me."

"Well whatever, you know your trade that's for sure and from where I sat it was well told. Thought the young lad was going to wet himself, I did."

He pointed at Grendel and laughed.

"Come on, your round laddie. Let's get a few more skegs in."

I knew it was a mistake and so I did it anyway. I don't recall much after that. I didn't get to my room that's for sure. I woke up, stiff, aching and frozen in the early hours. The bar was in darkness and I could smell the wood smoke and ash from the fire which was now pretty much dead. Another person was snoring loudly nearby but it hurt too much to turn around to see who it was. I staggered to my feet but only after doing indescribable damage to my screaming knees and on the unsure legs of an ancient fifty-two year-old I moved painfully towards the doorway and the passage to my room.

As I trod unsteadily in the general direction of the doorway there was an almighty yelp followed by a series of growls and grumblings as I stepped on something furry, large and warm. Hengest, the inn's mangy old dog leapt up out of sleep and scuttled off in the darkness to somewhere behind the counter where I heard it rumbling and mumbling to itself in a very human manner.

"Ja' bas, I'm tryin' a sleep 'ere. Gertcha...."

Behind me in the dark, the speech trained off into incomprehensible snarls and grumbles that sounded strangely like dog. Well at least the snoring had stopped.

Once more I reached the small dark and dirty little room and once more I gave little consideration to matters of hygiene or to the calymenes or to anything else for that matter. With just enough wit to get to it, I hit the bed hard and went out like a light.

It was pretty light when I was prodded into a sense of wakefulness by a large stubby set of fingers that punched at my shoulder like a hammer.

"Fawk'in, you's all right, Fawk'in?"

One of the ugliest faces I have seen for a long while loomed right into my vision with a look of serious concern in its brown eyes. The nose would have been mistaken for a wild mushroom if it had been seen on the ground in a wood. The eyes were uncharacteristically small though they still retained the cow-like look, possibly with a hint of pig in it.

It took me a while to gather my frayed senses but once I had done so I realized that this was probably my cohabitee, Maucum. I mumbled something incoherent at him and sat up. That was when I realized that I had a headache: not just any headache either, one of those ones that really get to you and remind you just exactly how much you have abused your body the night before. I had a growing concern that I was going to be sick and the longer I sat there the more worried I became.

It can't have been more than a few seconds before I decided that I needed some fresh air and so I rose unsteadily to my feet and, with a completely futile and ridiculous gesture, I attempted to straighten the shoddy bed. I then made a lunge past Maucum towards the dark opening that was the door and moved as fast as my aching knees would allow me down the corridor and, eventually and without mishap, out into the yard at the back of the inn. There in total abandon I emptied the contents of my stomach into the new fallen layer of snow.

Breakfast at Champneys that morning was a quiet affair for me, a bit of dried bread that tried to pass itself off as toast and a black coffee. However, it seemed that the rest of the world was determined to make as much noise as possible. Grendel wandered in coughing and hacking much like he did every morning but today he seemed to have adjusted the pitch slightly and it really got to me. He dropped a breakfast platter on to the teacher's table with uncalculated indifference and grinned at me.

"Morn'in Fawk'in," he said through his broken teeth.

Before I could nod even the semblance of an acknowledgement, that damned dog started yapping somewhere from beneath the folds of the teacher's voluminous skirts. You would have thought that the sound would have been muffled and perhaps it was but there it was again that subtle change in pitch that seemed to go straight in and bounce around inside my head.

Then Grendel's mother dropped a pan or some other heavy, noisy echoing thing in the kitchen which in turn made Hengest yelp in fear or pain before bounding off through the breakfast room and out eventually into the snow where he stared barking furiously. He had the sound of a dog who really didn't like what had just been done to him but it didn't help my fragile state.

Groaning with a combination of aches and pains in knees and back, not to mention a dull ache somewhere in the vicinity of my kidneys, I got up once more and went outside into the snow. There I found Hengest eating the contents of my stomach, deposited earlier. It was a bit of a struggle not to offer him seconds. A couple of deep breaths and I wandered off into the village in search of some quiet.

I spent a wretched time wandering about and looking for somewhere to curl up and sleep. There were however no options that did not involve the likelihood of frostbite or hypothermia and I had no desire to return to the inn for the time being. This meant that I was reduced to wandering aimlessly about for best part of the morning, nodding greetings and pleasantries that I did not feel to those people who were out and about. To add to the sense of misery, it began snowing again towards the end of the morning and the wind picked up a bit and took the temperatures down even further.

Even walking about, my fingers and toes began to go numb, or at least they began to go numb only after they had passed through the nasty, prickly cold phase. My breath, condensing in my scarf froze into beads of ice adding to the misery and I discovered that my right boot had a stone or something in it that began to make me limp slightly. How it got it was anybody's guess but I wasn't going to attempt the manoeuvre for its removal as it would mean bending down (in itself a challenge to my vertebrae and the slippery cartilage between them) to remove the boot and then hopping around on one leg whilst I shook out the offending object.

Then of course there would be the additional pain of trying to replace my foot into the boot (already tight) and tying up the lace once more with numb and recalcitrant fingers and thumbs. I didn't even think about what it would do to my headache. No,

71

even thinking about the task made me wince. I put up with the hurt and the limp, after all what's one more little hurt in the great scheme of things?

By the time I returned to Champneys my foot hurt like I could not describe and I was limping badly. I was chilled to the core and shivering uncontrollably. My fingers and toes, as far as I could sense, did not exist unless I wriggled them. That then reminded me that they too hurt quite badly. I pushed at the main door to find it locked. That was a bit of a relief because it probably meant that I had been wandering about longer than I realized and that the lunchtime session had finished. Hopefully at least the inn would be relatively empty and with a serious bit of luck would be quiet.

I went round to the back and across the yard, past the remains of Hengest's breakfast and stepped in through the back door. Inside the usual waft of stale air and smoke and the relative warmth seemed almost comforting. This feeling was helped along by the darkness inside. I had never before noticed how bright snow could be when you were looking out at it through bloodshot eyes with a million cells screaming murder at you for poisoning them so badly.

Inside I made for the warmest, darkest spot I could find. This was on a dirty and tattered rug on the floor by the fire. I had to evict Hengest before I could claim it and this was done without any style by stepping on his tail. He yelped out of sleep and slunk off with his tail between his legs, his eyes fixed on me as he moved with a look full of malice and accusation. I didn't care. With only the barest of thoughts for vermin and parasites, I lay down, curled up and slept like a dog.

Bang! Something was happening. Bang! There it was again. It started in the unpleasant dreams that I was having but then it moved up a gear and entered waking life. Bang! I opened one eye to see Grendel's mother lying on her side hitting the huge bolts on the front door with a mallet. After a few seconds I realized of course that it was me on my side and that she was standing upright. Partly common sense told me this and partly the pain in the left half of my body. Why on earth she had to be doing this was a mystery to me other than as a vindictive attempt to prevent me from sleeping.

"Fawk'in," she said by way of greeting when she saw me getting up off the floor. She seemed to take it completely as normal that I should have been sleeping on the floor where the dog normally rested.

"You've woken up in time to drink, eh?" she added and then grinned when she saw the look that must have been on my face.

"Hah! Esa skegs i'nt it. Appen yu'sabin a cup of tea?"

This offer was unusually kind for Grendel's Mother and when she brought over to where I was now sitting it took all my presence of mind not to thank her for it.

"Esa good stuffa," I managed to growl at her.

She winked at me in reply.

It's pretty obvious to say that I drank nothing but tea that night, my last night at Champneys. I think I pushed the limit of my hospitality by asking for tea time and time again but it was hot and it was wet and it had no alcohol in it and slowly I could feel myself rehydrating. I spent most of the evening talking to Markel about the tale of the Fire Dancers.

He also seemed a little subdued and I noticed that he only drank ale and kept off the skegs, even when offered. I got him to go through the two styles of the tale in outline for the most part but occasionally in detail. He also added a few additional bits that either I had not remembered from his original rendering or that he had forgotten to tell on that night. He expanded also on the more sinister tale and gave me a few pointers on how to give it that added twist.

Having said that, he was pretty complimentary about my own effort of the previous night and pointed out that he had a mind to add some of my own bits to his version of the tale. You see, ever the tales grow and change and reform.

I considered this again as I walked away from the inn and the village on the road towards the Trellsgut Mountains early the next morning, having let myself quietly out of the back door before anyone arose. I had paid in advance for the extra night that I now no longer needed and I was up in time to argue the case with Grendel or his mother and to reclaim my deposit but of course, as was customary, no one else was around to give it back to me.

However, it didn't really matter in the great scheme of things. I had collected this somewhat enigmatic tale as I had intended to do. Indeed, I had gathered more than I intended for I had two tales rather than just the one and I felt that for once I had added my own contribution to the repository of knowledge that now sat within Markel's skegs-hammered mind.

Yes, I had spent more than I had intended to but then what was new in that. Yes, I had drunk more than I meant to or should have but again sadly, that was not novel either. It was also true that I was not really any nearer to my understanding of the lost nation known now as the Fire Dancers but to be honest I thought it unlikely to find enough information in one tale to do that task. I had a basic picture though and it gave me a sense of the loss of them and a hint of what might have become of some of them. I was looking now to expand on this on my visit to the Trellsgut where I hoped to find out a bit about why they seemed to have disappeared so utterly.

PART TWO
ON THE ROAD

II
Welcome's Tale

The journey to Trellsheim could have been a particularly arduous affair but in the event it proved, by good fortune, not to be. Once I had got myself down from the village onto the main road I was fortunate enough to be spotted by the driver of one the fairly infrequent ox wagons that crawled along the road from the towns in the south bringing spices and other goods to the north. Trellsheim was in fact the most northerly town in this part of the known world (and possibly anywhere else for that matter).

Although fairly remote and isolated, still it had a good population of fairly wealthy families as a result of the mining and stone quarrying that was carried out in the mountains nearby. The black marble from the area travelled as far south as Xandria where it was the main building material of the famous libraries there and the precious metals, especially the copper and zinc were almost legendary.

I had just got to the road and had started to walk as best I could along the frozen and rutted way with that determined yet sinking feeling that this was not a good idea. Even the thought of that extra (and already paid for) night in that filthy bed in Champneys began to seem appealing.

I hadn't walked very far when I heard the unmistakable noise of badly oiled axles squealing away somewhere behind me and hidden by a thicket of trees away south near the river. I carried on walking as there was nothing more guaranteed to be ignored than a walker standing by the roadside with a smug expression on his face that seems to say, *"Come on, you've got to pick me up. There's no one else around for miles."*

I added a little extra feeling to my trudging as I went, careful not to add too much for fear of appearing too contrived. After what seemed an interminable time and all the while the noise from the axles (which was in essence comparable to the sound of nails being drawn over a blackboard) getting louder and closer and less bearable, I heard the heavy breath and snorts of the oxen. This was my cue to turn around and when I did so I was greeted with the friendly, smiling face of the wagon driver peeping out from an assortment of scarves and other garments. These didn't fully mask the turban wrapped expertly round his head which had been white once but now, I suspect with a combination of spice and dirty rain, was heading towards limestone grey.

"Yallusc nashz qu'arta Trellsheem?" he yelled at me with a wave of his hand.

Ok, so I had no idea what he had said but he was smiling and he had said Trellsheim and the intonation was definitely that of a question. I wasn't sure of the language and certainly didn't speak it, whatever it was. I went for the obvious and replied with a weary (but not too weary) nod of my head.

"Yes. I am mate."

I refrained from adding anything resembling a question (you know the kind of thing, "it is far?" or "nice day for a walk isn't it?") because I did not want him to think that I might be asking for a lift and I had no idea whether he spoke my language anyway.

He had drawn up alongside me now but had not reigned in the oxen. These were creatures that it was best not to stop as you could never be sure of getting them started again until hunger drove them or the scent of a female ox in season energized them. He looked down at me still grinning and nodded (disturbingly he appeared to be nodding his head from side to side).

"Trellsheem qu'arte fashook, atcha. Binad'en Yallusc sheeman?"

He reinforced this by whacking the board on which he was sitting with his left hand. It took no language to recognize this as an offer of a lift and of this I was truly grateful.

"Yes indeed," I replied nodding eagerly.

I was still careful to omit the basic courtesies in normal speech because whatever nationality this trader was, we were still in the north and anyone travelling alone was likely to be armed.

With his help I climbed up onto the moving cart. I threw my travel bag into the back of the wagon and made myself comfortable on the bench next to him. I use the word 'comfortable' rather loosely in this context. There were two reasons for this. The first resembled a bundle of black cloths in the back of the wagon which moved when my day sack landed on it. From its now visible mouth and backed up by some large yellow canines and rich red tongue came a whining sort of a growl.

"Atcha, Yallusc sterpa na boursa," laughed the driver as he saw the growing look of alarm on my face.

Of course I had no idea what he had said. I kind of hoped that he had said something about me waking up his pet (and very tame) black bear. Of course he could equally have said, *"don't move or he will eat your liver."* Either way I decided to turn around and face front. That way if the first guess was true it made no odds and if the second was closer to the truth I would at least be keeping still and I wouldn't see death approaching.

The second and more obvious reason for discomfort was the simple fact that the bench was hard and badly planed and very cold. I was soon to realize as the miles passed slowly by, that the position just a few feet above head height from the cold ground was considerably exposed to the chill breeze that was blowing.

Once the driver had recovered from his fit of laughter over my discomfiture he held out his hand and rattled off a series of words at me that I took to be a formal greeting with his name somewhere in it, possibly a statement about his family and where he came from. Of course he could equally have been saying something about how far it was to Trellsheim, that it was too far to walk and that he would be happy to drive me there for twenty trupps. I felt slightly reassured that the latter was not correct as I had not heard the word 'trupps' in any of his speech so far. Curiously, he ended the whole matter with the word, 'Welcome'. This took me by surprise and as I shook his hand I repeated the word. It was more of a question really from my perspective.

"Ah, Welcome, Welcome," he grinned at me shaking my hand vigorously.

As he pumped my arm with his surprisingly warm hand, I told him my name. Just the one word, as I wanted to keep it simple for now. In reply he repeated it a couple of times followed by a couple of Welcomes. I began to suspect that this was in fact his name rather than a greeting so I said it again, this time more of an affirmation.

"Ah, Welcome, Welcome," his grin seemed to get wider and his dark eyes sparkled.

"Atcha, atcha! Yallusc...." he repeated the name that I had told him. He was still shaking my hand and I was beginning to feel the circulation in my fingers struggling but I didn't feel that it was appropriate to withdraw. Physical actions are pretty important when you are light on verbal communication. Fortunately, he also decided that was enough and with a couple of "atchas" and some lively nodding of his head from side to side

he slapped me firmly on the back and then stuck his hand back under the covers that were over his legs.

My next thought was, "Now what?"

I could see rolling out before me mile upon mile of slow plodding oxen, squeaking axles, the bitter chill air freezing me to the core, aching bones and so on. Don't get me wrong here. I wasn't ungrateful. The thought of a walk through the snow and the cold to Trellsheim was not appealing but it was still a good day's travel by wagon and it was seriously cold and it was only day time. At night the temperature would drop off the scale. I was equipped for it as I had planned for a two day walk but then I had intended to set up a camp well before dark and get a fire going. I had no idea what Welcome had in mind and it was clear that we would not get to Trellsheim until well after dark unless we stopped for the night sooner.

I decided that the first task was to pluck up the courage to reach back past the bear in the back and get some of my spare clothes and my tarp to keep me warm. With a slightly worried look at Welcome (who just grinned and shook his head from side to side) I extended my arm out over the muzzle of the (apparently) sleeping bear and let my fingers hook the loop of the day sack.

Of course I knew that to retrieve the clothes would involve dragging the sack back towards me and over the bear. I had visions of teeth and snapping snarling sounds, lots of blood and pain. Nothing for it though. My fingers gripped tight possibly for the last time under my own nervous control then the muscles in my arm tensed and I gave a pull at the loop.

I had hoped to lift the sack clear of the creature but I should have known that this was doomed to failure given that it was hard enough to lift the thing onto my back even in normal circumstances. In the event, the sack collapsed onto the bear which grunted in its sleep and opened its eyes briefly before closing them again with a petulant sounding growl.

79

"Ah! Ah sterpa na boursa," chuckled Welcome on the seat beside me as I hauled the sack over into the front of the wagon. It took a while to extract what I wanted as a result of the cold and my reluctant fingers and whilst attempting not to drop anything off onto the road. I didn't want to have to jump off to recover it. Soon I had wrapped an extra layer of clothes over my legs and had spread the tarp over the top of it all, wrapping it with difficulty and with some discomfort around my back also.

Welcome seemed to have forgotten about me now as me drove the cart, chewing casually with much the same motion as a ruminating cow. Occasionally this action would be interrupted as he spat the red saliva at the road to the side of him. On one occasion he must have seen me watching him for he stuck one hand under the cloth covering his legs covers and a small packet wrapped in leaves appeared from somewhere. (I didn't really like to think where.)

"Atcha!" he said as he offered the packet to me shaking it slightly with a motion that reminded me of a man offering a morsel to a dog.

"Atcha. Betel, Yallusc farshoom?"

I took the packet from him. It was hard and disturbingly warm. Unpleasant images crept from the darker corners of my mind snickering at me with the petulant sounds of a sleeping bear. I sniffed the contents of the packet. This was betel. I didn't really want it but I didn't want to offend and I was at last at a level of relative warmth and comfort so I cut a piece off with my knife and stuck it in my mouth. I wrapped the packet as best I could and handed it back to Welcome who grinned at me and thrust it back into the warm depths of his covers.

"Atcha."

"Thank you," was what I should have said but for safety I settled for a polite nod.

We sat then for a while in relative silence. That is the silence of a cart with dry axles and two flatulent oxen and I began to wonder once more how I was going to pass the next few hours whilst we headed slowly for Trellsheim. The biggest issue was the communication. We could not exchange much information using half a dozen words including our names, the exclamation "Ah", the word "boursa" which clearly referred to the bear, "betel" and "atcha" which seemed to be used for anything or any time when there was the risk of a pause in a sentence.

None of the words I had heard had given me any indication of the language or the nationality of my host. "Atcha" was used in a number of languages in the Ruardean continent but that was pretty vast. The darker skin coloration and the turban also gave me nothing significant to work with other than a greater than average probability on religion. However, I tended to avoid any discussion on religion as it had the habit usually of over exciting my temper with or without alcohol. His style of clothing was nondescript. Well to be precise, the phrase "style and clothing" should not really be used here, not when the phrase "tattered remnants that he had flung about him to keep out the cold" was sitting there looking at me with bright dark eyes.

A few more miles had passed by before I decided to try a few attempts to communicate with Welcome. I started with a simple question.

"Ruardean?"

Welcome looked at me and stopped mid-chew.

"Ruardean?" he repeated, *"Ru-ar-deyn"* he chewed around the word. *"Ru-ar... atcha,"* he said, returning to his more animated form of speech.

"Atcha, atcha! Na Ruardan na. Welcome Bours-an-vacors," he punched the air with his right fist and cried out *"Bours-an-alibat!"*

Now it was my turn to look quizzical. I assumed that he had just told me what his nationality or tribe or family was but it

unknown to me. That was a bit odd as I prided
y knowledge of geography and on the fact that I was
ravelled.

;-an-alibat?" I asked.

"Na," he nodded up and down vigorously, *"Bours-an-vacors,"* he repeated and then followed this by the same gesture and shout as before.

"Bours-an-vacors," I repeated with a small voice in my head telling me that I was sounding a little dense here.

His grin seemed to get even wider, if that was possible and he shook his head enthusiastically from side to side.

"Atcha! Atcha!" he repeated.

"Bours-an-alibat?" I asked again.

He looked at me and, for a second or two, I think he also thought I was being dense but then his face lit up. He put his right palm to the middle of his chest and nodded slightly and slowly in a formal manner. Briefly he looked almost regal.

"Bours-an-vacors," he said slowly and deliberately. Then with a swift action he reached down beside him on the other side of the cart and swept a viciously curved tulwar (that made my knife seem a bit like a tooth pick) into the air above his head.

"Bours-an-alibat," he cried in a voice that would have made me wrestle with my bladder had I not already met the man. His face took on a truly frightening expression as he waved the sword about menacingly in a circular motion in the air above his head.

"Atcha! Atcha!" I said. I was forced into the language in part out of surprise but if I'm honest mostly out of fear. Now I understood. Nation, tribe or family: Bours-an-vacors. War cry or challenge: Bours-an-alibat.

He placed the weapon back from where he had taken it. His face returned once more to the relaxed, smiling and ruminating mode that it had hitherto demonstrated. He nodded, smiling and sighing to himself as if in some private joke.

"Ah, atcha! Welcome!"

He sighed once more, his smile back on his face and went back into his own private thoughts.

At this rate I was going to need a much longer journey if I was going to get anything out of him. We both settled back into our own thoughts for what seemed like hours but which was in fact probably only minutes. There was nothing to break the monotony except when the bear in the back woke up and jumped off the wagon, disappearing into a thicket of trees. Apart from a brief moment of concern, I gave little heed to it and the driver gave even less. Some while later the creature came ambling back to us and climbed back on board. He settled down again and started licking around his muzzle and generally cleaning himself. There was blood and other bits in his fur but he looked relatively satisfied.

We travelled more miles and the sun was at last getting up high enough in the sky to suggest midday. I had been lost in my own thoughts: part tales long told; part fire dancers; and, part all the usual rubbish that just sloshes around and seems to pop up unwanted when you can't think of something else to keep it at bay. That is the bit I hate most about redundant time: all those unwanted thoughts. Past arguments and outstanding debts, bits of grief that really have no place in your life and which you try to keep locked away and under control. I was just running through a particularly unpleasant row that I had had with a publican once when I heard an odd but yet strangely familiar sound.

It was Welcome and he was humming a tune that I recognized from a long time past. What was familiar was that it was an old school tune that I used to be forced to sing in the interminable periods of Latin with the school's robust and rather fearsome headmaster. I used to mouth the song most of the time as he would pace up and down the rows of boys and bend down now and again to listen in as we stood in varying degrees of attention. Occasionally, his gown would sweep around and strike the head or shoulders of an unsuspecting child to yell, "sing up, boy" or "who's singing in that deep voice?".

If you think about it that was particularly cruel in a form full of boys whose voices were breaking and whose pimpled faces and sprouting hairs in all sorts of places were setting them up for some terrible anxieties ahead.

What really caught my attention was the fact that it was a Latin song. Welcome was not singing any of the words and it was a bit of a long shot but I thought it worth a try even though my spoken Latin was at best poor and my only real knowledge was a reading knowledge of the language.

"Cacatne ursus in silvis?"

This was a phrase that I had read once although I cannot recall the context. I hoped that I had said, "Does the bear shit in the woods?"

Welcome looked up and replied almost without thinking, also in Latin.

"The bear is presumed innocent until proven guilty."

"Atcha," I said, grinning and followed this up with the traditional question.

"So you speak a little Latin?" I asked, my attempt at Latin

The question was pretty facile; given he had already spoken to me in the language.

Again, Welcome replied formally without hint of smile or nod of head.

"I speak a Little," he replied.

This was probably more to the point. After all I had no idea if he spoke it fluently or just a little (which, of course, he had now confirmed).

This put a whole new complexion on the journey. Welcome's Latin was spoken formally and deliberately and he almost seemed to change personality when he spoke it, taking on a grander and more classical persona that once again, made him seem regal. My Latin was typical school-boy with the addition of a number of years reading in the classical texts of the libraries of Xandria. However, I just about managed to keep up with him and where I struggled, he kindly re-phrased the sentences for me.

Now that Welcome had a language to talk to me in, he seemed not to want to stop. He told me that he was Ursian which, apparently, was a tribe located in the Ural Plains of Sardek – one of the southern territories on the Ruardean continent. They were nomads who crossed the great sand sea on camels carrying spices and fine fabrics from the far-east and bringing these to the "barbari" in the north. Although traders, the Ursians were fairly warlike, hence the war cry when they declared their tribe and their favoured weapon of choice was the curved tulwar of which I had already become acquainted.

Welcome was in a period of apparent exile from the tribe or his family for some matter or other. He didn't expand on this and so I didn't press it and let him continue the flow of his own particular story.

He had left the Ural Plains over about a year ago and had travelled north initially with seven camels loaded with silks and certain rare spices. His first significant stop had been in Xandria where he revisited the libraries and spent several days searching out rare books in the many markets of the city.

I have to say that my interest levels went up a few notches as he spoke and I stored the matters of 're-visited' and the search for rare books for discussion later on. Like I said, I didn't want to interrupt the flow.

When he left Xandria, he had travelled many days along the straight stone roads of the Thalians until he reached the capital city. He had first traded most of his silks and spices and had then sold the camels in Thalia for (in his words) a small fortune and far more than the beasts were worth especially as one of them was on its last legs. He had bought a horse and cart for a pittance and had transferred what was left of his goods onto this. After a few weeks of rest and luxury in Thalia he moved on reluctantly up into the dark countries.

He sighed and commented that for barbarians they (the Thalians) were remarkably civilized. He didn't talk much about his experiences in the dark countries other than a few rather angry and fast spoken sentences including words such as vermin, savages & filth that I could not keep up with and, given his irritation at this point, didn't really want him to repeat. I was also reluctant to let him know that in this particular and apparently (to him) unsavory part of the world was the place that I called home.

It took him several months to traverse the various squabbling countries but at last he crossed the great river Flava. This, he emphasized, only after he had sold the cart on the one bank and had paid to have his goods transferred to barge to cross the river. On the northern shore be bought an ox wagon and two mangy, half- starved oxen. He leaned forward on his seat and smacked one of the fat oxen on the rump with the reigns.

"These oxen," he laughed in Latin

I thought that now was a good opportunity to mention the Libraries and to find out a bit about his search for books. So I asked.

It turned out that Welcome had spent a number of years previously studying jurisprudence in Xandria under the tutelage of a lawyer named Cronos. Now, for the avoidance of doubt, this was not just any Cronos, oh no. This was *The* Cronos. Cronos of Mar. Cronos the Law Giver. The man who wrote two of the greatest legal text books of the age: "Discourses on the ownership of my horse" and, "Catechisms for legal analysis". He had also been responsible for drafting the "Thirteen Rules of Pollicis" which provided the principle Legal Code for the fifteen Xandrian city states.

I had read the Discourses myself, albeit in translation, and held it out as one of the best works of political theory that I had ever met. Then, who am I to say? Still, I carried a copy of it in my pack everywhere I went together with a less known work of fiction that he wrote in his early days.

This man, this spice trader, had met him and had studied under him. It was incredible.

"What happened?" I asked in my faltering Latin, unable to contain myself.

Welcome started to explain how his father had known the family and had met with them and so on. All the usual networking and contacts and where usable, as much nepotism as could be tolerated. However, that's not what I meant so I asked again.

"I mean, what went wrong?" I continued, testing my Latin to it's limits.

"Oh nothing went wrong," Welcome replied with a smile.

"You see there was this girl with eyes like sapphires and rich dark brown hair that shone like copper when the sun caught it. Her breasts...."

Part of me didn't want to hear about her breasts. That seemed a bit too much information for the purposes of decency. Yet another part of me wanted to hear just a bit more, you know the kind of thing: skin colour; texture; odour; taste. Fortunately for decencies sake, he came to a sighing halt and disappeared off into his own thoughts for a few seconds.

"There was this girl. We fell in love. Her family was rich. My family was richer. They hated each other: her brothers threatened to emasculate me if I ever went near her again. We eloped and were married and she died in childbirth within the year. My family disowned me and my own brothers threatened to emasculate me if I ever came home again. Her brothers swore eternal blood revenge against me. I lost the sun in the heavens. Atcha!"

He sighed.

"I also gave up an apparently promising career as a legislator. At least that's what Cronos said to me the night I told him I was leaving. Actually, he shouted quite a bit, from what I recall, and it wasn't all necessarily the kind of language you would want to have recorded in a law book."

He stopped and smiled at me again. He had just rattled off the most appalling series of tragedies in the space of a few minutes and yet as he looked at me sitting there in his dirty clothes and rags with the less than white turban and his betel stained lips he looked for all the world as though he was at peace.

"Fickle fate, fuck's us all," he sighed in Latin.

This was crude but to the point, I guess and if anyone had a right to say it then if he had been through all that, it would be him. He made it sound almost philosophical.

My mouth must have been open for an unusually long time because firstly, Welcome rustled in his garments for the packet of betel to offer me and secondly, when I shut my mouth it clicked in a most unpleasant and loud manner.

"Cheer up," he said. "It could have been worse. I still have all my parts."

"Of course!" I thought grimly as I carved myself another piece of betel from the too warm packet.

VII
Of Books

Some of our time together was spent in what I thought was particularly agreeable discussion. Welcome told me about his interest in old books. Apparently, he had a number of fairly rare books hidden about his wagon in various places that were both secure from ingress of water or any other fluids (given the proximity of the bear) and from damage by animals (also relevant, given the proximity of the bear).

I guess that it might not exactly be considered as a prudent thing to say to a relative stranger, given that books, any books, could command serious money in the right quarters. However, Welcome didn't seem bothered and with a bit of thought, the sleeping black bear and the tulwar at his side were pretty good insurance policies.

He told me that, at his last visit to the markets around Xandria, he had picked up a couple of interesting books. The first of these was a Latin copy of Jonas the Strangler's Lives (and Deaths) of the Saints. I was not familiar with this work although the writer's infamy was well documented in literary circles. This psychopath had written several books on the lives and gruesome deaths of a number of holy men and women. He was known to have written with considerable style and passion having successfully stalked most of his subjects (and victims) for years before their eventual demise and elevation to the status of, in his opinion, sanctity. His literary reign of terror lasted some forty years or more before his own slightly random but certainly poetic end when he was gored to death by a rampaging bull in an annual bull-baiting festival in a minor town in Visigon.

When he mentioned the second book, Legenda Terrae Borealis, I felt a sense of real excitement. This was a rare text indeed – I had never seen a copy of "Readings of the Northern Lands" although I had heard of the possibility of its existence from catalogues in the libraries of Xandria. He told me that he had found it on a back street market stall and had paid almost nothing for it.

I hadn't yet told him of my interest in the subject given the fact that I was researching the tale of the Fire Dancers. This was partly because it was almost impossible to get a word out with by temporary companion and partly because I was not as outward going nor as casual with information as this itinerant spice trader.

Frankly, it wasn't the kind of text that I would have expected to find in an ox cart on its way to Trellsheim. Indeed, I doubted very much that there would even be a copy in that town's library, although I had been hopeful. In brief, it was a text that I never expected to come across but seeing my apparent enthusiasm for the book, he asked me if I would like to have a look at it. My Latin rendition of the phrase "*Does a fish have scales*" was as erroneous as it was enthusiastic.

I am not sure that Welcome understood me for he looked pensive for a while. Then he spat out his betel and took a small bag out of a pocket in his coat. I thought at first that this was the book but it looked a little small. When he handed it to me it was very light. He gestured to me to spit out my fresh piece of betel and then told me to put on the gloves that were inside the bag.

Although this was pretty sensible I found it to be highly incongruous. Here we both were sitting on an ox cart in the cold heading for Trellsheim, neither of us dressed particularly smartly and both seriously in need of a bath and yet he was asking me to put on what turned out to be a clean pair of white linen gloves. I pointed out that my hands were not exactly clean but he waved this away.

I put on the gloves and then looked at him. He seemed to take a minute, perhaps it was a last minute change of heart about showing me the book. I guess I would never know. Then he leaned back and prodded the sleeping bear, saying something harsh in his own language to it. It grumbled but didn't move so he prodded it again a little harder, repeating the words.

The bear growled petulantly and rolled over onto its other side and went back to sleep. Welcome rummaged around one handed in cloths and blankets that had been beneath the bear and pulled out a large leather sack. It was too heavy for him to lift one handed so he handed me the reigns and turned around to pick it up. I wondered what he expected the oxen to do other than to continue their leisurely pace along the road.

When he had it and was seated back on the bench, he took back the reigns and then grabbed a blanket from the back and threw it across my knees, presumably to cover my somewhat dirty tarpaulin. He then handed me the bag.

I untied the drawstring and took out the book. It was about one and a half hand spans high and a span in width. The cover was black and slightly battered. It appeared to be some form of leather. The spine was plain and had a slice taken out of it about a third of the way down. I don't know why but the shape cleanness of it reminded me of a sword cut. Carefully I felt the leather and then lifted the book to smell it. It smelt musty, like old libraries with a strong hint of bear.

"May I?" I asked.

"Of course, go ahead. It's vellum."

His eyes sparkled with delight as he watched me. I turned back the cover and tried to read the handwritten notes on the inside sheet but unfortunately they were in a language that I did not have. I looked at Welcome but he just shrugged his shoulders. I felt the pages. Even through the linen gloves I could feel the quality of the material. Handmade, not machine, heavy and smooth to the touch. The print was simple and unadorned giving the title, author and the year of publication, 1573. Good sixteenth century books were not rare but they were not that common. This really was a gem of a book.

On the next page there was a dedication of some sort. It read, "Caelum, non animum mutant, qui trans mare currunt.[7]" It was a quote from classical text although I could not recall the source. As I read it out, Welcome tapped his chest.

"Hic," he said and grinned at me.

Whilst it may have seemed appropriate to Welcome and his peregrinations, I could see no obvious link with the subject matter of the book, given that it was from what I understood to be an account of the tales and legends of the part of the worlds that we were now travelling in, an area singularly devoid of obvious access to the sea.

Carefully, I turned a few pages, not so much reading as looking at the pictures of the words. There was something inherently beautiful in the relative order and structure of the texts and the Latin seemed to add to this in a way that vernacular text did not. Phrases that seemed to come out of childhood washed past my eyes as I continued to turn the pages carefully and slowly. I found a couple of dead moths between some of the leaves but other than that the condition inside was pretty good. The book must be worth a fortune.

"How much did you pay for it?" I asked, forgetting my manners in my enthusiasm. In my culture as in many, it was considered as rudeness to ask the price unless you were buying.

Welcome didn't seem to mind and told me with obvious pride that he had beaten the seller down to fifteen Marques.

"Fifteen Marques," I gasped.

I didn't often have access to that kind of money. That in itself was to all intents and purposes a bit of a fortune.

"Ah, but I'll get at least sixty for it at the book fair in Menthos in the spring," replied Welcome with what sounded like calm assurance.

Around this point in time, I have to say that my view of Welcome had begun to change. There was clearly more to this itinerant trader than met the eye. No one I knew would part with fifteen marques for a book, let alone talk of selling it for four times as much. In fact, very few people I knew would part with any money for a book, not to mention a good few who couldn't even read a book in any language, never mind Latin. He had mentioned wealth but I had assumed that he had left it all behind. Well, perhaps not. Any thoughts I had of trying to buy the book from him stood up and walked away.

As he watched me, I went back to the contents page to see what information was available. There were a fair number of different tales, some of which were interesting and some of which were not so interesting in the current context. Frankly, had I the time, I would have read it cover to cover. However, for now I was fixed on one thought and that was to get as much out of this on the Fire Dancers as possible (if any) whilst I had the chance.

To my disappointment, there was nothing obvious in the chapter titles but a couple of them looked as though they might offer something and another chapter, titled "On Wolves" was so obscure that I felt that if I had time, I would have to look at it.

My concern now was whether or not Welcome would let me read some of it rather than just look at it. I couldn't just sit there and read it partly because it was rude and partly because I hadn't technically been given permission. After all, apart from the interest factor to me this was a rare and, if Welcome's comments were to be believed, a very valuable book. The act of reading, technically, was a threat to its value – which I have to say in passing is a very sorry state of affairs and of course calls into question the meaning of the word, value.

Fortunately, once more Welcome came to my rescue. I had already told him in passing that I was a Collector of Tales and obviously the book was of great interest to me for its contents as much as the fact of it.

"You will want to read some of that," he said. *"Much of it is a bit bland to be honest and rather disappointing for the content but you'll find that chapter on wolves useful, if you are looking for interesting stories about this part of the world."*

He paused and looked at me.

"Fire Dancers, is it?"

"*A good guess,"* I replied with a smile.

"Oh no it's not a guess," he replied.

"I shared a fire and food with a wagoner heading south last night. He told me about a Bard who had told a story of the Illuvaqu'e at an inn where he was staying and how the tale had surprised even the village story-teller. It nearly caused a riot by all accounts."

"Not exactly," I responded and then queried, *"Illuvaqu'e?"*

"The Fire Dancers," he answered.

"It's in the book. Go on, read. Read! In return perhaps you would be so kind as to tell me the tale that the wagoner heard. I do like a good tale and you have to admit that spending most of your life looking at the business end of an ox is not the most stimulating of pursuits for an unemployed and slightly under-qualified legislator. Besides, it saves me having to charge you thirty trupps for the loan of the book."

"Thirty," I started but then he winked at me.

The book really was an absolute gem. I didn't read the chapter on wolves first but rather skimmed a few different tales before settling on one in particular that at first didn't seem to have much in common with my current search but in the end did in fact offer a few interesting pointers.

The Latin was clear and well written and I had relatively little trouble reading most of it. Admittedly I had to skip a few passages and probably lost some of the literary value as a result but probably no more than the standard transcription errors that would have taken place across the ages as the tale had been handed down. After all, each story is like a living organism, constantly changing and evolving at micro-level. All it takes is an agent of change: in this case, me.

Sadly, allowing for the cold, the fact of conversation and occasions when I had to get down and help push the recalcitrant wagon up relatively gentle if slippery inclines, I only had time really to read a couple of the tales before we arrived at the outskirts of Trellsheim. Welcome wanted to camp outside the town walls for the night so that he could prepare his goods for sale the next day. Also, I suspect, he wanted to hear my tale. Listen to me already! I make a couple of additions and a story that has been sloshing around in the wilderness for centuries suddenly becomes my tale. It sounds a bit like theft, even to my ears.

We arrived at a camp outside the town walls just as it was getting dark. Already there were about a couple of dozen other wagons at the site and here and there could be seen the smoldering beginnings of their camp fires. We drew up a distance from the other groups and Welcome explained a few points of etiquette among travelers as we secured the wagon and set up his camp for the night.

Apparently it was not considered acceptable to draw up too close to another wagon. In the first instance, the oxen tended to fall out with each other and in the second, it tended to restrict the space for a fire if one was to be made.

Whilst there was a general tolerance exhibited amongst the wagoners in terms of nationality, colour, creed and so on, they did not tend to talk to the lone riders and the stage wagons. Itinerant players and other entertainers were also shunned unless they were either good looking or the wagoners had been a long time in the wilderness, if you get my drift. They avoided the itinerant religious orders as though they were the plague.

They did however engage in some intercourse with some of the smaller scale travelling sellers (which included tinkers and travelling blacksmiths) as they tended to have a possible service value at some time in a journey.

The only group of people that it seemed that no one dealt with, so Welcome informed me, were inhabiting a small collection of wagons and occasionally a brightly painted caravan clustered together at one end of the encampment.

"We don't speak with them for any reason," he muttered quietly, sounding strangely intense about it.

I was about to ask why when he added an afterthought, "We don't even look at them! They are not there."

Now that didn't make a lot of sense to me as they were obviously there away from us in plain sight. Of course, you know how it is when someone says, "Don't look," You just can't help yourself can you?

Well I couldn't and my eyes caught those of a good looking woman of perhaps forty years with dark hair that was tied up in a tight bun. She had a heavy jumper and plain woolen skirt that should have hidden the size of her breasts and the shape of her hips but did not. The eyes that looked back at me were dark and inviting and wickedly intense.

I mean this in a purely sexual sense. It was a bit raw, for want of a better term and I was disturbed to find that blood was being shifted about my body without my permission. My cheeks were radiating a heat that I hadn't previously noticed and I found it necessary to make a quick adjustment in my nether regions to prevent any embarrassment. (Although, as I have remarked before, my clothing and physiology probably mitigated against that.)

"Tch," clicked Welcome as he stepped between those eyes and me, "we have nothing to do with those people!"

He was surprisingly earnest and he got my attention. I could feel myself deflating on several levels. Still, in the back of my mind there was this growing voice asking too many questions about these strange people and about this utterly fascinating woman. Welcome didn't explain who these people were and in all the excitement of that evening, I didn't get around tov asking.

By definition the camp was a polygot affair with people and languages of several variations being available. Generally, the language spoken amongst wagoners was that of the location but for those who could not speak it, or where circumstances were more suitable, they had their own particular language which they spoke only amongst themselves.

I had heard of this but had no knowledge of it and Welcome, although informative on almost all things, was clearly not prepared to share this with me. I have to say that from my brief stay at the camp (strangely enough my first ever in any such camp) all I managed to pick up was that it involved a mixture of various open or clandestine hand and body gestures and some guttural sounds that appeared to have no words in them at all.

However, it seemed to serve them well for in the time that I was there I saw one potential knife fight and a dispute over one of the camp whores (a pretty but sad looking lad of about sixteen years) diffused by a series of these guttural exchanges and gestures. Sadly enough, I did understand the basic thrust of the argument about the boy.

Welcome also advised me not to use Latin in the camp and also pointed out that he would be using his own native language and gestures to communicate with me whilst there. I was a bit non-plussed about this, particularly if he wanted me to tell him the tale of the Fire Dancers.

"Don't worry," he replied, "just use the vernacular. You can tell them all here (he meant the wagoners)."

"But you..." I started.

"Speak it perfectly well," he continued, adding as if in answer to my raising eyebrow, "Well you have to be cautious about strange old men that you meet on the road."

He smiled without a hint of embarrassment.

I asked him about the Latin issue and he told me that it was, after all, the language of scholars and was treated almost as a secret language by many. Both issues were the kind of matter to give rise to suspicion in the camps. It also gave the impression of learning and therefore wealth which he suggested was not a good thing to suggest in a camp full of hungry itinerants with barely a hundred trupps to their name. He drew his finger across his throat and grinned.

The last point made good sense to me but I thought it a bit rich for a community with a secret language made up of grunts, weird hand gestures and a few pelvic thrusts to consider Latin a subversive language (and by implication, shifty). However, I kept that thought to myself along with the fact that I actually fell into the category of hungry itinerants with barely a hundred trupps to their name.

I thought that I could help Welcome as best I could at first by trying to do what looked obvious. The problem was that nothing actually looked obvious to me. I had no idea what had to be done with the oxen. Presumably they needed feeding but I could see no sign of anything that they could eat. Also presumably they needed taking out of harness but the thought of trying to do that and getting trampled for my pains, really took any enthusiasm out of me. As initiative had fallen away dismally, I resorted to asking Welcome if I could do anything to help.

"Atcha," he replied loudly, *"yallusc sterpa aurachal."*

I looked at him blankly until he followed this up under his breath.

"See to the oxen. There are bales of straw at the north end of the camp. Go and grab a couple of those and bring them back. They are provided by the Town Authorities and are free."

He spat.

"Well, they are free to those who are about to pay their extortionate Gate Duties to enter the town."

I nodded and stared to walk away but he yelled after me.

"Yallusc sterpa na rauca!"

Then under his breath, *"don't catch any bugs!"* adding, *"the bales are heavy."*

IX
A Tale Of Bugs

I made my way to the north end of the camp, picking my way carefully across the mix of rutted, frozen ground and the all too frequent troughs of water and other liquids (and substances). I tried to look purposeful but I knew that I was being watched by every pair of eyes that checked ox harness or loosened saddles or was doing anything else in the camp that didn't involve looking the other way. No one spoke to me, neither word nor gesture on the first part of my journey.

I had no idea why Welcome had shouted out about the bugs. I assumed it was either some kind of joke or one of those meaningless phrases that people often use as a parting. The comment became clearer after I reached the bales.

The bales were heavy, so I could only carry one at a time and of course that meant another long walk through the watching eyes of the camp. I hoisted one onto my shoulder and headed off back to Welcome's wagon. The straw smelled mouldy although it was surprisingly dry and it made me itch. The sensation began almost as soon as the bale was on my shoulder and it got progressively worse as I walked. I desperately wanted to scratch but I had both hands supporting the weight and a small boy inside my head told me not to put the bale down for fear of looking weak. I carried on, traversing ruts and rivulets, the old man inside my head shouting at me to put the bale down and have a good scratch.

I thought at first that it was either the dust in the straw or perhaps the straw itself – I had a mild allergy to grass and so expected that possibility. The reality however told me the meaning and significance of the phrase "sterpa na rauca".

Something small and prickly crawled into my hair and made its way across that part of my head where the hair was thinning.

When I say small, I mean relatively small. It was not for example the size of a louse as I wouldn't necessarily have felt it. Nor was it the size of a mouse for example. But it was somewhere in between and I had a horrible feeling that it tended nearer to the mouse than the louse. I twitched and made an involuntary movement to drop the bale and get at the creature but at the same time I noticed five and a half pairs of malevolent eyes watching me and six nasty looking mouths all grinning at me in a way that was not comforting. For a tiny part of a second, man and boy exchanged arguments in my head. The boy won and so the bale remained on my reluctant shoulders.

I determined to carry on despite the unknown creature in my hair. I hoped that it didn't bite or have any nasty attributes like stinging, poisoning or infecting. That was before the next two clearly separate prickly things started moving in my hair. It took all my self control and a bit that I didn't know I had, to refrain from a squeal of horror. By now I couldn't drop the bale if I wanted too. My hands and arms flatly refused to accept any messages from a central processing unit that was only a few millimeters from those prickly and scratchy unknown creatures.

The wagoners who had been grinning at me were laughing openly now and calling and gesturing to others as they watched my discomfiture. I also heard a few familiar terms, "Faw'kin farners" was one of them but I have to say that I wasn't particularly focused on these. From my own experiences in the past I knew that to lose face in front of some of these brutes was dangerous and so my only option was to carry on.

My resolve was tested one more time when one of the creatures started to move down the hair on my neck. At this point I attempted a slap, quickly talking my hand away from its task of supporting the bale. I missed whatever it was and the bale wobbled precariously. This in turn caused me to lose my footing on a rut and I slipped into the oily mixture of liquids that were spread about the area. The most unpleasant aroma wafted up into my face and in normal circumstances this might have caused me to retch. These were not normal circumstances.

It is difficult to be picky about the things that make you sick when there are large (yes I think, with good reason, that I can claim that they are damned well large as far as I am concerned) creatures crawling about your upper body just out of your vision. I wondered briefly and somewhat objectively whether that was deliberate on their part.

With considerable effort I got back to Welcome's wagon and threw the bale down in front of one of the oxen. Welcome wasn't about so I had no option but to go back for the other bale and to run the gauntlet of wagoners and others one more time. First, however, I had to sort out the movement. I reached up with both hands and pulled out of my hair two large brownish beetles. They were pretty tricky to get out as they held on tight with their spiky little feet but after a bit of a struggle I got them out together with several strands of my grey hair. I held them in front of my eyes by their carapaces and they wriggled their twelve spiked feet in the air like clockwork toys.

Apart from being larger than the average infestation they looked pretty harmless. In fact they looked rather comical. Vaguely like the stag beetle from my own country. I flipped them onto their backs, still holding them the same way. They wriggled their legs just the same. Although I had every intention of wreaking havoc on whatever it was that had boarded me, I have always had a soft spot for beetles so I placed them back on the bales of straw.

That was a mistake. As soon as they touched the straw they started to wave about the pair of formidable pincers that they had on the head. They looked quite threatening now and then to make matters worse they gave off the most appalling stink. The ox, whose meal had just been immolated by these creatures, looked at me out of one doleful eye as if to say, *"Have you just farted over my food?"* That seemed a bit rich from a creature whose only form of intercourse with its human colleagues was the near constant escape of gas from its business end.

I was now contemplating the removal of the beetles from the bale. I didn't want to go for the bash-em-with-a-stick approach as I didn't particularly like killing things – even offensive little creatures like these that had even less sense of personal space than some of the indigenes of these parts. I decided on the flick-em-into-the mire-and let-em-take-their-own-chances option as somehow I felt less culpable for their demise (should it transpire). I watched them struggle in the oily surface tension for a second or two before they dipped beneath the surface and were gone without a trace.

"Itchy and scratchy little beast," said Welcome under his breath in Latin as he brushed past me lifting the third creature from my back and crushing it in under his boot. Then out loud for the benefit of the onlookers.

"Rauca festoor 'n da!"

He placed his boot in the patch of filth that I had dropped my own two bugs into. This was more symbolic than real gesture as I doubt that he actually managed to crush the two hapless creatures that I had probably already drowned.

He beckoned to me to follow him to the back of the wagon where he produced a small unlabeled bottle. He shook a quantity the greasy mixture from the bottle into his hand and then rubbed them both together vigorously. He motioned me to bend forward and then he rubbed his hands in my hair. There was a stinging sensation on parts of my head (where I suspect the beasts had scratched me) and then the pungent smell of fish. It was *feshstynkas bru* of course.

"It'll keep any more away," Welcome muttered quietly.

I wondered a little petulantly why he hadn't put the stuff on before I picked up the first bale but then he wasn't my keeper and it wasn't really his concern. As I walked back for the next bale I realized that Welcome had seemed a little different. It occurred to me that he had been a bit tense and his eyes had been looking about a lot as if checking or looking for someone or something. Then I considered that I hardly knew the man so maybe it was normal for him around crowds of other people or just maybe he was irritated at having to wet nurse me.

I collected the second bale with no further bug problems and a disinterested partial audience of betel spitting wagoners who watched me absently from their wagons as I passed. Interesting that generally they had same look and facial expression as their oxen. Even their eyes seemed to be closer to the side of their heads than was normal. Their heads (that is man and ox) followed me for a while as I passed them by, returning to what appeared to be a natural ruminating pose (for both parties) after about a couple of minutes.

Welcome told me that he had arranged for me to tell the tale of the Fire Dancers at the camp fire of one his fellow wagoners about three or four wagons way to the east. He said that there would be an audience of about a dozen but in the end it was nearer thirty. They were fairly attentive and there were few interruptions. I told my rendition, including the wolves. There were some open mouths at the end and a few expletives but no one tried to stab me so I rated the tale as a success.

Welcome woke me early next morning whilst it was still dark. The camp fires were out but everywhere people were moving about, checking harnesses and securing goods in the wagons. I could hear some children playing and laughing somewhere out in the darkness. There was a sense of excitement all about: like a holiday perhaps.

Welcome explained that the town gates opened at dawn, which was about an hour away and that it was important to get into the town early. The first reason was that the Gate Duties were discounted for the first hour after dawn and then got progressively more expensive as the day passed. He explained that the theory was that the less you could afford, the earlier you would get up. Those who could afford to lie in and wait or who stayed at the nearest village inn and travelled on could afford to pay more. I reminded him that the nearest village inn was Champneys, almost a day away and suggested that didn't really think that anyone with any serious money would pay to stay there. He looked at me as though I had missed the point.

"*Did you see all the rooms at Champneys?*" he asked.

"*Well no, I guess not,*" I replied.

"*Did you see the annex?*"

"*What annex?*"

"*Exactly. There you have it. There is more to that place than meets the eye.*"

Well that had me stumped. I had been there three days, seen nothing special or exceptional. I had seen nothing even hygienic let alone luxurious. Then it occurred to me that the teacher always looked clean and tidy and that I had never seen her in the wash house. Then come to think of it, did the tax collector stay in a room as filthy as the one that I shared with Maucum? Somehow I doubted it.

As I was mulling this over, I noticed that Welcome looked different. For a start he was wearing a clean white turban and beneath a cleanish looking thick woollen cloak I could see another white garment. His feet were no longer booted and he wore lightweight open sandals that seemed totally out of place in the snow. He was also clean shaven and looked well washed and groomed. He looked classical.

How he had achieved this transformation in the filth and grubbiness of the camp amazed me and I felt a twinge of guilt at my own shabby demeanour. The word 'barbarian' crept into my mind as I scratched the now five-day old stubble on my face and

105

surreptitiously sniffed in the direction of my armpit to determine the extent of the offence. By the state of my hygiene alone, Welcome would have known that I came from the dark countries.

A noise behind me made me turn around and there was the black bear sitting on his haunches with a red sash tied around his neck. His hair looked sleek and groomed and to make the point further, the beast started to groom its face. As he moved I caught a whiff of perfume.

"You groomed and perfumed the bear?" I said. It was part question, part exclamation."

"Atcha," Welcome replied, *"Novata boursa,"* he grinned back at me.

In my head, my mother's voice was berating me for my lack of hygiene. I felt like a dog. If I was capable, I would have howled.

We reached the gates within the hour and in time to pay the discounted Gate Duties. As we had approached, I started rummaging in my purse for some coin but he pushed my hand aside with a smile.

"It's not necessary," he said in Latin.

At first, the Gate Wardens were surly and offensive to him. This was not, I think, because he was Ruardean, they were probably rude to everyone more or less in equal measure. As we approached I heard a muttered exchange that was deliberately not a private conversation.

"E's a Ruad'n bastard in't 'e?"

"Why 'es one a'right. All that teeka marsala and chapartee stuff and all."

"Why there's a fawkin farner too. Ja bas!"

The last comment was directed at me and I considered this. The only direct insult had been thrown at me not the Ruardean and I was more or less their neighbour of sorts by geographic comparison. Then again, there were some pretty hefty laws against racial and religious discrimination in this part of the world, so perhaps they had opted for a safer attack. Discrimination against me was neither racial (sadly as I was like them 'barbari') nor religious as I was as much a believer in the old gods as I suspected they were.

Welcome drew the cart to a halt and looked down at the Wardens. He spoke to them in Latin, despite his comments to me in the camp the night before. As he spoke he brought his hands up to his face, bowed his head and then drew them away again. As he did so, he brushed against the right side of his cloak, exposing the white robe that he wore and the curved tulwar that I noticed he now had strapped to him in a bright and expensive looking scabbard.

"How much have I got to pay to you bastard sons of goats to enter your filthy little hovel here on the edge of nowhere?" Welcome asked politely in perfect Latin.

Whether it was the language or the tulwar I could not tell (I suspect it was the latter) but the effect on the Wardens was impressive. They sort of stiffened to a kind of rigidity and grew a few inches in height from their previous slouching position. When they asked for (not demanded) twenty trupps they added the word, "Sur" which in these parts is a courtesy afforded to the nobility or to warriors.

Welcome's olive coloured, manicured and clean hand dropped the heavy coin down into the dirty upheld paws of one of the wardens and when he offered back one coin.

"There's too much 'ere, Sur".

Welcome waived it away with a smile. The coin travelled with surprising speed down into a pocket.

PART THREE
INTO TRELLSHEIM

X
Trellsheim's Story

As the ox wagon followed the other wagons ahead of it up the gentle incline away from the gate, I got my first view of Trellsheim. I hadn't seen much of the town as we had approached it, partly because it had been dark at first. Then as we drew nearer the walls, which were unusually high, tended to obscure much of what was within.

The central road from the gate was quite narrow with only two lanes for traffic: one up and one down. The lanes were rutted by design so that the cart wheels fitted into the grooves and ensured that traffic moved in an orderly and safe manner through the relatively narrow streets. I wondered what happened to wagons that didn't fit the design but in the event, I didn't see any in my whole time in the town. Beside and between the lanes were areas for horses and walkers to move around and this looked to be a less organized affair as there was no clear 'up' or 'down' route.

Although early in the morning, the road was chaotic and packed and very noisy. On either side of the road were houses, official looking buildings and here and there an inn. These were built in the early modern style mostly, being big beams and uprights of black wood and in-filled with some form of mortar. Each of the three or four storeys overhung the previous by about two feet so that there was a sense of enclosure about the whole area. At certain points along the road, there were arched constructions across the road to the buildings opposite which appeared to be both functional and structural.

There were few windows in most of the buildings with almost none at ground level. Generally, these were small with small panes of glass, usually leaded. The windows in the high arches, however, seemed particularly large. Large enough for a person to fall through, I thought. I recalled that one of the less savory aspects that the town was known for was its underworld. The standard method of criminal assassination was by defenestration. This was unknown anywhere else in the northern world.

Looking up at the floating arches above, I could see the sense of it (as it were). I was also pretty sure that such defenestrations were unlikely to take place at this time of day on the basis that the victims fall would probably be broken by the heaving mass of humanity, oxen and goods wagons in the streets below.

The houses opened onto the road with no form of pavement and I saw that such doors were unusually stout and reinforced for buildings that lay within a town wall. There was very little snow on the ground here, a lot of slush and a foul smelling rivulet of liquid and solids running in two small gullies on either side of the road. Sitting some six to eight feet above it on the ox cart, the stench was appalling. It must have been breath-taking at pedestrian level.

Welcome had been completely silent as we travelled slowly up from the gate and I noticed that he had stopped chewing betel and had drawn a scarf across his mouth and nose. I could just about smell a perfume above the reek. It was similar to that on the bear. The bear was also silent and, unusually, it was not curled up asleep but sat upright and alert in the back just behind Welcome.

"Barbarians! Look at all this filth. In my country we have our excrement run in pipes beneath the surfaces to take it away from habitation. It is unclean and a sin against god to behave like this," he muttered in angry Latin to me.

At least, I think it was addressed to me although it seemed to be to the world at large or perhaps just an escaping angry thought. For my part, I briefly wondered where the channels carried all the sewage. I left the thought at that and decided to rummage in my pack for a scarf to cover my own mouth because I could sense that my breakfast was getting a bit rebellious in my stomach.

Once I had recovered a suitable garment cautiously from the pack beside the bear, Welcome offered me a small bottle of a clear liquid that smelled of roses and jasmine. I sprinkled some onto the scarf and offered the bottle back.

"Keep it, my friend. You will need it here and I have plenty more."

I thanked him and slipped the bottle into my day sack. I had never owned a perfume and, if I am honest, I was a little pleased to receive such a gift.

Eventually the road leveled and opened out onto a large central square. The houses followed the edges so that the effect was of a flat space the size of a small arena into which, it seemed, the human and bovine contents of the entire northern world was pouring like effluvia. Here, the snow still lay in small, shallow drifts and I noticed that the channels of sewage had actually disappeared. This was, presumably, because we were on top of a reasonable sized hill now and everything other than human activity was flowing the other way. This gave the whole expanse a much more wholesome feel.

This, Welcome told me, was the central market and this was where he was going to set up his stall. I noticed that the ruts that channeled the movement of carts and wagons had smoothed out now so that vehicles were free to move in any direction. I was surprised at the relative lack of chaos as wagons and carts started to make for what seemed to be known and recognized pitches.

That is not to say that there wasn't a bit of tension here and there. I saw one knife fight erupt between the men in a hide wagon and a rather thick set looking brute carrying eggs and cheeses. We didn't wait to see the outcome but a number of wagoners had stopped to watch and from what I could tell, were placing bets on the winner.

Welcome brought the cart to a halt and a spot that seemed to be almost as near to the centre of the square as was possible. The centre itself was marked by some form of memorial. It was some kind of miner with brutish arms a pick and a lantern all cast in a dirty looking bronze. Welcome's wagon drew up alongside it at its base.

"This will be my home for the next few days," he said, "and sadly here we must part for I need to set up the stall and get both myself and the bear cleaned up."

I wondered how much cleaner he, and indeed the bear, could get but I let that thought go.

"If you need me at all over the next few days you will find me here. That is unless of course I am trading at another stall or fulfilling a call of nature, but on those occasions don't worry, just ask the bear," he grinned at me.

I thanked him for his kindness and asked if I could help him set up or anything. He declined saying that it was best he did it all alone. Once the merchandise started moving, the bear got a bit possessive of anyone other than the trader. He told me that he had had one unfortunate incident a couple of years ago where the creature took a large chunk out of the shoulder of a well-meaning but foolish man who insisted on being helpful.

I knew it. All along I had been sitting near the beast and all along in the back of my mind both man and boy were yelling, "danger – wild animal," and I had been arrogant enough to ignore it. Still luck had smiled upon me and I was mercifully in one piece.

We shook hands, which to be honest, Welcome looked unhappy to do – no doubt the fact of my state of hygiene now that he had cleaned up for the market - but he did it anyway. His hand was warm and soft and he squeezed mine lightly and quickly. Then he took a step back and gave me a slight bow, which I took to be the parting of his homeland. He accompanied the gesture with some words that I did not understand and which were melodious and pleasant to the ear: easy to recall.

At first I took these to be a parting in his native tongue but later I was to find out that this was not so. It was a prayer. I asked once more if there was anything I could do to thank him or to repay him for the kindness that he had shown to me but he just smiled. I turned and had begun to walk away when I heard him call out behind me.

"*Atcha! Atcha. I had almost forgotten,*" he called. "*This is for you.*"

He handed me a parcel wrapped in waxed paper and smelling vaguely of rose water and lemons. The waxed paper was dusted in a coating of white powder, which I later found to be a form of sugar, although why that should be was beyond me. I took the package. It was heavy like a book.

"*It's not,*" I said as a hopeful realisation dawned on me, "*I couldn't,*" I trailed off, not really meaning it.

"*Yes you can. I have read it,*" he replied with a smile that accompanied the obvious lie.

"*But you said it was worth a fortune. I couldn't possibly,*" I trailed off again. I really didn't mean what I was saying but I just couldn't accept this gift.

"*No. Take it. I have more,*" he said, "*and I would probably only get forty marques at best for this forgery.*"

He winked and then laughed at the look on my face.

"*Well, no, it's not a fake actually but let's leave it at that shall we. Take it in return for the story. You will find it interesting.*"

What could I do? The boy said to keep it. The man said to give it back (but I knew that he was lying because the sale of this thing alone would keep my family for a whole season). I laughed, embarrassed and thanked him. With nothing to offer him in return I felt foolish (that would be the boy) and churlish (the man) in equal measures. I hugged him and patted him on the back. I couldn't help it was an involuntary reflex from bringing up children. He smelled clean and fragrant: beautiful, I would say. I must have smelled rank. He relaxed into the embrace, squeezed my shoulders and then stepped away.

"*Take care.*"

Those were the last words that I heard from him. I made my way across the wide expanse of the market square without incident, clutching the sweet smelling parcel in my hand. I felt a little guilty and a lot of pleasure at the gift. Admittedly, I wasn't sure now if it was a genuine copy or a fake but I'm not sure how important that was. The contents alone were invaluable and in a sense it didn't really matter if it was worth fifteen Marques or a hundred and fifty. After all, I wasn't planning to sell it. Well not right now at any rate.

The first task was to find a base that was comfortable and that I could afford: preferably somewhere with a bath. The inns and hostels along the market square looked a bit expensive on the western side and the ones on the eastern side that I had noticed as we came into the square had looked a little basic, if not rough. I decided on a standard tactic. Find the expensive hostels first and then get into the backstreets behind them for some of the better quality inns.

There were plenty of people milling about and so, despite my earlier thoughts on crime, I didn't have too many concerns about disappearing into some of the quieter lanes and alleyways that ran off the market square. Besides it was quite light now and with the snow on the ground, even where it was melting in the water dripping from the eaves, there was a general lightness about.

After a few abortive attempts I found a tidy little inn about three hundred yards further uphill west from the main square. The Sun Inn was the name on a rather neat sign painted outside with a once bright yellow sun painted in traditional style: a pointy star with a bright smiley face. However, this smiley face was winking.

Inside there was a young lad behind the bar, I guess about mid-twenties with a series of rings through his left ear and his nose. He was neatly dressed and although his clothes were old, they looked very clean. He was wiping a clean cloth over the even cleaner looking oak surface of the bar as I walked in.

"*Morn'en,*" I offered as he looked up at me.

"*Mornin,*" he replied.

This enabled me to recalibrate my dialect slightly and gave me an even greater sense of optimism about the quality of the place. The spectres of Grendel and his Mother started to amble off into the dark passages towards the rear of the building.

"'*Appen you've a bed?*" I asked.

"*For t'night?*" he queried.

"*No indeed. Ffor five nights or more,*" I answered.

By way of response, he reached down behind the bar and brought up an old book with a battered cover which he opened and consulted. Running an immaculately clean finger down a page half filled with tiny neat handwriting he came to a halt alongside the number fifteen – today's date – followed by another number, seven.

"*I've got room seven free for six nights and nothing else,*" and then added,"*you got a mate with you?*"

Ah, I thought, as the all too obvious penny dropped. "Mate" was a term for a partner but unless I was mistaken was used for partners of the same sex.

"*No,*" I replied trying to sound nether shocked nor too casual. This had all the makings of a good stay and I didn't want to screw it up, literally as well as figuratively, by appearing either too sanctimonious or too available.

"*But it'll have hot water for sure, no?*" I added in an effort to move away from my sexual preferences.

"*As a dog's got flees,*" he replied with a smile, "*all the rooms 'ere 'ave hot water, my boy!*"

"*Ah for sure,*" I replied with perhaps a little too much enthusiasm.

"*This smells good,*" I said sniffing the parcel that I was holding, "*but I stink of stuff, no?*"

I was mindful of the heavy dousing of feshstynkas bru that I had received the previous night to ward of those bugs. In fact, I wasn't entirely sure that those very same bugs hadn't propagated themselves unknown to me in my hair or clothes. In the back of my mind a grim little voice added "or skin" with a nasty little snigger. I chose to ignore that although I couldn't suppress an involuntary shudder.

He looked at me a little distastefully, for which I have to say that I was grateful if for no other reason than that it moved him away from any sexual interest in me – I hoped. Then he brightened up and sniffed.

"Well, I can smell flowers and something else," he said and sniffed again.

"Roses I reckon," he sniffed once more.

"Ah me," he exclaimed almost clasping his hands together, *"It's Jasmine!"*

Once I had worked out what he was on about, I took out the bottle of perfume from my pocket and showed him. He took it from my hand almost with reverence.

"O it's a beauty! And it's a glass bottle as well," he sniffed the stopper.

"Do you want some of it?" I offered, hoping that it wasn't taken the wrong way – well actually both wrong ways. It was the first perfume that I had owned in my life and I wasn't offering to give it to him, nor was I offering him anything else, as it were.

I didn't need to worry, he opened the stopper and dabbed a bit on the tip of his finger and then wiped it behind his ears. He then used a different finger (in this world that is seriously focused on hygiene, believe me) and tipped a tiny drop onto this and wiped it across his throat. He popped the stopper back and smiled a smile of genuine pleasure.

"That's truly kind of you, thank you."

I was shocked. I tried not to show it but I couldn't help it. This was a deliberate breach of etiquette in these parts and one I

116

worked hard not to fall foul of. He must have seen my disquiet for he added, in a slightly harsher tone.

"We use bruta speak here don't we? Well we don't have to behave like brutes as well. Thank you is as thank you does, so to speak. There's nothing wrong with a little politeness whatever the rest of the world thinks!"

Then, changing the subject he added, *"It's a gift from a mate, eh?"*

"O crap," I thought, "we're back to my non-existent partner."

I decided to try another approach and by that way, if necessary, make myself less available.

"It was a parting gift. He's a Ruadean."

It was probably a mistake and I had no doubt that it would return to savage me, but it seemed to work well. His face took on a sympathetic look and he smiled.

"Ah, the ways of love eh, the ways of love," he sighed.

That was the end of that conversation.

I got the room for ten trupps a night all in, which I was pretty pleased with. The room as I guessed it would be from the state of the bar itself, was immaculate. In fact, so much so that I took my boots off before stepping over the threshold. My host had taken me up to the room and I could see that he appreciated the gesture, even though one look at my socks could have told him that he was probably better off with the boots. He gave me the key and explained how the late latch worked in case I was out in the town – which from the wink that he gave me probably was a euphemism for having sex in the courtesan quarter – and after showing me proudly around the place, left me on my own.

The first thing that I did was run a bath. I feel that I need to point out a couple of things here, just to set all this in perspective. The world in which we live here is pretty basic and is a bit light both on amenities and in a lot of cases, the basics that some might consider standard for a civilized modern society. For example, the only forms of power available to us in the northern marches were wood, club moss (a poor form of coal), peat and sphagnum and where luck and geothermal vents existed, the planet itself.

Things were a little different in some of the southern lands and in the more organized and developed city states such as those in Xandria, Heros and Gypeta. Here there was also the technology of antiquity which had been passed on and honed to near perfection. In Xandria we could harness the heat of the sun and turn it into sources of power in ways that the ancients couldn't even dream of. In Heros, wind turbines of both colossal and micro scale harnessed the power of the maritime winds so effectively that the island of Cypria traded in energy with other parts of the civilized world that were incapable of deploying this resource. Households on the islands, with their own micro turbines installed on their roofs hooked into the city state grid and sold energy on the same simple basis as they also sold hens eggs from their garden gate. Gypeta led the classical world with its harnessing of tidal power and the conversion of saltwater to fresh using the phenomenal forces of nature.

Sadly, here in the north, there was no such capability and the basic and primitive method of combustion was used to squeeze out each inefficient therm of energy from more or less anything that stood still for too long.

So what I am getting to is that the action of running a bath (and a hot bath no less) was a serious luxury and not one to be scoffed at. Trellsheim had, in one sense at least, the incredible good fortune not only to be sitting on some of the planets biggest remaining and accessible deposits of minerals and ores but also sat at a major interstice of the North-East to South-West Caledonia and the Iapetus fault lines. As such, it had a superabundance of heated and very mineral rich water forced up under pressure from the superheated rocks below. Thus I could walk into a bathroom in the town, almost any bathroom, no

118

matter how poor, and by turning on the tap have instant access to heated water.

There were down-sides to this abundance of course because the planet itself occasionally took payment in return. Trellsheim and its entire surrounding area had been leveled something like eighteen times over the past seven hundred years by the kind of earth movement that probably hasn't otherwise been seen since the planet was in its infancy. The loss of life on the most recent occasions had been phenomenal. It was pretty near total on the last earthquake about one hundred and fifty years ago.

So that is how I was able to be standing naked, dirty and smelly in a bathroom in the barbaric north with a steaming bath before me full with all its promise of warmth. All that was really missing was something sweet-smelling to add to the mineral rich brew before me. I searched around for a short while and found, in a cupboard in the bedroom two stone jars: one labeled, "Es'a stink as good"; and the other "Es'a stink as nat so good".

I sniffed inside the first one and it smelled sweet and lemony. The other smelled vaguely of leather with a hint of something else (although what the something else was I could only guess: it had a hint of the spice cumin probably). Thinking that I was better safe than sorry on all counts I added a bit of both to the water which then fizzed away for a while rather vigorously slowly turning the water to the colour and cloudiness of milk. Putting the jars back from whence they came, I climbed into the water and slipped comfortably and luxuriously below the surface.

I don't know what it is about baths but they are guaranteed to put me to sleep within a very short space of time. Obviously I hadn't stayed under water for long but I was soon fast asleep and probably snoring loudly. How long I had been there was anyone's guess. I was awakened by the sound of loud banging on the bedroom door next to mine.

At first I thought that it was some form of complaint about me as I struggled back into wakefulness and wrestled myself from the now tepid water. It soon became apparent however that this was some other matter: a bit of a domestic, by the sounds of it. There followed a lot of shouting between two individuals together with a third voice chipping in now and again calling for moderation although it has to be said that the various terms for "moderation" had a certain colour in them. After about ten minutes of almost constant dialogue (with interjections, bangs and expletives) and by the time that I was dressed, there came a sudden silence. Whatever it was, it was over.

When I checked the time, I found that it was well past midday so I wrapped up and went out in search of the library. I knew that it was somewhere in the district known as "above town" which I understood was where the principal church or cathedral was located. When I left I could find no one around to ask for directions and so, standing outside the Sun Inn with the snow starting to fall again, I chose the uphill direction of the alley on the basis that above town meant exactly that. It crossed my mind briefly that there could be more than one hill in Trellsheim but I was in no real hurry. I had arrived there earlier than planned so technically I had an extra day or so to spare.

The alley was steep and cobbled and treacherous with ice and snow so the going was slow and it took me best part of an hour to reach the top. Here I found the church, which was in fact a simple affair of wood and mortar in much the same style as the houses that I had first seen. It was small and badly windowed like the houses that lined the steep alley that I had just climbed. Somehow I had expected something grander for such a famous place and this gave me little comfort for the quality and indeed the content of the library, wherever it was. I had expected to be able to ask someone for directions at some point in the walk or failing that once I got to the district but I had seen no one in the past hour. The place seemed completely deserted.

XI
The Young Mother's Tale

I don't mind isolation on the open road and I have no particular worries about being alone in the wilderness (other than the usual and sensible ones such as the fear of bandits, bears or wolves). However, I find an empty town - or in this case empty streets - a cause for serious concern. Somehow, it doesn't seem natural and I start to get spooked.

As I had walked up the steep cobbled alley, I had started to imagine that I was being followed. On a couple of occasions I had stopped, ostensibly to gather my breath (these stops being in addition to the genuine rest stops) in order to listen out for the unwelcome sound of someone following. All I had heard was the dripping of melt water from the eaves above and the quietness and sense of peace that seems to accompany falling snow.

There hadn't even been any animals about. No dogs or cats; not a rat or trilobite; no birds; in fact, nothing. As I had walked on however, the feeling of being followed or being watched had grown on me again. Hairs had started to rise on the back of my neck.

This discomfort had remained even at the top where the alley opened out into a broader area where the houses and the church were spaced apart.

There were a couple of trees growing in what looked like a small area of grass that was now covered by a blanket of unmarked snow. Again I looked around. This time I was more obvious about it. Firstly, I was actually looking for the library and the only way to find it was to look around the wide expanse of the square in which I now stood. The second reason was because, apart from being generally rattled, I was beginning to get a bit irritated. It has to be said of course that the irritation was with myself rather than person or persons unknown who was, or were, probably not there in any case.

There was no obvious sign of the library and I didn't want to walk back down the alley without having satisfied myself that I was not being followed. I decided to walk around the perimeter of the open space, checking for a sign or label of some sort or for evidence of books within the few windows that were visible. This also gave me a chance to check for possible assailants in any alleys running off this area. Of course, it probably escaped my mind that to seek out a potential assailant was in fact to create exactly the confrontation that I was afraid of, but no matter: that's how I am.

The strategy was also slightly flawed on the basis that walking around and peering into people's windows was not usually the kind of action to promote anything other than aggression. In most cultures it wasn't exactly acceptable unless of course it was family or relatives where for some obscure reason all the usual barriers designed to give us time and space seem to be discounted.

I didn't find anything resembling a library in my search and peering in through windows like an ancient and nosey relative revealed not a single book nor, I would add, did I see another person. This latter fact was probably a good thing because, as already commented, it would be difficult to explain why I was generally poking about in a fairly shifty manner. Looking for a library?

"Yeah right!"

Slightly downcast (but not too much - it was only a library and I could always ask at the Sun when I got returned) I decided to walk back. First however, in a childish whim, I decided to cross diagonally the virgin snow in the centre of the open area. It doesn't really matter how I got to this point in the square – I had obviously doubled up on my searching of the houses without noticing it. More importantly, from a self-analytical point of view was why I wanted to do this at fifty-two years and a quarter. I don't know why but I did and so I stepped out onto the blanket of snow. That was when I decided that I was definitely being followed.

There on the grass – I could see it through the snow crushed beneath the large footprints – was clear evidence. When I had arrived, this was virgin snow. Now there was a trail of prints laid down by a hastily moving biped wearing boots heading from where I stood across the square to a point where my alley came out opposite.

In the brief time that I allocated for analysis as my heart rate increased and my breathing became shallower and all sort of complex little chemicals started whizzing around my bloodstream, I considered a number of points. I ruled out time travel for, as I understood it, all research into this had ceased some centuries before on the basis that such travel was too challenging intellectually. Most attempts had apparently resulted in total loss of the subject as a result of Mandelays Paradox: moving backwards in time and space from a point of origin results in the displacement of the exit point where the origin and the exit are the same. In other words and by way of example, you walk out of one door into a predetermined year in the past and then when you return though that same door you find yourself back in Jurassic Gondwanaland looking down the throat of a small tyrannosaur.

I also ruled out amnesia, absent mindedness and dementia for obvious reasons (from where I stood). This left the simple fact that someone had crossed the square whilst I had been here and that I had not noticed.

Even scarier was the fact that this person was now in my alley and that this was the only way that I could see that would get me back down to the rest of the town and more importantly to the Sun Inn.

I am not a total wimp and the only way was back so I crossed the square to the alley without any of the anticipated pleasure of sloughing through the virgin snow. I had my knife in my pocket but it was only a small blade and was (I shamefully confess) rather rusty at this point as I had recently used it to slice an avocado pear.

Other than that, I had no other form of weapon – though it has to be said of course that I wouldn't have known how to use one anyway. Suppressing thoughts of defenestrations, throat slitting and general beatings, I tried to make myself look as large as I could by breathing in as far as I could, swing my arms about and walking as slowly as was reasonable – if I had a tail I would have fluffed it up.

To reinforce this rather doubtful position, I massaged my mind into an aggressive state, took another breath and plunged into the relative darkness of the alley. I headed down towards the Sun Inn trying, and probably failing, to look as though I wasn't running away from an unknown fear (which I was) and whilst trying to move at a pace that said I was afraid of nothing (which of course was untrue). I also had to avoid slipping on the treacherous surface underfoot which, according to the man in my head, could result in broken bones. He was probably the only one with any sense here but I decided to ignore him on this occasion (as, sadly I have done and will do on many more).

I made it to the Sun in good time but frankly I must have looked ridiculous. Fortunately for me no one saw me (or rather I saw no one else) and the probably mythical foot-pad or assassin or just plain bandit did not materialise. I reached the door of the inn, which was closed against the cold and slipped at the last minute, catching my head on the door frame. I don't know what it is about me and doors that often I seem to make contact with them and frequently this is by way of my head.

I opened the door and went in, stamping my boots on the mat provided for that purpose. No one looked up at me although there were a good few people in the bar. That was pleasant. It was nice not to have your every move watched. I also noticed that quite apart from various beers, a number of people were drinking hot drinks. There was a strong smell of coffee in the room. The background noise was lively but moderate. I dropped my day sack on a chair (for some reason that attracted attention) and walked over to the bar. There was a different lad behind it. He had one ring in his ear and tattoo of a rose on his left bicep. He wore a black vest that showed off a muscular physique. It has to be said that for a man, even to me, he looked pretty good.

I asked him what hot drinks he had and was told that apart from various coffees they had a number of herbal teas, some honey drinks and various flavorings. He winked at me at the last point leaving me to wonder what exactly that meant or indeed what exactly the flavorings were. Sometimes ignorance is bliss and so I left it at that ordering a mint tea.

"You'll 'ave pastries with 'at?" he asked automatically.

Now there is something that I really hate about ordering food and drink which I can only attribute to my age and disposition. If I order a drink, I order a drink. If I want food with it, I'll damned well ask. Even with half a brain and a tongue I could manage that much. True he was a big lad but I couldn't help giving him a look that said more than I was prepared to do to him.

To his credit, he looked a little sheepish.

"Sorry, pet," he said, *"It's the Bo'sun. He likes us to make extras."*

The last bit was lost on me as my head was working on the *"sorry, pet"* bit. I could see that I was going to have some problem with the courtesies here.

It isn't that I am an impolite person but when I head up this way for visits I try to adopt a different persona in order to ensure that I fit in and that no one tries to stab or otherwise injure me for insults imagined or otherwise. The risk here with

126

this excessive use of routine courtesy is that I am likely to relax and walk into another hostelry, say thank you and get beaten to the ground. The fact that the boss, presumably the multi-ringed laddie, had probably worked in one of the great franchises of the southern cities (mercifully not present in the farther reaches of the north) didn't cut any ice with me but I stopped glaring at the boy.

"I'll take it over there." I said and went to sit at the table where I had left my day sack. Here I took out the parcel that Welcome had handed to me and placed it on the table, having first checked that the surface was clean of fresh or otherwise stale sticky beer or any other liquids (or indeed solids). I needn't have bothered. The table was immaculate and shone with a new layer of well buffed wax.

I un-wrapped the paper, trying not to spill any of the remnants of sugar (if that's what it really was) onto the table or the floor. In my head the man said something like, *"god what do you care, you're in Trellsheim and you're was in the northern marches. The normal rules of society and intercourse are more or less on temporary suspension!"*

Once the paper was put back in the sack I placed the book on the table and opened it up. On the inside front cover, someone, presumably Welcome had written a note in Latin, "What we obtain by asking isn't really ours."

The man must have read my mind. I really wanted this book but wasn't even going to offer to buy it. (That is even before he told me of its potential value to him and before I realized that I wasn't in his league on this matter.) Of course, it could be that he just saw the desire in my eyes.

By this time, my mint tea had arrived, neatly contained within what at first I took to be a glass. In fact, it turned out to be crystal and beautifully made at that. A small bowl was set down on the table for me to place the leaf-holder in and as he did this I asked him whether the library was up the top of the alley above town.

"*What, this alley?*" he asked. "*No one goes up this way beyond the Sun.*"

Then he added, "*That way goes up to the plague quarter!*"

Well that was good to know. I had just casually wandered up into the plague quarter and walked around snooping and peering into the windows. No wonder there was a church up there.

I should point out that there was probably no actual risk of catching the plague by going into the quarter. This plague, as such, was not like those contagious diseases of antiquity, carried by rats and fleas and the like. Nor was it like the great diseases of the twenty-first century as these had been contained, in part by human intervention but mostly by the co-evolution of virus and host to merge with our mammalian DNA to become an integral part of all of us.

This plague was the great virus of the twenty-first century that had jumped ship from its original hosts and had latched onto common genetic material that we shared with those unfortunate creatures inducing a disease in humanity similar to myxomatosis in rabbits.

Within the space of a hundred years or so it is recorded that over eighty percent of the population of the planet had been killed off by it or associated diseases. No amount of research could accommodate the disease or halt the inexorable advance through all populations. Of course, the consequences had been dire in social and political as well as in human terms but it had managed to sole one pressing problem of that day. With a planetary population of some ten billion reduced over a few tens of years to around two billion, the pressing matter of human devastation of the planets very finite resources, had been put on hold for a while. Time enough possibly for most optimists to think that the species could work out where it went wrong the first time.

As the remaining custodians of the human gene pool, this decimated population went on to breed up humanity as it is today in all its glory. With the privilege of hindsight one can say, with confidence, that so far it is only by luck and a relative decline in sperm count that we are not yet back to our glory days of ignominy and climate change. Well that and the fact that we had already put much of our fossil fuel carbon back into the atmosphere before the plague had struck.

There were however, occasionally in populations, genetic mutations that made individuals susceptible to the disease. Where these occurred the poor creatures were placed into plague quarters where they could live out their days as the disease took hold of them. Frankly there was no reason to segregate them as they posed no threat at all to the rest of the population but I suspect that we have learned very little about how to deal with social attitudes to disease over the ages.

I learned that "above town" was to be reached by way of another alley that ran off the central market square about a couple of hundred yards to the north of the alley on which the Sun Inn was to be found. However, Jimas (the name of the lad that served me) had no knowledge of any library although he did suggest that maybe the Bo'sun would know about this. He was, it would seem, a bit of an avid reader when he wasn't "*trying to get his leg over*". This was just a bit too much information for me and I was a little relieved when someone called out for the lad from over by the bar.

So it looked as if I had more or less wasted the day. It was now heading towards early evening and I had done no research whatsoever. I sipped my mint tea and started to leaf through the book a slight sense of deflation mixed with a certain amount of frustration evident in my slightly erratic movements. Perhaps I could recover some sense of achievement by looking for information on my quarry in the book.

Some of the text was a little difficult to understand but I managed to read a fair bit about the Illuvaqu'e in one of the chapters. Here I learned of their origins in the steppes and grasslands of the east 'before the world was changed' whatever that meant. I read of their mythology – interesting - as they were in their own right mythology to me. I read on into the evening, knowing from the feeling in my stomach that I was moving well past time to eat and not caring that the mint tea in my crystal container was now cold and untouched. It has to be said that in most inns of this part of the world I would have had some surly landlord wander over to demand in a tone that took no prisoners.

"You wanna drink or summat else, ja bas."

This didn't happen here and for that I was grateful. In a brutish world, here was a little space of quiet and peace, seemingly devoid of the usual noise of men (and I do mean men the sex, not man the species). It was a breath of absolute fresh air in an otherwise stinking world.

I heard tell of the Fire Dancers gods and in particular their great god, who gave them life and then sacrificed himself so that they could grow and multiply over the land.

I had started to read a particularly interesting piece and was about to turn the page to a new chapter when a face dropped uncertainly into my field of vision. She startled me and so at first I failed to realise for a few moments the true, as opposed to the obvious, strangeness of this incident.

So far I had seen only men in the Sun Inn and generally speaking the only time that you would have seen a woman in a bar in this part of the world would be if they owned the place or were serving in the place or selling their services in the proximity (well usually in a bedroom or a doorway nearby) and sometimes both of the last two and rarely all three.

130

"You a'right, mate?" she slurred ever so slightly as she tried to bring her eyes into focus on mine.

"Indeed," I replied cautiously.

I wasn't in the habit of procuring female company for my evenings away from hearth and family and I didn't want to get myself into a position where I was either going to offend, insult or find myself in a situation of compromise.

"I've been here fer three weeks, no more nor less," she paused and swayed a little uncertainly in front of me.

"Where a' you a comin' to?" she asked and then belched.

I saw a couple of faces look over in our direction at her noise but they soon returned to their own matters and, regrettably, I was obliged to return to her.

"Not 'round 'ere. Down south no less," I said, hoping that she would be satisfied and go away. I was wrong.

"'tcha got?" she asked, looking with a slightly unsteady expression at my book.

"It's a book," I replied keeping it short, obvious and not too familiar.

"What's it about then?" she persisted.

"O crap," I thought, *"this could go on for ages."*

"It's a story for my kids," I tried.

I was hopeful that the mention of children would do the trick and send her away thinking that either I was sad and espoused or a weirdo that read kid's books. I should point out here that the words for brothers and children are the same in the language of the North. It is a measure of the development of social perspective and culture that there is no word for sisters or girl children. Context tends to be used to determine the sex of the children and given that the assumption has a bias to the male, mistakes are often made. This is not misogyny on my part: I am simply recording what I know.

"Kid's eh?" she repeated and then added, *"I've got three kids."*

She sounded both sad and proud at the same time if that were possible. My hearing was not great and her words were rather slurred but looking at her I felt pretty certain she meant three and not five. She can't have been more than twenty-six. Although I tried not to, I found myself looking her up and down. She wasn't particularly pretty in the face but she was quite shapely: nice legs beneath a wide skirt that was cut to enhance the shape of her hips. Nice waist. Lovely breasts... Oh dear, perhaps a little too much! Whether she noticed or not, her next question half read my thoughts – fortunately the ones before I started looking at her in a sexual context.

"Can you tell how old I am?" she asked coyly.

It was the way that she asked it that said that she wanted someone to appreciate and to praise her. I began to feel a little guilty about the sex bit and so I looked at her in an attitude of considered appraisal and replied.

"Twenty-six, no more nor less," I said as though making a bid at auction.

She smiled and her eyes sparkled with a new light. She looked both pleased and (sadly) grateful and as she responded she brushed back her hair with her hand.

"No. I'm twenty-eight and no more," she demurred.

When someone is that desperate, it is wrong to be too blunt. Do the young really have any idea about the insignificance of year measured in less than tens?

"No way," I said with a hint of astonishment mixed with part incredulity that I hoped she would take as genuine.

"You don't look it, and that's a fact."

Funny how we try to reinforce lies with data. Some popular "science" and much political discourse seems to be written that way also.

She smiled. I don't really think that she believed me any more than I did but she was, I could see, grateful for the kindness. Of course I have to say, she was a good looking woman, whatever she thought of herself.

"And you? What would you give me?" I asked her. This was, I should say, more by way of conversation than with any ulterior motive despite the unfortunate innuendo.

She looked at me for a while as if studying me. Then she looked me up and down in much the same way as I had done her. I did not feel all that comfortable about it and it crossed my mind only briefly (that is, before the man inside my head reminded me of the truth) that perhaps she had thought the same about me when I was eyeing her up and down like an old lecher.

Eventually she answered me.

"Pretty old," she said with simple finality.

I was crushed. That was a killing blow and no mistake. I had expected at least a stab at forty from one so young (well I was hopeful) but I really hadn't expected to be beyond count.

She must have seen the hurt look in my face.

"I'm not good at ages with old folks," she added.

It went from bad to worse. I decided to end this before I was deflated any further (as if that were possible).

I smiled.

"It doesn't matter," I said to close the conversation off.

I was gutted actually.

I really didn't want a post mortem on the matter. After that however and at a great cost to my own self-esteem, she seemed to become disinterested. Shortly afterwards she wandered off and started a conversation with a couple of men sitting at a table in a corner of the room. They weren't over excited about it I deduced from the looks on their faces, but at least she was no longer in my face.

I spent the last part of that evening in the Sun, eating a well presented meal there in a neat and sparsely decorated dining room with a dozen other guests. Other than me, the guests were in pairs and with one exception chatted away quietly about their own business.

The exception was the couple that I took to the couple from the room next door who had been exchanging a few heated words earlier that day. A dark cloud seemed to sit over their table and they ate their food in silence, occasionally throwing a meaningful and sometimes bitter glance at the other when the other was studiously not looking in their direction. One looked truly upset and the other looked defiant, angry and resentful. It called to mind a comment that Welcome had made in passing when discussing the love of his life.

"The Lover's sickness" he had said in one of his sombre Latin phrases, *"The disease worsens with the treatment."*

After the meal I dropped my things back upstairs in my room (where I noticed that it had been cleaned and the bed had been made) and then returned to the bar with the book to read quietly. This I managed to do without interruption and after a couple of hours and a reasonable quantity of the Sun's excellent ale, I headed unsteadily back to my room for the night.

XII
The Paper Seller's Tale

The book that Welcome had presented to me gave me some interesting insights into the lives of the Fire Dancers but although parts of it were well written, there were some chapters that made little sense at all. This was not only because my Latin was not fully up to the mark, nor was it because the writer had himself been a little limited in his knowledge of the language and was in any case using the vernacular rather than classical Latin. Some of it just didn't make sense.

What was even more peculiar was the fact that I hadn't noticed anything unusual when had first read parts of the book when I was sitting on Welcome's wagon. For example, within a passage setting out the origins of the myth of the Cor'moran there was what appeared to be an inventory of household goods set out in a single continuous sentence. In another chapter on wolves there was a passage setting out instructions on how to roast lamb. In another chapter, there was a note about how to repair socks. Later in the same chapter a piece on how to thread a needle if you had poor eyesight – that was at least informative and potentially useful to me.

Whilst each bit made perfect sense it its own content, it made absolutely no sense whatsoever in the context in which it was placed. The last piece I came across before disappearing into sleep was a passage that seemed to be made up entirely of groups of numbers of differing lengths (or sizes of magnitude) with no separators other than spaces and none of the usual mathematical symbols. I could only assume that these were forms of transcription errors that had crept in as the documents had moved from one language and or medium to another over the very many years since the first story was told.

Yet, if so, these were pretty weird copying errors as they seemed to represent extracts from completely separate documents. It was as though at some point in the evolution of these tales, some copying agent had either randomly, or otherwise unconsciously, drawn text from one document and copied it into the other. My last conscious thoughts were bizarre as the book slipped from my fingers onto the bed, creasing pages three hundred and fifty-five and three hundred and fifty-six, and my mind was released from constraint to wander the realms of my subconscious.

I overslept the next morning and woke up with the sunlight streaming into my room, the candle had burned down to a random mess of wax on the table and (to my horror) had dripped and melted off its holder and over the neatly polished surface of the wood. That might cause an upset on discovery, I thought as I tried to pick off the determined and resistant substance without much success. It would have made little difference for I already knew the damage underneath to the beautifully polished surface was probably irreversible.

Outside I could hear a few people moving about in the alley below but there were not many and as I didn't yet know what was normal for the time of day I had no idea of the real time. I couldn't smell breakfast and that was a bad omen.

I washed and dressed quickly and went down to the dining room to see if I could recover something to eat. There was no one there and the tables although empty and clean had the distinct look of tables that had been eaten upon recently. There was a vague smell of bacon and slightly burned toast in the air. I picked a small table set for one person and sat down.

As I was considering my next action, as if by request the Bo'sun appeared. I decided that he wasn't a morning person because he was fairly offish with me and had a singularly unpleasant look about him that I hadn't noticed when I arrived the day before.

"Ja missed it," he said, putting down a vase of fragrant yellow flowers on a table near the door.

"Breakfast's at sun up today and no later."

He gave no thought to the tense as he said this and inferred that the meal times changed on a daily basis. However, he looked so angry that I decided not to challenge this. I also managed to refrain from apologizing, partly because I didn't think I had done anything to be sorry for – after all I had paid for the missed breakfast – and partly because I didn't want to fall into the trap of apologising in this part of the world too readily. That really was a risk of personal injury despite the unusual manners in the Sun Inn.

I have always considered (and made good use of) the value of the long silent pause and in this case it proved useful. As the missing speech dragged on between us, I could see a slight change in his face. He seemed to soften slightly and then finally, after a moment of subconscious tidying at a nearby table, offered to get me bacon and eggs and some bread.

He moved off into the kitchen at the back of the inn, leaving me at the table. I waited feeling a little conspicuous and with nothing to do I simply looked around the room like an idiot at all the everyday items that were there. Before long he returned with the food and a steaming mug of coffee.

As he put these down in front of me on the table I took the opportunity to ask him about the library. The news wasn't quite what I was expecting. Yes, the library was above town and could be reached by the alley that his partner had described but, and this was a very big but, the library had burned down some months ago.

"They've still got some books up there though," he added quickly, seeing the look of disappointment flower on my face, *they're kept in a house nearby."*

Oh that was a comfort. No library and the books gone up in flames. Those rescued were now in some house nearby where no doubt the damp had been creeping and the vermin had been feasting for the past months. I chose not to think about the combustible nature of the medium that was always useful to light the odd fire in the cold.

"There's a lot of stuff up there, is there?" I asked with more cynicism in my voice than even I had intended.

"No, it's all shyte and stuff," he replied, going on to explain that the library had been full of local histories and tales but that most of the books salvaged from the fire were from the reference section which contained mostly historical monologues and law books. He said that he hadn't been up there since the fire and that he wasn't sure which house now held the books but that it was definitely nearby and bound to be signposted.

After breakfast, equipped with that information and with about as much optimism as a dying man, I decided to wander up "above town" and find out just how bad things really were. Firstly, I headed down towards the central market square joining a large crowd of people who seemed to be milling about expectantly. I had no idea what was going on and to be honest I didn't really care. The problem was that I couldn't get through the mass of flesh and it was blocking the way onto the square. I tried to ease my way through but people just refused to move. I pushed a little harder but there was absolute resistance.

"Ere, what you's a pushin fer?" asked a rather large, troll like individual as he peered down at me from a height of about seven feet. God he was an ugly brute, huge snout pushed sideways on his face with a mass of warts and other fleshy protuberances covering it. He had small dark eyes: no teeth to speak of; small ears set back flat on the side of his head and his hair was in tufts about his otherwise bald skull. Yes, there was some troll blood in there somewhere.

"Wos 'appen'in?" I asked trying to keep it simple.

"It's a killin' or summat for sure," he replied.

In truth he must have been able to see something for he stood a good head or more above almost everyone else. On the strength of that and on the basis that no one was going anywhere fast in the near future, I decided to hang around nearby for a while.

It seemed a little odd that an apparent killing should command such an amount of excitement in a town that was notorious for all forms of murder and violence. Still there was nothing for it but to wait patiently for some movement. After a short while this followed.

With the same surge as bath water moving after a blockage has been cleared, the whole body of the crowd suddenly flowed forward as one. It was quite scary as there was no option but to move with the current or otherwise fall and who knows what then. We roiled and washed into the market square for quite a way before dispersing in the greater, open space. On the way we passed a number of military types with batons, staves and halberds. These were the creatures that had been holding us all back. They were now lounging against the walls or against various wagons that were pitched near the outer perimeter of the square.

From the look of it, all the routes onto the square seem to have been closed off for a while and then all released at once. The result was a lot of very curious people wandering about expectantly in the market square looking for signs of blood in the snow, slush mud and all the other substances lying about. By some coincidence I soon found myself near the centre of the square. I could see perhaps fifty feet away the statue of the miner.

I thought that as I was here I might as swell say hello to Welcome so I headed in the direction that I recalled he had set up his stall. Here the crowd seemed thicker for some reason and it took me some while to get to him. When I did, I wished that I hadn't.

The crowd parted unexpectedly before me as it moved around a wagon and I saw an area that had been roped off. The area was around what I recognised as Welcome's wagon. The remaining snow on the ground had been stained red and lying in it was a shape covered in a dirty blanket that was not large enough to cover the feet which were wearing sandals.

Alongside it lay a heap of matted black fur. Blood pooled from a huge wound in its head that looked to have been made by some blunt instrument. I felt sick and shocked. I just stood there like an idiot whist people moved about with almost casual indifference.

"E's a faw'kin farner for sure," said a voice close to my ear.

"'E won't be sellin' books no more,"

I turned to see who had spoken but it was too late to tell. It was just a conversation between a couple of the onlookers. As I understood it, Welcome sold spices and not books. It was true that he had suggested that he would be selling some books but I didn't get the impression that it was his main source of income. Then again, who was I to know who had spent so little time with him. However, for some reason it did catch attention.

It was a big crowd on the marketplace that day and I felt very alone. As I stood there I found myself mulling over the matter of the Spice Trader. I had met Welcome a couple of days ago. I had never seen him before and in all probability would have never have seen him again with or without his unfortunate demise. He was to me a total stranger, almost as much as the nearest person standing next to me now. Apart from the shock of what looked like a brutal murder, the only other reason that it hit me hard was that I knew a bit about his life and history. He had after all come to life in my memory.

Then again, who said it was a murder. For all I know, the bear could have savaged him and then itself been killed by someone else coming to his aid (albeit a little too late). That thought was killed off almost immediately when I heard a couple of soldiers nearby discussing the matter. They were there to watch over the corpse and the wagon until such time as the assessors arrived, I would imagine.

"'E got a bashin' for sure!"

"That's for sure," repeated the other "Es'a faw'kin farner, he was. What d'ya think 'appened?"

"Do you think thieves nabbed 'em?"

"No way! What was taken, eh! Nothing for sure, I reckon," he paused, " 'es an 'onour killin', thats what it is."

"You think?"

"For sure. I've seen it 'a fore."

"Maybe. Perhaps the bear did it?"

"No way, ja bas! The bear don't know anything about 'onour killin's! He was protectin' him and got bashed for good elsewise."

"You think! E didn't survive for sure!"

"'E didn't."

Honour killing? I thought at first that this had to be absurd. Who would want to kill a spice trader in a god- forsaken town like Trellsheim for honour? Then on consideration, I reminded myself that I knew nothing really about Welcome than the brief snippets of his life that he had let me see. Obviously, his dead wife's brothers could have travelled into the far north with the express intention of killing him but it seemed pretty unlikely.

He was after all a trader and wagoner and this was a pretty dangerous bunch of people. It would be pretty easy to fall foul of someone in this environment and end up dead. It was all pointless speculation. I kicked a piece of ice at my feet and started to move away. That was when I saw a piece of paper on the floor.

When I picked it up I saw that it was the page of a book that had been torn out. It was wet and crumpled and had blood on it. I decided that I wasn't going to look at it here so, with a look around me that was more shifty than anything else, I slipped

141

it into my pocket and turned away. I headed back towards the alley that was supposed to lead to the library and when I got to the point where the alley met the square this was confirmed by a signpost. With a bit more confidence, I started up it.

There were a lot of strange looking people in Trellsheim. Now whether that was specifically true of the town or whether it was simply my own misconception, I have no idea. However, to me, wandering around this place it seemed a fact.

One such oddity thrust a strange looking sheet of paper at me as I walked slowly up the increasingly steep hill towards what was left of the library (I hoped). She said something unintelligible to me when I ignored her. Then she thrust the paper harder at me and spoke again. I could not ignore her now as she had more or less moved to stand in front of me. For some reason I didn't feel threatened in any way, despite the events of the morning, so I stopped and took the offered paper.

It was a folded sheet of newspaper with a couple of pictures of someone and a few columns of print. I didn't attempt to read it but I did look at it quickly. The woman then said something to me and something about the voice made me look at her for the first time. I found myself looking into the eyes of the woman I had seen in the camp outside the walls. Close up they really were wickedly appealing eyes and a blush swept up into my face at about the same rate that blood started to course in other parts of my body.

I hadn't felt this confused since I had been an adolescent but I had no time to consider this further. She spoke to me in a language that was wholly unfamiliar: a rich language full of life and passion and thick with sexual undertone. Her voice was like a fine wine full of body and her smell, which had only now started to pervade my other senses, reminded me of things that I would prefer to keep to myself.

I pride myself on language, but this one was alien to me. I couldn't offer a plausible guess at what it was that she was saying. In my confused mind it sounded like an offer that I could neither refuse (because I am a man) nor commit to (because am an aging man, not to mention married). I didn't know what to say. I didn't know where to look. To make matters worse I found that my eyes were fixed on a space below her mouth, below her throat, above the line of her dress that gathered her breasts together, disappearing down into her cleavage. I was a drowning man. I swallowed painfully and asked her if it was for me, ignoring despite my confusion and some of the less obvious innuendo.

She nodded.

I asked her if it was free and she nodded again to that, and followed it up with a throaty laugh that really should not be allowed in any woman. My eyes managed to find hers and my mind wished that they hadn't. I gazed into bright, moist deep brown inviting eyes with pupils that seemed to dilate as she looked back at me, opening like...

Confusion took control of most of my head and radiated round the visible surfaces of my skin. I swallowed and tried to thank her, hoping to move on.

That was when she placed her hand on my wrist. It was warm and it was wet with sweat, even though in the cold air our breath showed as mist.

"*No*," she said, "*enjoy. We have but one life!*"

She had said this in my own language. No hint of accent or error. I looked at her and was about to ask who she was when she laughed once more and turned away, waving her hands in the air in a gesture that was half goodbye and half abandon. As my eyes followed her of their own accord, she headed off down the alley towards the market square.

I looked at the newspaper sheet. It looked like some kind of religious tract. On the top of it on the front page were the words "One Life!" and below this it read, "New readers turn to page four." There were only two sides to it. I thought this a little

143

bizarre and yet it was not as strange as the fact that again, the words that littered the page were in the language that I call my own.

Shaking my head and muttering inaudible comments to myself, I pulled off my day sack and stuffed the paper into it. Then, replacing the bag, I headed up the alley. To those passing me by, I must have looked as mad as they get.

XIII
A Felon's Tale

After a while I reached the place known as "Above Town" and found the partially burned out shell of a building that I presumed was the former library. I say this because it looked no different to any of the other buildings around the top of the alley which, as with the plague quarter, had an open space in the centre of a square of buildings.

This time however there was no church but there was one of those strange external urinals in one corner and nearby what looked like a small lock up for felons. There was also a set of stocks raised up on a stone platform. These, it appeared were occupied. As my movement caught his eye, the man in them looked up as best he could and peered at me from under his eyebrows. This was partly the result of the way that he was secured and also partly because he was equipped with a prodigiously heavy forehead, the like of which made me consider whether Homo sapiens had in fact originally interbred with Neanderthals.

"Water matey," he shouted out at me.

He offered me a leering sort of a smile that I think was meant to be disarming. I might have been a stranger in these parts but I knew the rules. If you helped a person in the stocks, you replaced them in the stocks. I could see a couple of soldiers crouched and leaning with their backs against a wall watching me and hoping for some sport. I must have disappointed them.

"*I'm not the faw'kin farner here,*" I shouted back at the soldiers rather than the man. (I won't go into the protocol of talking to – or rather not talking to - convicted criminals here but it is another of those oddities of the northern marches.) One of them spat a red juice into the snow and they turned back to a game that they had been playing. It looked like bones but it could equally have been something far less savory from where I now stood. The convict in the stocks slumped back to his enforced position of rest.

I went in search of the temporary replacement for the library. All the houses looked the same which of course was no help at all. Furthermore, all the buildings in this place had very small windows and what with the absence of any form of lighting inside, it was impossible to see into the rooms without more or less sticking your nose up against them. This of course is what I was obliged to do and I made my slow way around the area on a house by house search peering in at each window and probably looking for all the world like a burglar. The soldiers, though, paid me absolutely no attention and so I assumed that this was seen as normal behavior whether I was seeking out the library or not.

Most of the rooms that I peered into were empty both of people and books. One of them had people sitting at a table eating a meal. They ignored me and I moved away pretty quickly. In another window I saw a couple having sex. The man was naked and very skinny but the women mostly clothed. They weren't that young and somehow I felt that sex that early in the morning on admittedly a warm day in a very cold part of the world was a bit over enthusiastic if not a bit tacky. They were too engrossed to see me and I have to admit that I took longer to move away from that window than I should have.

It has to be admitted that after a certain age – I regret I cannot recall when - one comes to regard the sexual act as a little ridiculous. I would suggest that this applies not just to primates but quite honestly to all vertebrates and indeed possibly many invertebrates. If one chooses to believe in the gods, then it is surely a jest in bad taste. If we go for the more scientific approach, one can only consider that it might have been better for some small creature many millions of years ago to have chosen a more subtle form of procreation. It would be tempting to suggest that it might have been better to stick with binary fission but then we would probably all be swimming about with our one cell in the sea still.

I guess for the younger of us it is only the rush of hormones into the system and blood to the peripheral parts and away from our brains that stops us from realizing just how absurd the thing is, even if we consider what copulating dogs look like for example. Thrusting buttocks look daft from any angle unless they are integral to you (and then they don't look any less daft, it's just that you don't necessarily care). For someone of my age of course the blood doesn't necessarily rush quite so fast (in fact rush is probably not the right word: maybe 'slip' or 'flow' would be more appropriate or then perhaps 'cajoled') and so one has more time to study form. I have to say that I probably preferred the rush of ignorance and youth.

In one window there was a very large fat cat, possibly one of the biggest and fattest cats that I have ever seen. It looked at me out of half-closed eyes as it squatted on what I took to be a woman's large fur hat and soaked up the little bit of warm sunlight that was trapped by the window glass. Beyond it in the room there were some books on a shelf but not enough (I hoped) to be classed as the replacement library.

In the end I found that the soldiers were lounging on the steps of the temporary library. I had almost to lean over one of them to look into the window and nearly knocked over the halberd that had been left carelessly against the doorframe.

"Hey, you be careful o' ma pike, yer tus putt," growled one of the men.

"You's a touchin' it and you's in the stocks."

He added, *"ja bas,"* for additional emphasis and then spat on the ground.

With my recent experiences at the Sun Inn, I damned well nearly apologised. Fortunately, I managed to retrieve the word as it was beginning to form in my head.

"Why it's a daft place to put it i'n it," I replied, and also added, *"ja bas,"* for additional emphasis myself. I did not spit.

"Why 'es a good'un," replied the soldier almost affably and he grinned at me.

Frankly I'll never get used to the etiquette of these parts. Retorts, tones and phrases that would nearly get you knifed in other places were considered friendly banter here and yet the risks of being polite, I have already over laboured.

"Is there a book-place nearby?" I asked, using the colloquial term in case they didn't understand.

"Search me," the soldier replied. "I'm not a reader, no ways."

He paused for what I guessed might be thought.

"You is, Maeket?"

This latter comment was made to the other soldier who so far had been indifferent to my presence.

"No more 'en you. Read a book once though: lots a pictures of girls 'nd stuff," he replied.

"That's not a book, ja bas. It's faw'kin," he let the comment die off in flight.

"Ye'sa," replied Maeket with a broad grin and a couple of pelvic thrusts.

"*Ye'sa mon!"*

Leaving these two talking and making various suggestive gestures amongst themselves, I knocked on the door of the house. After a while (quite a while) a rather timid looking person opened the door, after first opening and peering out through the viewport and then shutting it again with what seemed like serious attitude.

Appearances can indeed be deceptive. Timid, this person was not. Although wearing trousers and a very large jumper of some description, I could not tell immediately if it was a man or a woman. The jumper was hugely baggy and hid any possible suggestion of the presence or absence of breasts. The face was

148

craggy and the wispy hair was cut short in a bob that could have been for a man of a woman. The general build was of a short overweight person. The speech didn't really give me much of a clue either.

"D'j want?" this person demanded.

"D'ja got!" I replied with as much bad humor as I could muster.

"Books, a curse," was the reply couched in tones of irritation and contempt.

"Books as a'want," I said curtly, *"'Appen I'll be commin in, ja bas!"*

I got that in quickly to try and get the upper hand here. It didn't work.

This creature looked me up and down in an appraising sort of way for a few seconds and then sniffed. The sniff said more than the words that came in to finish me off.

"Why's a faw'kin farner 'nd j'a smell like a girl."

"Bastard," I thought.

I had forgotten about the perfume that Welcome had given me and obviously it was noticeable to this woman – well after all, how sensitive is the average male nose anyway?

"Look, you're 'avin me in here or no?" I persisted.

"I'm looking for a book or two." I said in my best business-like tone and added, *"Is this a book-place or not?"*

"Aye, aye, it's a library," she replied using the word as though to correct my ignorance, *"and you can keep your hair on."*

She added this, I think as an attempt to appease slightly, seeing out of the corner of my eye that the soldiers had stopped chatting and were leering at her somewhat obviously. They presumably had no problem spotting her as a female and clearly age was no barrier to their lust.

"Well, are you commin' in or not?" she said, now ushering me into the room with a sense of urgency and with the same kind of gestures you might use to move an animal into a pen.

"Come on. Come on in, that's it!"

She almost pushed me into the room behind her as I caught one last gesture from the now grinning soldiers outside.

"You're nothing but beasts," she hissed at them as she closed the door.

There was laughter outside and I heard a number of fairly graphic comments shouted out in the street now beyond the door about what they would like to do to her, where, when , how many times and in what positions.

"Y'animals," she screeched at them.

More laughter.

I didn't laugh nor did I smile, for one thing I don't think that I dared when I saw the look on her face as she came into the room and for another, I could hardly condone such brutish rudeness even in this brutish part of the world.

"So you want some books?" she asked in a more subdued voice.

"'Appen so," I replied.

"Many of the books were toasted in the fire," she offered and then pointed to a largish box on the table in front of me.

"'Ere is a list of our books. If the title's scratched out it means it is burned. The books are in three rooms and upstairs."

She pointed to an odd and strangely ornate little spiral staircase in one corner of the room. She then gave me another of those appraising looks with a hint of feral in it.

"Standard tax, no more no more, no less."

Having set the terms of hire she then turned and left me, disappearing quickly through another doorway. She looked sad and weary as she walked off into the darker corridor presumably towards the back of the building.

I sat myself down at the table and took a notebook and pencil from my day sack. I then started looking through battered and slightly singed cards in the box that was now the library's catalogue.

Although not a very large library (even before the fire) there were some pretty good books listed. Sadly, some of these were scratched out (i.e. burnt in the fire) but on a first quick flick through I saw a few remaining titles that caught my attention. I noted these down and also noted the rather idiosyncratic referencing system. It consisted of a square box drawn on each card which was divided into four, being the four rooms of the library, I assumed. In one box on each card there was a tick and a letter (one of the letter equivalents of N,S,E or W being obviously the directions of the compass) and a tally mark, representing a number between one and six . There was never a tick in the bottom left box which I took to refer to the reading room. Fortunately, I always carried a compass on my day sack and so could determine which wall was which and the shelf numbers were obvious (I hoped).

Having jotted down my list, I went in search of the books, many of which were in one of the downstairs rooms of the library. From one room, I could hear other noises in the house. It was an ordinary mixture. The sound of pots rattling on a stove and of young children chattering. Occasionally adult voices could be heard. The sounds and words were an interesting insight into the lives of the ordinary people of this town, if indeed these people were ordinary.

I have to confess that I hung about in that room looking for books that I had already found for longer than I needed to, just to listen to the sound of life going on around me. With the older woman and the young children and another female voice, it sounded very much like this was an extended family. The children certainly weren't the librarian's, if indeed that was what she was.

I managed to listen in on a fair bit of conversation at one point. Some of it was about the meal that was being prepared but they were also discussing the murder of a foreigner in the market place that morning. Word obviously travels fast in this town and the death of Welcome and his black bear now seemed common knowledge. What also appeared common knowledge (not necessarily that it was true) was that he was killed by some mysterious persons who were part of a secret society that was prevalent in this part of the world. They referred to them in hushed tones.

I couldn't hear a lot of what was said but I heard references to travelers, something about children, the words *"no better en vagabonds"* but the words that caught my attention were *"dancin' in the fires,"* which came at the end of a virtually inaudible paragraph of what sounded like explanation by the librarian.

Pressing my eavesdropping abilities to their maximum I managed to pick up a little more of the sense of the conversation. By all accounts, Trellsheim was a gathering point before some event, a festival or something. There was a fair amount of guesswork because the dialect was a bit off, the volume was a bit too low; and, my auditory senses were not what they used to be.

I couldn't establish why they thought Welcome would have fallen foul of these folks. This was not just the difficulty of spying on them but also because it was pretty obvious from what I picked up that they really didn't know. It was all pure speculation and absolutely no substance. The idea that Welcome would have been slaughtered by these folk seemed a bit far-fetched to me. Then again, what did I know?

According to the two women in the other room, the murdered trader had been asking questions about this group of folk. According to the two hushed voices somewhere off in the house, Welcome was killed because he was suspected of being an official of some sort, probably a Shreeve Tax collector.

In the informed opinion in the other room, he had obviously poked about too far into their affairs and had suffered the consequences. Apparently he had had his head bashed in by a spiked mace and that the bear, as it attempted to protect its master had suffered the same fate. Then the deed being done, the perpetrators had simply walked away from the wagon leaving the corpses where they lay and the contents of the wagon untouched.

No one apparently had seen the attack despite the fact that it was in the early morning (one of the busiest times in Trellsheim) and in daylight and, not to put too fine a point on it, right in the middle of a busy market square.

Apparently a group of soldiers had turned up within about five minutes of the attack, having been alerted to it by someone who had heard that there had been a killing in the market place. They asked a few questions and pushed a few traders about for a few minutes before cordoning off the area and closing all exits to the square for a while to see if anyone covered in blood was trying to get away. Having covered the bodies and posting a couple of men to watch over the wagon, they then departed. It was now a matter for the assessors.

I must have either spoken without realizing it (as I was prone to do) or have made some other noise (which I am also prone to do, it must be said) but the conversation in the other room stopped. There was a moment of silence and then I heard footsteps coming towards me along a passageway.

"Found the book you want?" asked the librarian with a tone that said something about not trusting any foreigners and certainly not ones that were prying around their town on clandestine, if not unsavory, business.

"Yes, some o' them," I replied as casually as I could, trying not to blush. I guess that it is a bit unethical to listen in on other

persons' conversations and I guess that must have been getting to me somehow. Either way, I was unsuccessful and I could feel the tell-tale warmth in my cheeks and face. The more I felt it, the worse I suspect it got.

"You been in the market place recently?" she continued, now with the air and attitude of an interrogator.

"I been down there," I answered quite truthfully.

"Ah. You saw the killin' then?"

This time she had an eager tone in her voice. It was almost hungry.

"I heard of it," I said.

This time it was a little less than the truth. I wasn't sure of the direction that this was going and I was worried about getting in too deep into something that I might regret. After all, I needed access to the library for my research and if I got banned it could ruin the whole thing.

"So what d'ya know about it then?" she asked and this time I understood that it was interest not threat that was driving her. That made the matter seem a little safer so I relaxed a bit and proceeded to say more than I should have. Sometimes I just depress myself with my stupidity.

I went on to explain about how I had travelled up to Trellsheim with the murdered trader having met him on the road. In fact, I just carried on speaking and the words just tumbled out until I got to the point where I walked onto the market square earlier that morning. When I stopped talking the librarian nodded and looked me up and down again as if reappraising me.

She sniffed and said, *"'Appen 'es a mate then?"*

"No," I said, slightly shocked.

I failed to see how this interpretation could be given to my tale. I was just glad that I hadn't told her where I was staying. I needn't have worried about this however, as in the following breath she came in with the obvious.

154

"You'll be stayin' at the Sun Inn, I expect," she said immediately.

I guess it was part statement and part question.

"No! No! No way," I said emphatically, realizing as I did so that I had made a mistake. Quite apart from the excessive protestations, it was obvious that a stranger would not know of the Sun Inn and its particular market niche?

She looked at me triumphantly. This was a game of chess that I was about to lose.

"Hah! Thought as much."

She turned and went back to the other room where after a while an animated and slightly excited conversation started up. No doubt my modified, or rather twisted, tale would be all over Trellsheim by tea time. I was seriously angry, not so much with my interrogator but rather with myself for being so seriously stupid. In a vague attempt to rationalize, I managed to convince myself that at least I hadn't offended her or been banned from the library and so I convinced myself that no real harm had been done.

IV
The Latin Texts

It turned out my various assumptions were wrong on several counts as I was to find out later that day and the next. I left the library soon after I had finished disgorging my stupidity as I was so angry with myself that I couldn't concentrate on the research. I left the books on the table in the reading room with the customary tax payment for each book (in this part of the world, one trupP) and shut the door, none too quietly on my way out after a rather feeble exit text.

"I'll be off then!"

Outside, the two soldiers looked up as I came out. I detected a new sense of interest in me as I walked by and I distinctly heard one of them sniff. I ignored the comments that were muttered none too quietly to my rear as moved off from them with perhaps a little more haste than usual.

I don't know whether it was paranoia on my part as a result of the upset of the past hour but I felt certain that as I stepped down into the alley, that I was being watched by persons other than the soldiers. I looked around quickly but could see no one obvious (other than those two soldiers who were now openly leering at me and making various gestures to me that left very little to the imagination).

My eyesight wasn't good enough to see into small windows from a distance and I could see no other obvious signs of movement. I felt sure however that there were many pairs of eyes watching me. As I carried on down the alley towards the market square, the paranoia increased and I had that feeling that you get when you think that there is someone walking behind you. I turned quickly on several occasions but saw no one and was relieved when I reached the comparative safety of the market and its crowds.

See how ridiculous we can be? I was relieved to reach a crowded place rather than walk along a deserted alley in broad daylight. It obviously slipped my attention that in this same crowed place not a few hours before, a man and a bear had been beaten to death in the middle of that anonymous and uncaring mass of humanity!

I made for the alley leading up to the Sun, which I noticed for the first time was called Sun Alley – well that was original. Several people were coming down the alley into the market place and I could see a small number of others heading up towards the plague quarter. My fear of pursuit had dissipated by now, reassured by the carrion comfort of the crowd and the proximity to the inn, my room and my temporary, if fictitious, sanctuary. I failed to see one particular figure in a broad hat and scarf turn as he or she had passed me by a few yards and then return back up the hill behind me a few dozen paces to my rear.

As I walked into the Sun, I looked for any signs of disclosure but detected none. No one seemed to notice me come in and thinking discretion the better part of valour, I decided to make straight for my room. It was the one wink that the Bo'sun gave me as I passed him on the landing that told me all I needed to know. Word indeed travels fast in this town. I closed and locked my door behind me, threw my day sack onto a chair and then slumped onto the bed – without removing my boots.

It was dark outside when I woke up cold and uncomfortable and with a depressing sense of loss – I can't explain it. How long I had been asleep I had no idea but it was pretty quiet outside and I could hear no sound of movement in the alley below other than one pair of footsteps hurrying down in the direction of the market place.

In the darkness of the room I could just about see a slip of paper that had been pushed under the door and now lay on the floorboards. I picked it up and unfolded it.

"There was a stranger asking after you a while ago."

I read this with a further sense of unease. I had no idea who had written the note as it was unsigned but I assumed that it was the Bo'sun or one of his staff. That wasn't the issue. What was a concern was that now, through my own stupidity and a little bit of being in the wrong place at the wrong time, I seemed to be attracting a certain amount of attention to myself. (It didn't cross my mind that this could be entirely illusory.) I could not help but feel that most forms of attention were an unhealthy thing in Trellsheim.

I sat back on the bed and lit a couple of candles that at least chased away the phantoms and shadows in the room, sending them off into the extremities and corners to mumble to themselves and chew nervously at finger and toe nails. I turned the paper absently over and over in my hand as a whole wash of thoughts and images went sloshing around my mind. I also took out the paper that I had found near Welcome's body and flattened it out. It had at least dried out now and the blood stains were moving towards a less startling brownish colour.

I couldn't make out all of the text as it had been damaged in the various liquids and the ink had run. It wasn't printed text but a series of handwritten notes in a very neat hand. Written in Latin, they seemed to be a series of quotations. The kind of thing you might write down as you read a book, hoping to store them for another time but somehow never remembering enough of the quote to make it worth the repeating. The writing was probably Welcome's but I couldn't be certain.

The first of them, I recognised as a quotation from Horace's Epistles. *"Those who run off across the sea, change their climate but not their minds"* I had seen it before in the front of the book that Welcome had given me. I guess that it must have been important to him, given that apparently he also had run off across the sea (admittedly in this case it was the sand sea). As I looked at the words it occurred to me that I could check the writing against the dedication in the book that Welcome had given me. I retrieved it from my day sack and was surprised to find that the scripts were completely different. On the assumption that the dedication was Welcome's script, this note clearly was not.

The next quotation was also known to me. *"Fallaces sunt rerum species."* The appearance of things are deceptive.

There then followed a series of fairly bland and obvious phrases which I glossed over quickly, arising eventually at a couple more vaguely interesting ones. When I say interesting I should perhaps really say something like 'pertinent', as that is what they were to the circumstances in which I, or rather Welcome, had found himself.

"Multum in parvo, memento mori" which I took to mean 'much in little, remember that you will die."

"Mendacem memorem esse oportet," which was something about liars needing good memories.

Then there were several others that I did not understand or seemed to make no sense at all and then the one, *"Let the punishment fit the crime."* Finally I read *"Unam vitam!"* One life: the last words that the strange woman in the alley had said to me.

Frankly none of it made a lot of sense and the quotes didn't really seem particularly relevant to anything. I wondered casually whether it was some form of code or coded message. Certainly, some of the phrases were pertinent to Welcome and the bits of his life that he had told me about but then again I had no idea if any or all of those bits were the truth or just an accumulation of stories designed to pass away a tedious journey. It seemed to me that I was collecting more tales on this journey than I had intended to.

The reference to "One Life" had reminded me of the newspaper and I rummaged in my day sack for the religious tract that had been thrust into my hand earlier in the day. Once I had opened it out I saw that it contained all the usual stuff about salvation and about prophets and significant events that no one else it would seem had ever heard of. There were also the calls for money to be given and an advertisement for some form of retreat. The bit that really caught my eye was a few lines of text under a smiling picture of a child on the back page.

"We are everywhere and we are waiting for you to join us. Become one of us: make this life a crowning achievement. We ask you to do this because you have come here for a purpose, not by chance. You may have come here with one intent but you will find many great opportunities. Come to us now. You will come to realize that we are all travelling together on a voyage of discovery."

Sometimes you read things or hear things and you think to yourself. This is a message meant for me. This could have been one of those moments had I been younger or more impressionable. Yes it had potential meaning for me if I chose to look for it in the text but in truth it was about as relevant to me as a fortune teller's mystic whisperings.

There was the fact that it was all printed in my own language however and that I was many many miles from my homeland. That bit I could not get out of my mind so I read on. In fact, I read the tract form start to finish and I found the bit about new readers that was meant to be on page four. Actually, it was a third of the way down page two and was nothing more than an invitation to send money and to some unknown place and name.

It had seemed to take longer to read than I would have thought and when I had finished it really felt like it was very late (or in fact early). Nothing and no one could be heard outside and the silence was that kind of quiet that really says that just about everyone is asleep and only those who are up to no good or who

160

are feeding babies are awake now. To add to this, one of the candles was burning low and the other was guttering. These, together with the fact that I was tired, my eyes were probably bloodshot from reading in the poor light and my back and shoulders ached with a combination of the cold and general age, were enough hints to suggest to me that sleep would be good now.

That is what I tried but too much had happened today (or yesterday if appropriate) to permit this easily. I lay there in the darkness with a whole series of images rushing through my mind, none of them pleasant and all of them seeming to hold some form of sinister meaning for me. I tried shutting them out but they just kept coming back until I found myself in the library above town, spilling out my life story to the old woman who was standing before me nodding and prompting me to continue whenever I seemed to be faltering. After a while I came to a point when I stopped talking and she looked at me and said simply.

"You are lost, boy. I suggest that you try to find a way home."

I asked her how I could do this and for a while I thought that either she hadn't heard me or that she wasn't going to answer. Then in a voice that seemed more like a man than a woman, she replied.

"There are two paths and the true way is obscured but you must take this."

"How will I know," I asked.

She looked at me in that up and down appraising way that could be used for so many messages and she sighed. Then after a few moments of her own in thought she started to speak and I woke up to the sound of someone banging on my door.

XV
The Cook's Tale

It took a few seconds before I was awake enough to call out but the banging just continued. I got out of bed, intending to dress but found that I was pretty much dressed already. I had at least removed my boots which I stumbled over on my way to the door. The banging stopped more or less as I got to it and by the time that I had fumbled with the key and opened the door there was no one outside or in the corridor.

It was still dark but obviously heading towards dawn and as I stood there in the doorway groggy and dishevelled from sleep I began to realize exactly how odd this really was. Then it got odder because I heard the door of the inn close loudly and the sound of footsteps making off down the alley as fast as the snow and slush would permit them.

I have to say that I was a bit worried about all this and a part of me was glad that I hadn't got the door open in time to meet the person who was knocking. All sorts of unpleasant visions ran through my mind once more as I stood there staring vacantly at the empty corridor until after a while I woke up fully and realized that even with my clothes on, I was cold. At more or less the same time, a light appeared at the far end of the corridor and round the corner just after it came a candle, a hand and arm and then the Bo'sun. He looked tired and a little cross. When he saw me standing in the doorway of my room he stopped, looking a little surprised and then spoke quietly.

"There was a stranger asking after you a while ago."

The same words as the note.

"Really?" I replied then added, *"Who's that then?"*

"Someone I've never seen before, I reckon." he said grinning at me and winking. *"You'll perhaps be asking to pay for two beds then?"*

He obviously thought that I had had someone (in at least two senses of the word) in my room.

"No!" I said, slightly offended, *"it's nothing to do with me. I was sleeping when I heard banging and crashing at the door! I didn't see 'out though so he's obviously gone."*

Why I had assumed that it was a "he" rather than a "she" was a bit beyond me but I had no further time to consider. The Bo'sun looked at bit worried and started back down the corridor shouting out as he went.

"How did he get in then?" then even louder *"Jimas. Get the dawgs out!"* then louder still, *"Jimas the dawgs!"*

Jimas, I assumed, appeared from the room next to mine. He was pulling on his trousers over his boots – so he obviously slept in them. This was proving to be a bit of a challenge and he fell down onto one knee. A voice called out from the depths of room to him and he growled a rather crude reply. All right, so he wasn't necessarily *sleeping* in his boots.

He soon had his trousers on and went after the Bo'sun who could now be heard rummaging around downstairs, opening a shutting various doors. I decided to follow them to find out what I could about my early morning visitor. Shortly before I got to the bar, Jimas appeared with a couple of fearsome looking dogs of some indeterminate breed. The only significant features were the muscular frame, the powerful jaws and the large canines.

They were probably called Grip or Fang or similar such names. He shouted something to them and then to my horror let them off the leash. They rushed past me without even so much as a sniff and disappeared into another room whilst Jimas unlocked the front door. As if in response to this the two dogs suddenly came bounding back into the bar and almost flew out into the cold air baying and barking as they ran down the alley in the direction that I had heard the footsteps go a little while past.

Jimas winked at me.

"They'll 'ave 'em, no worries!" he said and then closed the door and went off in search of the Bo'sun.

I don't think that the dogs did get the intruder, as the nocturnal visitor was becoming known. They came back after about an hour or so looking smug and self-satisfied but there was no sign of any blood (theirs or anyone elses). Jimas took one look at the expression on their faces (do dogs have expressions?) and then grabbed one of them by the ears and sniffed its breath.

"'Es been tampered with, I reckon. I can smell Bartle Bane!" he said with a seriously aggressive tone.

I had no idea what Bartle Bane was but Jimas was indignant and so it was obviously foul play. However, he wasn't fretting too much so it clearly wasn't life threatening to the dogs. Grumbling noisily about how *"some folks have no idea about dawgs"* he took both of them out to the back of the building where there was a small courtyard. Having nothing particular to do I followed him and watched as he hosed them down.

He explained that Bartle Bane was an extract from the yellow root of a type of nettle that took away aggression in certain animals. It had to be administered orally and although it tended to stain the skin of the person applying it, it was more or less unnoticeable on the softer tissues of a dog's mouth. It was usually fed to them in pieces of meat.

Once he had hosed them down, he gave them large bowls of water into which he had poured a few drops of a thick dark liquid from a small bottle that he produced from his trouser pocket.

"It's a tincture. Tincture of Mahmeet." he said when he saw me watching him. I shrugged and made a gesture that in any language meant something along the lines that it was all a mystery to me.

164

I will admit that he certainly knew how to handle the dogs. They were pretty fearsome looking beasts and I wouldn't like to be on the business end of those canines and yet he treated them like they were his children. In response they played with him as though they were, bounding around him and making mock attacks at him wagging their tails and holding their mouths open with that sloppy sort of look that dogs have when they are playing the fool.

I left Jimas and his dogs and went back into the Sun in search of the Bo'sun. It seemed likely that he had probably seen the first visitor or he wouldn't have specified a foreigner in his note. I found him in the kitchen forcing copious amounts of pork and apple stuffing into the cavity of a large capon. The kitchen was incredibly warm and above a roaring fire in the range, there was a large pan of bubbling liquid. It was a rich reddish colour with a hint of orange to it and it was viscous looking. The bubbles seemed to burst reluctantly on the thick surface and there was a smoky and sweet smell in the air.

The Bo'sun looked up, a small bead of sweat running from his forehead and down his nose before dropping with clear intent onto (or rather into) the capon. At least it was being cooked I thought, making a mental note to avoid anything including chicken tonight. The expression on his face looked murderous as he looked me up and down with one of those expressions that could be used for anything and usually meant something very specific.

In order to appease him I offered that I had no idea who the visitor was and that they had certainly not spent the night in my room.

"Ah no worries my dear!" he replied sounding far more pleasant than he looked. *"It's not good for folks to be wanderin' about my yinn at night."* He continued, the growl in his voice seeming to grow as the sentence progressed.

It was a statement of the obvious to say that it clearly upset him that there had been someone wandering about the Sun without his knowledge or permission. As he was speaking he was pushing the stuffing into the capon with increasing vigour and by the time he had stopped talking the motion became more one of forcible entry. The bird looked fit to burst and a short while later did so with the legs dropping lasciviously apart.

"No problem!" he said and reached into a table draw to pull out string and a wickedly thick and curved needle.

"I've got the thing to sort 'im out."

Almost against his wishes, a grin erupted across his face and he set to work repairing the torn flesh of the bird.

As he worked he seemed to regain his composure and after a while I decided that I might as well ask him about the note. He looked up at me as though I had said something offensive to him. Yes, he had seen the person and it had sounded and looked like a man and had walked like a man as well. Apparently that did not make it a man for certain as far as the Bo'sun was concerned. He had been caught out before in some very peculiar situations it would seem.

He had not seen the face as it was covered with a scarf and broad brimmed hat that was tilted low over the eyes. Long hair, slightly reddish looking: smelled of a perfume that he could not quite place but had smelled before; spoke with the accent of a southerner, a bit like me apparently.

As he had been talking, the Bo'sun had moved on to another task and was now busy chopping carrots without even looking down at his hands. He seemed to be in a talkative mood so I kept going and asked him if he thought the first visitor and our intruder were the same person.

"No way of knowing." he replied as he scrapped the now diced carrots into a large pan with some onions a few herbs and spices.

166

I followed him across to the range as he started to sweat the vegetables, he didn't seem to mind and asked me to get the salt for him as he stirred the pan. Perhaps use of the word, ask was a bit passive: it was more of an instruction. Anyway, I obliged him and soon he was busy throwing in salt and herbs and other bits and pieces into the pot as he stirred the vegetables.

He offered that the first visitor had asked for me by description and he laughed as he gave me the words that he had used. Oldish guy: middling height but a bit overweight, long grey hair going a bit thin and looking a bit unkempt; unshaven for a new days and in need of a bath; hiding it all under a blanket of perfume . I wasn't over amused but it was actually a fairly reasonable description of me when I arrived a few days ago.

"*Didn't say what he wanted, then?*" I asked.

"*No, he had a drink and then left.*"

This was a bit weird as I had no idea who might be looking for me in this place. Clearly he didn't know my name or he would have made reference to it when he asked after me and I knew no one in this town as it was my first visit here.

"*Ow ah!*" the Bo'sun said as he tipped a collection of bloody and chopped pieces of flesh into the pan with the stewing vegetables.

"*'Nd he said that you'd 'ave some books about you as well.*"

Of course, it was probably known in the Sun that I had something to do with books as I had asked Jimas about the library the day before. I had also spent much of one evening camped in the bar reading the book that Welcome had given me.

"*Ow ah!*" I replied as though it were of no particular matter to me which, as thing stood, was just about true.

"*Well, seen as you're a book scholar an all, that's one thing, but it's none of 'is business either way!*" said the Bo'sun in a manner that I found reassuring.

Then he added, *"And it's nobodies business but mine to be nosin' around my Yinn in the early hoursl, ja bas!"*

I thought that he was going to spit as he added the last part but I guess that he remembered that he was in the kitchen in time to stop himself. He really did not like the idea of people snooping around his inn.

By now he had added water and some rich gelatinous amber stock to the pan and the whole thing was bubbling merrily away as he stirred it occasionally giving off a very pleasant aroma of herbs and onions and just a hint of rotting meat. The Bo'sun must have seen me sniff because he grinned and with a very boyish wink at me.

"You'll be 'avin capon after all?" he said.

"It's currish else wyse. Currish is good stuff where the meat's getting on a bit."

He added this last bit without any qualms or concerns about my point of view as a prospective customer or possible complainant.

He placed a lid over the curry and moved the whole pot to a quieter part of the range so that it could simmer for a few hours in time for lunch. Then he wiped his hands on the rather neat apron that he was wearing and crossed the kitchen to where a side of bacon was hanging. He grabbed it and with a strength that I would not have imagined in a person of his (or indeed any) size, hauled the whole thing down onto a black platter and started carving off thick rashers for the breakfast.

"Full breakfast eh?" he asked over his shoulder to me.

"That's good stuffa." I replied.

"You'll 'ave bludpoden?"

"For sure!" I said, *"it's very good stuffa is a bludpoden."*

I made my way back into the dining area whilst the Bo'sun prepared breakfast for those of us who were up and about. I noticed that instead of the usual bare wood, the tables were today all covered with blue and white checked table cloths and

168

on each was a small vase of yellow flowers. I later found out that today was the anniversary of his founding of the Sun Inn and each anniversary he dressed the tables in this manner and made the bar look a bit special. The last point, I hadn't noticed in the excitement of the early morning but I decided to keep that for later.

Breakfast was in, tabled and eaten and in a depressingly quick time. I don't know why it is but the older I get, the faster the food seems to go down. Usually I barely even remember eating the meal. The blood pudding was out of this world as I guessed it would be. These parts of the world were renowned for their use of offal, herbs and spices in the most amazing charcuterie.

After breakfast I went back to my room to collect my day sack and Welcome's book. The room was already tidy and the bed made. All my papers were neatly arranged on the table, which looked as though it had been polished and new candle stumps were placed in the candle holders. Someone had left their tinderbox beside them on the table, presumably by accident. It was an old, once ornate, silver looking box (probably silver plate) with some engraved words on it. Rather than wander back downstairs with it, I decided to leave it there for when its owner realized the loss.

I had chosen to head back up to the library, partly to have a look at some of the books that I had found on the Fire Dancers, partly to get a return match on information handling with the librarian and partly to see if I could find any clues as to the nocturnal intruder in the Sun. However, for some reason wholly unknown to me, having turned right outside the door and headed down towards the market place I carried on forwards rather than turning left for the alley to Above Town. I only realized my mistake after a few moments when I noticed all the bustling crowds of people around me.

As I was already in the wrong place, I decided to take a bit of time to have a look at the various stalls and wagons on the site. I could never resist a look around a market and setting aside the brutal murders and the brutish collection of wagoners with their weird sign language and secretive customs, this one was no different.

There were a fair number of stalls selling meats of various types. These included more exotic meats such as squirrel and bush pig, wild boar and coypu.

The last of these a kind of large rat like animal that was originally brought in from overseas and farmed for its fur. However, the enterprising creatures had tended to escape into the wetlands where they built extensive tunneling systems to live and breed in. These in turn caused a number of the irrigation channels of some of the low lying lands to fail and occasionally burst with all manner of consequences. The consequences for the now wild coypu however were that they were hunted as pests, stripped of their fur as a luxury item and then (because nature hates waste) they were identified as a palatable if somewhat gamey meat that was cheaper than lamb but would curry anyway.

There were a few spice stalls and wagons but Welcome's wagon was nowhere to be seen. In its place at the pitch beneath the statue at the centre of the square there was a wagon selling cooking utensils, knives and other sharp and somewhat nasty looking metal objects. It was whilst I was looking over a rather solid pan for frying that I caught sight of a movement that startled me.

I had seen a reflection more of light than shape in the dull base of the pan as I turned it over and instinctively I looked over in the direction of its origins. I saw someone at another stall who, to all intents and purposes, was examining a few cheap balls of knitting wool but was quite clearly watching me. I felt as if my heart had missed a beat and I became conscious that I had started to sweat slightly and my breathing had become shallower.

As I had turned, I had seen the face move down from a position where it was looking at me to one in which it was inspecting the wool with an intensity usually reserved for precious metals or undergarments. The figure was wearing a tight fitting woolen cap that came down over the eyebrows and wrapped around the face was a dark scarf. There was nothing unusual in that in particular.

The coat came down more of less to the ankles and then as I looked I realized that he or she was wearing lightweight sandals. Now that was weird. Most of us were wearing heavy boots and one or more layers of grimy but precious socks, the kind that knock you over backwards when you take them off. The only other person around here that I had seen wearing sandals was Welcome but he was dead.

I considered briefly and then foolishly acted on the idea of walking over to the stall and see if anything happened. Now, one has to say that this was potentially a stupid strategy and one that could well have ended in bloodshed (mine that is, as I am no warrior and that is for certain) but I was prevented from this course of action by the strong arm of the wagoner whose stall I had been browsing.

"Ere, ja bas! You's a nickin' ma pan is ya, ya faw'kin farner!"

Well that was rich coming from a peripatetic salesman who was only half a dozen levels up from a vagabond. I was about to say something to this effect as I turned back to face him, trying at the same time unsuccessfully to shake his hand off my shoulder. He was another creature of excessive height. In one hand he held a huge saucepan that he looked about to use as a weapon and in the other hand. Well in the other hand he held me. Despite the cold he was wearing a kind of string vest only the material wasn't string: it was a heavy chain mesh and in the words of some people I know, he was ripped. In the words of others, he was buff. He looked about as much a warrior as I didn't.

I grinned, a little foolishly, man and boy inside my head screaming and pleading with me not to apologize. Oh well, nothing for it I guess. I took a deep breath, hoping that it wasn't my last and fired a reply.

"Why would I want to be nickin' your faw'kin pan, yer great big girl's blouse? Why, there's mankin' rust all over it and anyway what are you gonna charge me for it?"

I may not be a warrior but he was no word-smith.

"Wha' sat yer sayin'? Where's there rust?" he said dropping me and grabbing the frying pan to inspect it for rust. A huge finger scraped across the surface and then came back up in front of his face. He looked at it briefly where I could see the faintest hint of red and then his cheeks coloured up. I thought *"oh crap, he a berserker too and I'm going to die for telling the truth for once".*

"Aw for sure, mate, there is as well." he sounded a little abashed and then added *"It's the hair you know. It's getting into the riron. But it's good stuffa, the riron is and it'll polish up if yer seal it and treat it well.*

He paused.

"Fifteen trupps."

We we're off! No more risk of death but it was a contest to the end that I could not walk away from.

By the time that we reached that end I acquired a really good frying pan with a slight amount of rust for eight trupps. That was pretty much a bargain. The giant got eight trupps and managed to get rid of a heavy pan. The exchange had also gained the attention of some of the crowd and when I left him he was in a vigorous exchange with another would be customer. I hope he got a better price than he did with me. I also lost sight of the figure watching me. He was of course long gone by the time I was able to return my attention to where he had been standing.

I should make one point here just in case it is not that obvious. I imply that the follower was a man. Actually I have nothing to base that on. All I saw was a figure of about my height and build with sandaled feet. Now you might think the feet would have given the game away but don't forget that we are standing in a market square in the northern marches with snow, slush and other filth all around us. Those feet were pretty dirty. Then there is my eyesight. At twenty paces distance much is lost in translation between the retina and the cortex. As for smell, let's not make any mistakes here. Just be grateful that I can only hint at the various aromas that were hovering about this place. Don't forget the oxen and other animals that were hanging around here and I don't think that I have mentioned the offal cart yet. In fact, I don't think that I will.

XVI
The Swift's Tale

Now that the excitement of buying the frying pan was over, I decided that I needed to look around a bit more. This time however it was to try to catch another glimpse of my unknown follower. I took it as likely that either they would have hurried off on being discovered, possibly be replaced by another person (but why?) or that they had backed off for a while to keep watch from a distance. This being the most likely course, I decided to mill about looking at anything and everything until such time as they brought themselves to my attention once more.

It took some while but eventually they made a slip and I caught sight of them watching me from a spice wagon. This time I was cautious to make no movement to attract undue attention or to give any hint that I had seen them. I made some passing comment to a wagoner whose goods I had been inspecting and then doubled back towards the spice wagon where I purchased a small packet of red pepper spice. With a sense of satisfaction, I had noticed my follower fade back into the crowd as I approached but they did not go far.

Having now found him (this is still an assumption of course) I decided to head off back towards my original destination: the library. I removed my day sack from my shoulder and dropped the spice into the top of it, looping the handle of the pan onto a rope and flinging (well, more like placing) it carefully back over my shoulder so that it rested on the outside hanging down at the back. In that position I thought, rather lamely and without much confidence, that it might prevent a knife into the back should that be the purpose of my follower. I then made my way back across the square to the alley leading up towards the alley to Above Town.

It was difficult trying to watch what was going on behind me without turning round too obviously. I stopped a couple of times to tie up deliberately loosened boot laces and I used the opportunity to look behind me after some of the younger women who were coming down the alley towards and past me. However, it is difficult to be convincing about this when the women were wrapped to the full in winter clothes and in fact all of them more or less had the same basic shape whether young or old: a badly rolled rug. On one occasion in fact I realized just a little too late that one of these "women" was in fact a man who had the same approach as me. Our eyes met across the street. Mine, I hope said something like *"No, no, no! My mistake."* His unfortunately said a whole lot more. I just hurried on hoping that he didn't decide to follow.

Eventually I got to the top of the alley and out into the expanse of the small square. The stocks were still occupied and the occupant looked up wearily at the sound of my footsteps.

"Water mate!" he shouted out at me once more, offering me the same leering sort of a smile that he had attempted once before. I didn't even give him the time of day. Two soldiers were still there. I had no idea whether they were the same two or not. They might have been but either way they were there, playing a game just like before and watching anyone moving about in the street. I had to approach them to get to the library as they were more or less sitting on its steps. One looked at me in a disinterested sort of threatening way and threw the dice once more on the ground with grubby yellow stained hands. The other winked and blew me a kiss. OK so this one at least as probably one from the other day.

I climbed the steps trying not to look or feel discomfited by the loudly whispered conversation that was taking place behind me on the street and involved no doubt numerous references to me and my alleged sexual proclivities. I knocked on the door and waited. In the corner of my eye I could see a dark figure enter the square from the top of the alley and head off in a fairly slow manner towards the other side of it.

The librarian did not answer the door. It was a younger woman with a pretty but tired face who I took to be her daughter and probably the mother of the children that I had heard on my last visit. She smiled at me and made some indeterminate gesture with her hand that I took to be an invitation in. It was interesting to notice that neither soldier looked up at her or made any kind of comment but I left it at that. I followed her into the reading room where, again with another vague gesture, she left me to my own devices.

Once I knew that she had gone and that I was alone, I checked the window to see if I was still being watched. I could see the soldiers on the steps but they were still at their game. Across the square the hatted and scarved shape of my shadow was standing against a tree. As I watched I saw a brief shake of the arm and a slight and quick bending of the knees. Why they couldn't use the public urinal nearby was of course another matter. No doubt now about whether it was a man or a woman, I thought. He was however alone and that at least was reassuring.

I went back to the catalogue and started looking for the books that I had intended to read on the Fire Dancers and the myths of this part of the world. There were a couple in particular that I had intended to seek out as I thought that they might add a bit of value to the matter of the double ending of the tale. As I was flicking through the card index I started thinking about the muttered and muted conversations that I had overheard on my last visit here. That is how I found myself looking through the index with absolutely no purpose whatsoever.

This approach offered up an interesting observation. Each of the books that I had intended to review and indeed others that I hadn't known about but also related to the Fire Dancers were listed as "*Gone*" or were scratched out. Even the books that I had viewed at my first visit were "gone".

"Coincidence or what?" I asked myself out loud and was not surprised to find that there was no response. I decided to test the hypothesis by picking another couple of subjects at random to see if they came up with a similar result. The language of wagoners yielded only a couple of references (after all it was meant to be a secret language) but both of these were in the library, according to the catalogue. Wolves and their habits produced a large number of references including the book that Welcome had given me but which was recorded, as "Gone". Some were crossed through and some were not but there was sufficient distribution to demonstrate to me that there was nothing odd about that subject.

This was all a bit weird and I guess that I was beginning to get a bit carried away with some kind of conspiracy issue. To give myself a break from all this I got up and went to the window.

There across the green were two dark figures talking to each other, or at least in the posture of people talking to each other as I could neither see movement nor (obviously) hear voices. One of the figures, I was pretty certain was the one that I had labelled as my shadow. The other, although similarly dressed was slighter in build (or at least shorter and with a less bulky coat perhaps).

Now this was starting to get to me a bit. It was bad enough having one person following you for reasons that you cannot even guess at. It was quite another to see that they had accomplices or co-conspirators involved in the game. It crossed my mind to go out and speak with them and to find out once and for all what this was all about. However, I also knew that this was pointless. Either they would be gone into the alley before I reached them or they would be standing there five minutes after I had returned to the library discussing the strange antics of an old man with serious paranoia before returning to their respective homes and families.

I decided to return to the business of the catalogue and went in search of a few books Wolves, given the temporary lack of availability on the Fire Dancers. I deliberately chose those books that were in the upstairs room as I wanted to be able to take a look at the two persons that I now thought were following me. I left the reading room equipped with my list and headed off to the spiral stairs. These took me to a rather forlorn room at the front of the house crammed untidily with books without any sense of order. I had to ignore the directional instructions of the catalogue as there were multiple piles of books against each of the walls and in some areas these had toppled and slid down to merge with other equally displaced books in an untidy mess on the dirty carpeted floor.

The room was incredibly dusty and smelled damp. There was a dead bird lying in a corner of the room on top of a pile of books with small dried pieces of its final defecations littered on the cover. It looked almost as though it was resting but I knew from my travels that these birds rarely made landings other than when nesting and that their legs were not really well equipped to land and take off again other than by dropping from a height. It was one of those long distance migratory birds that travel from these parts of the world down to the shores of the Azure Seas each year. Not this one. Dead in the cold north and looking strangely desiccated. Not a feather out of place and only the sunken eyes to indicate at a glance that it was in fact dead and not asleep.

Why this room was so different from the others was a complete mystery. Downstairs was so orderly and clean. I started looking for the books but without much expectation but found a couple relatively easily. I also found, to my complete surprise a couple of books that I knew had been listed as "Gone" in the catalogue. After a short while I bundled together the four books that I had found and took them carefully back down the circular stairs to the reading room.

178

Only when I had got back down did I realize that I had forgotten to see what was going on outside. I took a quick look through the reading room window. There were now four people all dressed darkly and with various coloured hats and scarves all standing on the far side of the square. I decided at this point that I was not going to look outside anymore. I also wondered briefly whether Trellsheim had any laws against conventicles as existed in many of the other towns in the northern lands. These laws were brought in once civic authorities had regained control following the great Plague Riots a couple of centuries ago, in those regions that were particularly hit by the disease. Although couched in terms that implied religious toleration, they were in fact intended to prevent crowds of people forming on the streets other than in recognised market or assembly areas.

The size of the conventicle permitted varied from town to town but was generally in the region of six to eight persons and no more. In the worst hit towns, it could be as few as two which was to all intents and purposes a permanent curfew for anyone with a family, as children tended to be included in the poll count.

I have to say that I was becoming slightly alarmed at the number of persons who appeared to be interested in my activities, if indeed that was the case and it wasn't just random chance. Admittedly the presence of a couple of soldiers suitably tooled up on the doorsteps of the library gave me some sense of comfort but if the numbers increased any more I think that this scrap of comfort would be blown away.

In what proved to be a vain attempt to stave off the growing anxiety I tried to read the books that I had picked out. I failed to concentrate on all counts and after a decent period of time during which I achieved nothing but a series of moderately sharp intakes of breath, I gave up the task and stood up. Dropping the last book onto the table in irritation and four trupps into the honesty box, I gathered my day sack and unused notebook and went out into the hallway. I thought that it was ill

179

mannered to leave without making my exit obvious even in this ill-mannered world and so I wandered down the corridor into the depths of the house. I guess that I was also damned curious about this place, if I am honest.

The further into the house I went, the darker it became and the corridor went quite a way before it turned a corner and went at right angles off to the left. I had already passed a couple of rooms that were empty and in a third room there were two youngish children playing. They had small figures in their hands and one was directing the other in some kind of war or battle. I passed their doorway quickly as I didn't want to disturb them or to give them cause for concern and as I headed away I could still hear the urgent voices and the conspiratorial tones that they were using.

At another doorway I found the entrance to the kitchen. It was dark and quiet, the only light coming from a small window high up on the outer wall. Light streamed down through the dust laden air onto a table where a book lay open. Before it was the young woman, her hands clasped on her lap and her eyes red and wet from crying. She was sobbing openly now as I watched her but she seemed not to see me. In spite of the voices, there was no one else present.

I crept past trying not to be noticed. A part of me said that it was time to leave: that would be the man in me I guess. Yet the boy part of me said to look a bit further. I took the boy's advice (as I often did) and turned the corner of the corridor.

I was brought to an abrupt halt. In front of me was the iron face of the old librarian. She was standing there in the dark. I don't think that she was doing anything and I don't particularly think that she was walking along the corridor towards the kitchen or the library or me. I felt that she was waiting there in the dark, just around the corner. That she was waiting for me.

I had stopped dead in my tracks with all the guilt of a boy up to no good written all over my face. I looked down at her and in the poor light her skin seemed terribly solid and where it caught the light it seemed to radiate. Parts of her features were obscured but her eyes were dark and bright and angry. For what seemed like an age she stood there. She didn't speak, she didn't seem to breathe and I don't believe that she blinked once. I could feel a pulse beating in my neck and a small bead of sweat forming on the side of my head. I felt it run down part of my jaw and I shuddered.

"You found the upper room, then?" she said without any emotion.

"I did." I replied quietly, searching her eyes for sign.

"We *'aven't had time to fix it up yet."* she said her voice harsh with no hint of apology.

"Seen the bird?" she asked.

I nodded.

"Sweftes." she said.

"Probably." I replied woodenly still looking for the attack that must come.

She lifted her arm and pointed behind me towards the kitchen door, her index finger still and stiff and lit from above so that the skin looked oily or waxy.

"And you've seen our shame?" she said quietly, again no emotion.

I was silent. I wasn't entirely sure what she meant or even where this was all going. I didn't know what to say. I just looked at her and tried to communicate with her that I was just looking and to say that I was leaving: that I didn't mean any offense.

"And our joy..." she continued and as if on cue I heard the boys playing in the other room.

She didn't give me time to reply but continued, taking two steps forward and pressing me back.

"You can close the door on the way out."

Again, she gave no hint of emotion.

"And never come back!"

Her last words to me were hissed, full of venom and anger and bitterness. After a moment's hesitation, as my heart pumped somewhere behind my ears, I moved away. I backed from her as if from a threat and continued to walk backwards for a few paces before turning sharply and walking, almost running, from the house.

As I shut the door, the guards looked up and at the same time four coins were thrown from the reading room window to fall like stones into the remains of the snow and slush outside. The window closed like a prison's doors. There was a moment of silence.

"'Appen there's a storm a commin," said one of the guards looking up at the sky and the dark clouds forming.

"Aye, that there is," I replied, forgetting language as I watched now eight dark figures looking back at me from across the square.

I was reluctant to leave to relative sanctuary of the library steps and the comforting proximity of the soldiers. In my head there were a mass of emotions and anxieties washing about. Partly this came from what had just happened and from which I felt a sense of absolute failure and partly this came from the whole uncertainty of this growing crowd of people who seemed to have an interest in me.

To gain some thinking time I cast about for something to say to the soldiers. Strangely it came to me as I thought oddly about the stains that I had seen on the soldier's fingers. The one soldier had yellow fingers and Jimas had said earlier that day that Bartle Bane caused a yellow discoloration on skin.

"Have you seen any dogs about here at all?" I asked him.

"I've seen some for sure." he replied looking animated suddenly. *"Two dawgs came yammering up the alley this morning. They were snuffling and snapping about near the doorway here. We had to stop 'em from scratching the paintwork."*

182

He stopped and rummaged in his pocket and brought out a packet of something.

"Ah's give them some Bartle Bane," he said, *"I had to put it in my meat pie: the one I was savin for me breakfast."*

He paused long enough for me to catch up and then added a bit more that managed to lose me slightly once more.

"Makes 'em less snappy, does Bartle Bane," he grinned, *"it's a good stuffa for snappen dawgs!"*

I grinned back at him but inside thoughts were racing. The intruder had come to the library but surely it hadn't been the librarian. I had heard the sound of running and I could not imagine a woman of her age running along a corridor or up an alley that was slick with snow and slush. Were these people in the library in league with my pursuers and were the others still watching me from the other side of the square?

I pointed to the group of people opposite us (which I was relieved to see was still a total of eight) and asked the soldiers who they were. One of them looked up as though he hadn't even seen them gathering.

"No idea. I expect they're faw'kin farners, ye was!"

"Somethin's goin' on though." Added the other soldier with a sense of finality that I could not leave alone.

"It's all ok though?" I asked – I would like to think that I asked hopefully but I know that there was a reasonable bit of anxiety in the question. It was wasted on these two though.

"It's all ok?" They repeated, stupidly, as one voice.

"I guess so unless you's a faw'kin farner!" they grinned as one.

"Some as don't like fawkin farners, you know!"

I could see this conversation going fully over the wrong way.

"You're not a faw'kin farner are you?" One of them asked with a slight hint of threat in the voice.

"And ladybodys, they don't like them neither!" The other one added enthusiastically.

"You're not a ladybody are you?" he added with a strong hint of menace.

This was going pretty much the wrong way and it didn't seem to matter what I said, it just got worse.

Yes, I was a stranger (we can leave out the expletive) so I seemed to have a problem but no I wasn't a ladybody. Even so, if what they said was true, I probably had a problem even if they weren't interested in me specifically. I decided that there was no point postponing the inevitable. I just had to head back to the Sun and deal with whatever came up along the way.

I wouldn't consider myself a brave man but nor would I consider myself cowardly. There comes a point at which routine fear cuts out and you have to step over into the next zone. This next zone, the man's voice in my head tells me is stupidity. It's the one where, as the motivational words say, you go and face your fear. The boy in my head thinks that's great because you get a rush of adrenalin and he really loves that kind of thing. I am fifty-two, on the other hand, and my knees suspect that I might be a bit older. The thought of moving quickly to zone three, which is fight or flight – and in my case it would be flight, I can tell you – and having to run with a howling mob of pursuers hot on my tracks down a treacherous alleyway (to ... well to where ever, I don't really think that I want to consider that right now...) really did not appeal much. Still, what choice?

Sometimes the absence of options is an advantage. I left the false sanctuary of the library steps and walked towards the Alley. The felon in the stocks looked up.

"Water..."

"Shove it up your arse!" I hissed at him under my breath and with the confidence of someone who knows that he can't retaliate and in any case probably didn't speak my language.

I had worked out that there was no point going over and confronting the eight of them. Either they were interested in me or they were not. If I headed down the alley, they would either follow or carry on about their business oblivious to my petty actions. Having crossed to the head of the alley without looking at the figures, it took all my willpower not to take one quick peak as I disappeared out of the sunlight into the shade.

I now had the issue and all the anxiety of getting down the alley at a reasonable pace without slipping or falling and fast enough without looking as though I was in headlong flight. Behind me in front of the library, the soldiers having first sought out and found three of the discarded coins thrown from the library, started up their game of dice again and carried on their conversation about the *"faw'kin farner as what likes dawgs"* as they sniggered at the various less savory implications of that concept.

Opposite at the far side of the green six hatted and scarved figures carried on the conversation that they were having in hushed tones about a subject that no one outside their circle would ever know about. Storm clouds were slowing blowing in from the East, chasing away the bright blue sky and bringing with it a greater chill and the promise of more snow. The felon in the stocks lay limp and quiet as though he was asleep.

In the upper room of the library, the desiccated, brown swift lay on a dusty book, its sunken dead eyes hiding the story of its last minutes of life some months now past. In the relative quiet of the rooms behind the library, the small boys continued their game of soldiers. In the kitchen the woman, their mother perhaps, continued to sit with her limp hands on her lap, palms up and slightly cupped as if she held a shallow bowl into which the tears of her bitter sadness occasionally dripped.

The wax skin around the face of the old librarian that reflected the small amount of light from the tiny kitchen window stood out in relief against the darkness of the corridor whilst her breath came and went slowly and with measured pace, seeming to draw in entirely with each one, the world in which she stood.

XVII
A Bath Tale

I made it back to the Sun with no intervention whatsoever and slipped as quickly as I could through the narrow, brown painted double doors. Jimas was behind the bar and he looked up briefly before returning to his own business. A few people sitting around drinking coffee and chatting or reading but the place was generally quiet. I went to the bar to get myself a drink and, whilst waiting for Jimas to finish serving another person, I watched for signs of movement outside through one of the narrow windows that looked onto the alley. I saw one of the hatted and scarved shadows walk past without even checking his pace, heading up towards the plague quarter presumably. There were no others to be seen as I watched.

"Mint tea?" said Jimas, making me jump slightly.

"Eh up, you're a bit jumpy?" he said with a grin. *"Perhaps it was all this morning's excitement?"*

"Perhaps it is, Jimas." I said automatically.

"Ye was!" he replied, equally automatically, and went to fetch the tea.

When he came back, I told him about the soldier and the yellow stained hands up at the library as I paid him three trupps.

"Soldiers!" He said. *"There's only one thing they're good for!"*

He smiled lecherously and made a gesture that clearly demonstrated what soldiers were good for.

"The dawgs are ok, though." he added seeming pleased that all ended well for his pet monsters.

I went to sit at a table in a quiet and uninhabited corner of the bar. I needed a bit of space so that I could spend a while trying to blot out all the activities and mysteries of the morning (and it was only just turned noon). There is a surprising numbness that I can achieve when things just seem that little bit too much. Perhaps if I had grander views on life in general, I would call this some form of meditation or achieving some higher state but in truth I don't think so. It is just as I said, a form of numbness: of switching off.

The tea was hot and refreshing and, as I sat there numbed and sipping the drink, I could feel a familiar sense of relaxation permeating my veins.

I woke up some time in the late afternoon. My mouth was dry which could only mean that I had been sleeping (and most probably snoring) with my mouth open. In a public place like this it was, by definition, embarrassing. I looked around but no one present seemed to be watching me and I could only hear the activity of the Bo'sun or Jimas who were working in the galley just out of view.

It seemed like a good idea to head off to my room and catch up on some proper sleep. I didn't feel much like eating and I was in no particular mood to be sociable. I left the teapot and tea on the table (rather than taking it to the bar). This was done out of a sense of petulance on my part although it wasn't particularly directed at the two guys who ran the place. It was more towards the world at large, the world that seemed to be stalking me for some obscure reason and which, beyond my utter comprehension seemed to be closing in about me. In my utter ignorance, I had absolutely no idea how enclosing it was all about to become.

As I fumbled as usual with the lock to the room (or rather with the location of the key in whichever pocket I had dropped it) I caught the faintest whiff of some perfume or scent. It was so fleeting that it might even have been a hallucination, if that is the correct term when applied to smell. I assumed, if it was real, it had come wafting up the stairs on the breeze or had insinuated itself from under one of the doors along the corridor and thus made its escape.

This changed as I opened the door and the scent came wandering out on the air that tumbled out of my room into the colder, heavier air outside in the corridor. The atmosphere was heavy with moisture and there was a hint of warmth about it also. I thought that perhaps I had left the hot water tap running earlier that day and that by some miracle, the bath had not overflowed.

The sound of the tap being turned on gave the lie to this possibility and started up in me an increasingly familiar sense of dread. Perhaps I was sharing this room with another night watchman! I had expected better of the Sun, somehow, when compared to the grubby stay in Champneys, but I suppose that I was in the north and things were a little different to the world in which I . The thought of another huge and ugly night watchman or some similar other half-troll wandering out into the room (my room I had thought once more) naked and dripping was not pleasant. Then again there was the perfume and that added another dimension to the matter, a particular bent that I didn't really want to expand upon right now.

The long and short of it all was that I really didn't want to be sharing a room with someone else. Rather than confront the individual at a disadvantage (I hoped) I decided to go and remonstrate with the Bo'sun and get him (the individual), or me for that matter – I wasn't proud – installed in another room. I was about to head off down the corridor when I heard a gasp from my bathroom (I still thought of it as my bathroom you notice).

The gasp did not sound like that of some giant oaf of a man, in fact it didn't sound like a man at all. This pricked my interest slightly and I decided to hang about and see what was going on, rather than involve the lads downstairs unnecessarily.

With hindsight, that was arguably a mistake but I have to say that the jury is still out on this, even today.

Rather foolishly, I tapped on the door to the room (my room) and then leaned a little further forward and said in the rather exaggerated way that people do when sticking their bodily presence into places that they think perhaps they should not be...

"Hel-lo!"

I used my own language, rather than the local vernacular though I don't know why. Still I got no reply other than some slight splashing about in the other room. Clearly they hadn't heard me and so with the exaggerated steps of some giant wading bird I walked further into the room towards the bathroom door.

Then I made the second of those ritualistic and totally pointless challenges that people make in such circumstances.

"Is anybody there?"

Even I knew the answer to this. Either there was a person or persons unknown in my bath or otherwise some unfortunate creature had fallen in the water and was splashing about in its death throws and gasping what was most likely its last.

Obviously I still had not been heard and as there was now silence from the other room, I decided that perhaps enough was enough and I ought to go in and find out. There was of course the risk that this person or these persons unknown having now realized that they had been discovered were now lying in wait to beat me senseless the minute that I put my head around the door.

It occurred to me that this was actually the only sensible thought that I had had since I walked into the room and so I looked about for some impromptu form of weapon with which to defend myself in the event. I found nothing obvious but what I saw as I looked around the room made me stop dead in my tracks and made my heart race. There on my bed was a dark broad brimmed hat and trailing off the bed and across the floor was a long scarf. In my new heightened sense of alert and alarm, I sensed rather than saw a dark shape behind the door and in a panic I swung around, throwing up my arms in defense across my face and head. The large black coat that was hanging there paid me pretty much no attention whatsoever.

Now we were talking serious here. The idea of my pursuer or pursuers being in my room and even more so that they should be in my bathroom was bizarre beyond belief but it did nothing to detract from the real sense of concern that I had, nor take away the risk of possible attack and injury. There were two options: fight or flight. I am not a brave man but nor do I consider myself to be cowardly and perhaps it was the idea of catching someone off guard in the bath that strengthened my resolve as it were. It could also be that I was sick and tired of being followed about all day by unknown persons and not to mention the personal affront (if not pretty much an assault) by the old librarian but I decided to go for the fight.

I picked up a small wooden chair that was by the window and, holding the rather cumbersome thing in front of me, stepped into the steamy bathroom. I made as little noise as possible now and didn't say a word as I advanced into the thick warm air. I think that is why the person in the bath probably didn't notice me.

Her eyes were also tightly closed and her whole head was under the water. She had the most amazing bronze red hair that floated around her head like copper seaweed and she was totally submerged. Well technically not totally, her nipples floated on the surface like pink cherry blossom in a pool and further down her body, slightly lighter curled red hair surfaced occasionally. Even further downstream, some of her toes also surfaced and, even as I took in a full view of what was a very beautiful naked woman luxuriating in my bath, I couldn't help but notice that her toe-nails needed cutting and that there was dirt between some of her toes.

I stood there like an idiot and a pervert just soaking in the beauty of it all before me. She really was lovely, white skinned and with boyish hips (and I really like women with boyish hips although I wouldn't admit that to the Bo'sun and his mates downstairs for fear of confirming their already unreasonable suspicions). I said that she was beautiful (and she was) but I would also point out that I think that almost all women are beautiful without fail or effort and that it really takes some significant action (or lack of action) on the part of an individual to prevent them from being so.

Whether this is just because I am a man and equipped with my own supplies of testosterone and desire and all that goes with it, or because my culture has led me to define beauty in the female form or, simply that women are in fact beautiful, I have no idea. I like to think it is the last option but I suspect that there may be other factors that I just don't want to admit to. I have rarely in my years seen a man that I consider beautiful for example (and in fact I can recall exactly the one time that I have) and never in my life have I ever wanted to sleep with, or rather have sex with, a man and yet there are many, many women with whom I would love to have had sex with (at least in my head).

I had managed to get my focus back onto her face at just about the right time and was looking at a beautiful mouth with light pink lips tightly closed against the warm water when she suddenly surfaced and opened her eyes.

It must have been a strange, if not ridiculous sight and I would have thought a little worrying to her. There was this old man in the bathroom looking down at her. Let's face it, no matter how I tried, the lust and the desire must have been pretty obvious. I am sure that my mouth half open like an idiot (it's a wonder that I wasn't dribbling) would have been enough, quite apart from the obvious hunger in my eyes (which fortunately of course, I could not see). Then again, I was still holding the wooden chair in front of me , my arms stiff and erect so that it must have looked, for all the world, like an abstract simulacra of my penis.

Perhaps that is why, instead of panicking or calling out or even trying to cover herself she simply looked up at me. For my own part, I was unable to move my gaze away from her eyes for fear of embarrassing myself further and could see her eyes sparkle whilst at the edge of my vision I saw her mouth also break into a broad smile that let her teeth show through.

"I'm awfully sorry..." I started to say, still holding the chair out straight in front of me and unable still to take my eyes from hers. *"I must be in the wrong room."*

I was on auto pilot and this was just crap. I was obviously in my own room and had just come into the bathroom to sort out an intruder. The only difference was that instead of some brutish man with a club ready to beat me to death, here before me was a beautiful and naked woman who was smiling at me. If she had pulled a dagger from under the water and plunged it into my chest I would have been none the wiser and would have died just as brutally.

"It all right" she said, still smiling and speaking my name, *"I was waiting for you."*

Perhaps I had died after all. The voice that spoke my language and then my name was one that I had first heard over forty years ago. If it were at all possible my mouth dropped open further and the chair, which was starting to get heavy anyway, started to lower at more or less the same rate as the erection that I haven't yet admitted to started to collapse.

"Do I know you?" I asked her, the chair now on the floor.

"No, not yet." she said pushing herself backwards and upwards in the water so that in addition to spilling water out over the back of the bath and onto the wooden floor where it ran towards me across the uneven surface, she had placed

herself into a sitting position with her breasts in full view. I was now staring hopelessly at her.

"But I know about you." she said still smiling and without a hint of embarrassment. In fact she looked as though she was enjoying my discomfiture.

"Do you have a towel?" she asked and then continued almost without interruption. *"You are the Collector of Tales."*

"Yes." I said and then recovering slightly *added "Yes, to both. I'll go and get you one."*

I turned and left the room and I have to say that I was glad to get away from her for a while as I really needed to recover my composure somehow and to get the blood pumping around to the parts that really mattered rather than to recently unused peripheral organs. I rummaged around in my things to find a towel that I could present to her with the least sense of embarrassment.

I only had two, so my judgment was made on the basis of look and smell, the latter being more significant to me for some reason. I tried also spraying a little of Welcome's perfume onto the preferred option and wafted it about in the room vigorously to disperse it. I knew however that even to my aging olfactory organs I could still smell the stench of my feet on it.

I had just about got myself under control when I heard water moving in the bathroom and recognized the distinctive sound of someone rising up out of a bath. My imagination went into overdrive. A few seconds later she appeared at the doorway and my erection came back with even greater vigor than ever.

"It's a bit colder out here," she said, wrapping her arms around herself (but still leaving a lot that didn't require imagination).

"Have you got that towel?"

I looked at the offensive rag and threw it towards her. She caught it and sniffed it with one fluid action before flinging it in the direction of the bath. I heard a slight splash as the thing hit the water and no doubted started to sink.

"*I think that it's seen a bit too much action,*" she said.

"*Have you got anything clean that I can throw on for a while and perhaps you can get a fire going? You have a spare shirt or a jumper perhaps?*"

I failed to notice that she had immediately taken control of me in the way that women seem to do and that I was now busying myself about my room on her instructions. It took me no time to whip out a cream coloured shirt from my pack: my favourite shirt in fact. Worn only on special occasions and clean as of now, it had a round neck with stud holes where I could vary the collar style (when I could get hold of the collars). It was a coarse kind of cotton but I suspect that there was a fair amount of nettle in it also.

This I handed her as she approached me. It must have looked as though I was warding her off because a slightly puzzled expression passed across her face before she started to dress herself. Let's face it though. It was hardly dressing and although the shirt covered all the essentials, there was still the simple and let's face it, glorious, fact that there was a really good looking woman standing more or less naked in my room.

Sadly (and I say this because it demonstrates obsessive behavior) I noticed that she had, since I left the bathroom and before she got out, cleaned her feet.

I was conscious that it was in fact cold in the room but I was not over keen to turn my back on somebody who was after all a complete stranger to me, even though she owned a voice that I could have sworn that I had heard before.

"*Why don't you sit on the bed,*" I said,"*then you can keep yourself warm with the blankets until the fire offers a bit of heat.*"

I said this without really thinking and only once it was out, did I realize exactly how it sounded and, in all honesty, exactly how I was thinking.

"Is that a proposition?" she asked with a smile.

"No, of course it's not," I replied a little sharply, *"I just thought...."*

"That's very kind of you," she interrupted going over to the bed and doing as I suggested.

This meant that I could get on with lighting the fire whilst she remained just on the edge of my vision. The fire had already been well laid by the Bo'sun or his staff and I was moderately expert in lighting fire in all sorts of circumstances (well perhaps not this circumstance). I soon had the fire alight and as the dry kindling took, the flames began to dance and crackle in the hearth.

"That was quick," she said.

"It's a knack. It comes with experience and age," I replied.

"It'll take a while to heat up the room though so I would stay there if I were you."

I added a couple of the logs to the fire, a little too early I knew but I was keen to move this on and hopefully get this woman on her way, wherever that was. I hoped at least that the logs were well seasoned and would light quickly.

There is something wonderful and comforting about a fire and for a while I looked into the flames and they danced and waved about. I hadn't forgotten the woman and was sort of watching for any sudden movements or hints of threat but regardless of this I gazed into the light trying to work out what to say next.

I felt that I was on safer ground now that she was clothed or at least, covered. I guess that she was mid-twenties, which makes her younger than two of my daughters. When I hadn't been staring at her various attributes as she stood in the doorway of the bathroom I had noticed that she was a little bit shorter than me.

She was now sitting on my bed and was watching me as I moved about the room with an expectant and almost childlike expression on her face.

"Do you have anything to eat?" she asked rather plaintively and at those words she moved from being an object of sex or desire in me, to something rather different and I remembered my age and the fact that she was quite literally young enough to be my daughter. I felt a deepening sense of shame that blossomed in the coloration of my face as I recalled my earlier thoughts and if I am honest, aspirations. She did however remain to me a beautiful woman. Before I could answer her, she spoke again.

"Are you all right?"

"Yes, I'm fine. Why do you ask?"

"You look a little flushed in the face, that's all."

"Well, my dear, it's a bit like this. I find a beautiful woman in my bathroom and, oddly enough she is naked and looks like my wife when she was your age. God's ear, she even sounds like her when she speaks. Now add to that the fact that I haven't had sex since I can't remember when. I am not sure if you can imagine the thoughts and imaginings that ran through my mind and if I am honest, still are and yet I have two daughters and a son who are older than you. So in answer to both questions, I would have to say no, I don't have any food other than a cheese that I bought a couple of weeks ago in a small village down south and no, I am not all right because I am pretty put out by the thoughts in my head right now."

Oddly, she smiled at me again. It was a disarming smile and it was wholly effective.

"But you haven't done anything or said anything to me and I am not ashamed. Believe me, I did need a bath and the opportunity was too good to miss. I hope that I haven't upset you. I do like cheese though."

I laughed.

"No you haven't upset me and if you like cheese, then let's get the thing out and see if it's up to the promises that I was given when I bought it. I also have a flask of..." I stopped because a thought, an obvious thought, had just struck me. "How is it you are speaking my language?"

"I'm speaking my language actually," she replied.

"I came here a few years ago with a trader from Xandria who promised to marry me and make me a woman of leisure. As it happens he didn't marry me and I had to become a different kind of woman of leisure than I had originally in mind in order to survive in this wretched place."

She paused and sighed before continuing, "If you have a flask of red wine, that would go really well with the cheese."

She smiled once more, and this time it was the unashamed smile that I had seen in the bathroom earlier. It had the same basic disarming effect. I laughed once more.

"As it happens I always carry a supply and I think that you may be right."

The cheese was a relatively unknown variety from a pretty limestone region just north of my country, made from sheep's milk and beautifully matured. As I un-wrapped it from its cloth, a delicious smell began to pervade the room. Placing it on the small table, I removed my knife from my pocket but then hesitated to leave it on the table with this unknown woman. She must have seen the gesture because she giggled, got up off the bed and reached into her coat which was hanging up behind my door.

"That's not much of a knife," she said. "Anyway I have my own here."

She took out a weapon from the inside of her coat. I use the term weapon' specifically because it wasn't any form of domestic knife. The handle looked to be of bone or something like it and was beautifully crafted. The blade was about seven inches long with a slight curve to it. It looked wickedly sharp.

"It keeps me safe," she said grinning, "and I keep very sharp in return."

I wasn't sure whether I liked the idea that I was now in a room with a complete stranger who seemed to have no fear of me and was waving a dangerous looking implement about as if it were a pencil. Admittedly, she hadn't cut my throat yet but that was not really a massive matter of reassurance. Anyway I dropped my knife onto the table with a somewhat petulant look on my face and went to get the wine out of my pack.

As I was doing this, she got back under the covers and watched me (I think) with interest.

"I have no intention of hurting you," she said, as I put the wine down alongside the cheese on the table.

In my head, the man's voice snorted loudly and said "she's a woman: of course she's going to hurt you!" I ignored him. I was relieved to hear the comment and was reassured by another beautiful and disarming smile that she gave me as I sat down.

Does that make me gullible?

Well I guess that it does, but then I am not a young man and whilst I have already said that I don't seek out the company of others, that is not to say that sometimes I don't just get lonely and want to hear the voice of, and speak to, another individual.

I cut the cheese in half (with my own knife) and then cut a couple of small slices out of one side, separating them to allow the cheese to breathe a while. Then I opened the wine and poured some into the mug that was already on the table and then filled the copper container that was the top of the flask for me. I motioned to her to drink but she refused, saying that she would let the drink breathe a bit along with the cheese.

That was exactly what I had intended to do. Against all the warnings in my head, I was beginning to like this woman.

"I'm sorry that I haven't got any glasses," I said. "They are a rare commodity and besides they don't travel very well."

"That's OK," she said lightly, "It's not a problem. If it's good, it's good and if it's vinegar, it's vinegar. There's not a lot more to it really, is there?"

I was really beginning to like her. She was saying things that I could have said myself. To change the subject, at least in my own mind, I went over to the fire, which had started to burn fairly well, to give it a prod and to put on another log. The room was not a lot warmer but at least it was not as cold.

"So how did you get in here?" I asked.

"I walked in," she replied simply as if there was some other way.

"No, I mean how did you get upstairs and how did you get though the locked door. I have enough trouble as it is getting in with a key."

"Oh," she said and smiled, "I made myself un-noticeable, walked through the bar and up the stairs and gave the door a bit of a shove."

I failed to see how a woman this pretty, even in a place like the Sun could not be noticed. If she came in wrapped in hat, scarf and coat she would have stood out just as much. As for the door, it was as robust as any other and the lock looked good.

"Really?" I said.

I think that the scepticism was clear in my tone.

"Yes, really," she said, adding, "it's a knack."

She smiled.

I left it at that.

"And you were looking for me?"

"No. I was following you. I have been since I first saw you in the plague quarter. Before that I was looking for you."

"Why?"

"I was asked to."

She was either unwilling to expand issues unless asked or was not a particularly keen conversationalist. This was a bit like trying to get blood from a stone. I continued anyway.

"Who asked you?"

"A friend," she replied simply.

"Just a friend?" I asked and then blushed further at the innuendo that I had not intended.

Whether she picked it up or not, she ignored it.

"A trader from the marketplace."

"A spice trader?" I ventured.

"With a bear," she replied as though we both knew how the conversation was supposed to run.

I could not imagine what Welcome's link was with this girl and why had he asked her to follow me.

"So why did he ask you?"

"Because he wanted to keep an eye on you and I was available."

I refrained from asking why he wanted to keep an eye on me. I began to wonder - and admittedly it was uncharitable - whether in fact the requirement was to keep an eye on the book that he had given me. That thought lasted until the spectre of the crowd of people on the green by the library had come back into the room to resurrect some of my anxiety and it sat now somewhere in the dark corners of my mind picking at any sense of comfort that I could wrap about me.

"Do you know what he wanted?"

"No not really. He said that you were the Collector of Tales and that he wanted me to keep an eye on you."

"So who were all those people outside the library earlier today?" I asked. It was a random question, I knew, but I thought that it might yield something

"Which people?"

"The ones that you were standing with whilst I was in the library. There were at least eight of you when I last looked."

She had started to look at me as if was being weird now.

"You were up there today weren't you?" I asked, sounding, I knew, a lot less certain of myself.

"No. I came straight here this morning just after you had left."

"But I thought that you were supposed to follow me."

"I was, but I thought that once I knew where you were staying the best thing to do was to go there and speak to you."

"But why?"

"To get to know you of course and see if I could find out why I was being asked to chase around on a fool's errand," she said.

"I may be stranded here in this god-forsaken town for the moment but I do have other things to do than follow some stranger about all day. I wanted to know what was going on and the best person to ask was you."

This had now gone full circle and I was none the wiser and it looked as though I was not going to get any wiser. I decided to try a different approach but first I reached for my wine. It seems that we had a similar view because she did the same.

The wine wasn't bad. It wasn't great either but it complimented the cheese. I cut us both a piece more, this time not waiting for it to breathe any further before devouring it. In this manner, more or less in silence other than the sound of munching and sipping, we demolished the cheese and a fair quantity of wine. I topped up our respective cups with the last from my supply and leaned back against the wall. (I was sitting on the floor – I have never really liked sitting on chairs and didn't feel that it was right to be sitting with her on the bed.)

"So you know already that the trader with the bear was killed yesterday morning in the market place."

I made this a statement but I suppose that really it was a question.

"I saw there was a murder in the square but I don't think it was him. I think you saw me there didn't you?"

I ignored the question and went straight to the point about Welcome.

"How would you not think it was him? There was a bear there as well," I offered.

"Oh it was his bear for sure but I don't think that he was at his wagon that day. He said that he was going to get someone to mind it for him as he had some business in the town to sort out. I heard that the bear attacked the minder and killed him before someone could kill the creature."

"How do you know this?" I almost demanded.

She ignored the abruptness and continued as though I hadn't interrupted.

"He asked me if there were any of us in the town who were Ruard'an so that he could get someone to mind the wagon and not upset the bear. I said that there wasn't so I guess he used someone else and the bear got upset."

That didn't make any sense at all. I had sat for a day on the wagon with the bear and had even dropped a heavy pack on it without undue consequences or even the slightest hint of attack.

We seemed to be at an impasse and so I decided to tell her what had happened to me from the time that I had met Welcome on the road until I found her in my room. At least that way she might be clearer about what was going on and perhaps then, she might be able to enlighten me. But first I had to know a name.

"It seems that you already know me but I don't yet know your name," I said.

She paused and looked at me for a while as though thinking of a suitable response.

"I have no name in this place."

There was, no doubt, significance in this statement but I had no idea what it was and I was in no mood to ask so I continued.

"But I have to have a name to call you by. I can't just refer to you as 'you' and somehow it seems impolite not to ask."

"I have no name. You can call me what you like: any name; any term. That is the nature of my trade."

This didn't sound very good to me. The nature of a woman with no name was beginning to dawn on me and I wasn't entirely sure that I was happy with the implications of my interpretation.

"Whoa there! Hold on now. Are you propositioning me? If you are then I have to say that I am not in the market and if that is the purpose of all this, then it is time for you to go."

A slightly different slant appeared to be developing here and it was one that I liked even less than most of the other interpretations that I could offer right now. I stood up and was heading to the bathroom to retrieve whatever clothes she had left there.

"I'm sorry," she called after me, *"that was not a proposition. I am not here on that kind of business. I've already told you that."*

She sounded genuinely distressed and when I returned from the bathroom with a small pile of clothes I could see that the smile had gone and that she was now looking at me with the kind of anxious look that you might see in a small child when you are about to tell it off. She had put down her cup of wine and was clasping her hands together in front of her anxiously.

I stood there for a while looking at her and saying nothing. I guess I was weighing it all up and under my scrutiny she fidgeted and looked now for the first time, embarrassed.

"Are you judging me?" she asked after a while.

"No, why would I be? If you want to know I am deciding whether I believe you or not. I think that belief is a little distant from judgment, is it not?"

That was a little severe, I admit. I paused but then added, in an attempt to be more human, *"I found your clothes. They need to dry out by the fire though as they are all soaking wet."*

"Yes," she said, *"I know. I washed them before I bathed. They were seriously in need of a wash as well."*

Involuntarily, I sniffed the damp pile: they didn't smell particularly clean.

"No soap for them, you see," she said, *"I only had enough for me."*

She giggled, *"cleaner than they were though, believe me."*

I put the chair by the fire and draped some of the heavier clothes over it before poking the fire into further action. As I felt the warmth start to radiate into the room once more, I took myself back to my position against the wall on the floor where I had left the sad dregs of my wine.

"Those might take some time to dry, you know," I said.

I was very conscious that that could have been taken in much the same manner that I had taken her comment about names.

"I'm not suggesting anything," I added quickly, *"I'm just saying that they won't dry quickly, even near the fire."*

If I had any sense, I would have stopped at that but I couldn't seem to stop and so just kept on going.

"It's going to be very cold outside by now, " I could feel myself colouring up, *"and I think that you should wait until they are dry before you leave, don't you?"*

I was dropping further and further into the hole. I could tell the depth of it by the burning sensation in my face and when I looked at last at her, the expression of amusement that had returned to her eyes.

"Are you asking me to stay the night, sir? "

She asked this slightly formally although her eyes were all out laughter.

"Good grief no!" I replied trying my best to regain some sense of control and composure. "I was just saying that ..."

I hesitated trying to find the right words.

"I was just saying ..."

Oh god this was awful. I took a breath and blurted out.

"I just think that it would be more sensible if you stayed here until your clothes were dry."

There, I felt as though I had propositioned her but I don't think that that is how I meant it.

"If that's all right with you, that is?" I added lamely.

"I am quite happy to sleep on the floor," I driveled on like a fool, "In fact I prefer to sleep on the floor usually."

This last comment was, thank god, my concluding point.

The girl with no name was laughing at me now, her hand in front of her mouth as she tried without success to stifle her amusement.

For my part I was furious with myself. I was behaving like some schoolboy, not a man of middling years with nine children spread out over   the past thirty odd of those, three of who –as I have already said - were in fact older than the woman now sitting on my bed naked but for my best shirt.

"I think that that is possibly the nicest proposal that I have had from any man in a long time," she said, smiling at me.

"And," she added, "for the sake of clarity, I don't mean an offer of sex."

We looked at each other for a while and I could feel some sense of control and calmness returning to me.

"After all, "she said, "you are old enough to be my father!"

"Yes, indeed," I mumbled, feeling more downcast than ever, "I am old enough to be your father."

We were both silent for a while after this exchange. I was lost in various confused and troubled thoughts as I watched the dancing flames of the fire and the strange patterns that they made on the clothes now draped over the chair. What the woman with no name was thinking, as my son would say, I have no idea. I don't really know how long we were like this.

I heard someone stumble along the corridor outside and then the sound of a key inexpertly wrestling with a lock. Whoever it was dropped they key twice before finally I heard the sound of a door as it closed. I guessed from this that the Bo'sun was locking up downstairs and pictured him calling time and scowling and vigorously rubbing the tankards clean as the dawdlers hung on to their last drops of ale before the return to their own homes.

I have never understood what it was that drives a person to spend hours in a place like this when their home and family is barely a short walk away. I guess it must be a form of loneliness. On those few occasions that I have worked behind a bar, now in the dim and distant past, I have seen these sad men sitting: sometimes alone, sometimes in groups, all clean and dressed and tidy despite a day of work. I guess it is some form of escape from a loud and otherwise chaotic home with children running about and crying and the woman that they thought of once as a goddess, now tearing her hair out with frustration, boredom and exhaustion: no longer the song of a Siren but rather the screech of the Harpy.

"What are you thinking about?"

The words slipped almost unnoticed into my thoughts as I remembered my wife, now far away with the younger ones of our brood. We used to ask each other that question: wanted to get into each other's minds to try to understand a bit more about the other. Perhaps in the end, it is good that we could not. It is not often now that we ask each other the question.

"My wife," I replied quietly.

"Oh," she said.

There was another silence between us during which the fire chose to crackle and spit out small bits of burning wood onto the floor. I got up and scraped them back to the hearth with my

207

knife and took the opportunity to add another log. The room was actually quite warm now.

"What is she like?" she asked as I sat back down on the floor and reached out for the wine that I then realized was gone.

"You said that I reminded you of her," she offered.

"She is beautiful. And she is a great soul," I said.

"She's never really understood that though and now that the weight of the years bears down on us even more, she understands it less. She gets very angry with me."

I continued, rambling a little with my own thoughts beside me, *"Sometimes, I don't really know why."*

I added the last bit as an afterthought. It didn't seem appropriate.

"Are you," she hesitated, *"separated?"*

"In the matter of geography, we are some three thousand leagues apart. In another sense, I don't think that we are as close as we were. We are both very busy people in our very different worlds. But no we are not separated in the legal sense."

She looked away from me as I was speaking. I could see her taking it all in but she was off somewhere else and I was left with my own memories. I watched her staring into the fire as it coughed and crackled before us but in her eyes she was walking in other fields and places. For my own part, the flames had started to dance before me but I was away in another part of my life talking to the woman who had shared her life with me.

"What are you thinking?"

I thought at first that she had not heard me but I refrained from repeating the question, preferring just to sit and watch her for a while. There was silence once more between us. She watched the fire, caressing the skin on her neck with the back of the fingers on her left hand, a tear forming in the corner of her eye. I watched her with all those pictures of times and aspirations gone by as they floated in and out of my mind. I felt sad and I felt very alone.

"I'm sorry," she said,"*it was never meant to be like this. We had such hopes and dreams. We were going to do so many things. What happened to us?*"

"*I think we did them,*" I replied quietly, getting up from the floor where I had been sitting (as I always did) and reaching out to take her hand.

"*Did we?*" she asked, the tears now falling, "*then why do I feel so ... empty?*"

I sat beside her on the bed, still holding her hand and with my other hand stroked her forehead and temple, watching the tears run the little paths down her skin. We sat there, the two children that we once were, in the darkness of the room with the firelight dancing and gamboling around us and for a long while neither of us spoke another word.

I don't know whether we made love at that time or had sex or indeed whether there was any carnal activity whatsoever. My mind was an orgy of images that came and went uninvited and could have come from one or many days or nights of the now distant past. I recalled tastes and sensations: the softness of the skin of her breasts; her nipples swollen for me to lick and suck; the smell of sweat and the taste of salt; the comfort of a body next to mine; the warmth of her leg across my thigh; damp and coarse hair rubbing against damp and coarse hair.

I heard you gasp or sob and like so many times before, I came to my senses alone and in the morning light, my bed disheveled and the fire now cold and ash, some of which had spread like a fan into the room. One of my hands was numb from sleeping on it and, as I struggled to rise up, something heavy fell off the bed behind me and slumped to the floor, leaning heavily against the back of my leg. Had I turned around I would have seen my day sack lying there on its side, a small and growing stain of dried lentils spilling from a bag within it to mingle with the dust and ash now on the floorboards.

"The Bo'sun is not going to be happy with this mess," I thought.

The chair was on its side by the fire but there were no clothes there. I saw through poorly focused eyes that the peg behind the door was empty. I could hear no sounds in the bathroom and all that was left to me was the throbbing in my temple and the pain with each pulse of my heart. On the floor just below the bed and painfully level with my eyes I could see a scrap of paper. I thought at first that it was the one that I had found at the market place but as my eyes struggled to focus on the writing I could see that it was different.

It was too far away to read (and sadly that was not very far for me) so I reached out with my right arm to recover it. That was a more complex task than I realized partly because both my shoulder muscles and the muscles in my arm seemed strangely reluctant to comply with my instructions. Then once I had in fact managed to reach the paper I found that my fingers appeared to have locked up.

I tried quite hard to retrieve this paper and only managed it after a considerable struggle with erratic and fairly mechanical movements from three of my fingers and none at all from one of them. My thumb seemed to move but had seemed to have forgotten how to form a grip with any other digit. All those millions of years of evolution lost in a moment.

As the paper moved up towards my eyes and came into focus I could see that it was written in a small flowing script with a fair number of attempts to restart the flow of the pencil, brush or whatever implement had been used to write in.

"You are asleep and snoring on the floor and I have to leave so I don't want to wake you. Thanks for helping me dry out (and clean up!). Fortunately, most of the garments are pretty dry now but I seem to have lost some underwear. Don't look for them, as the offending garments never made it to the bath

water. I think the wine must have gone to your head because you went out like a light."

There was a bit more added on hastily at the end and for a while I could not manage to get the script into focus. After a while however, my eyes managed to catch it and I read on.

"If you don't remember much then remember this. Nothing happened. It never would."

So she had gone. I lay back down in the chaos that was the floor and listened to the sound of my blood pumping through the dusty wooden boards.

PART FOUR
THE FIRE DANCERS

XVII
A Viral Tale

I was lost. How long I lay there, I have no idea. I know that at some time there came a knock in my dreams and someone stepped into the room, swore under their breath and then went back out again. A while two people were standing in the doorway talking in hushed but animated voices.

"It's got 'im for sure, Jimas."

"That's a truth!"

"D'you think 'e let anyone in ere?"

"Aye, but I don't know how. Why didn't the dawgs sniff 'em out or bark and growl about it then?"

"You're right but it don't look like anything's been taken."

This voice I finally recognized as the Bo'sun but somehow I couldn't seem to open my eyes and when I tried to move the numbness that had been in my hand earlier seemed to have spread to a good part of my body. I was frightened now but even fear couldn't move me. I couldn't even sense my pulse racing as I knew that it must be.

I don't know when it happened but some time as I was trying to move, they had gone and had closed the door behind them. I just lay there unable to move, listening to the sound of each breath and hoping that each one wasn't the last. Eventually I must have slept or lost consciousness because I was vaguely aware of falling in and out of strange dreams that were not dreams and that now I could not recall other than the sense, if sense it can be called, of turmoil and floating.

It was night overhead when I finally opened my eyes and I could see the bright stars of the northern constellations in the clear black sky above. I seemed to be moving slowly and I could gather, from the noise and the screeching of the raw axles, that I was in an ox wagon once more although what I was doing here was yet to be made clear. I made as if to sit up but something was wrong with the messages to my muscles and nothing seemed to respond to command. Then, with a renewed rush of panic, I remembered the numbness of my limbs before in the room and the hushed and urgent voices of the Bo'sun and another.

I called out, or rather I tried to call out but my mouth was incredibly dry and no sound came but a sad kind of strangled gasp. I tried again but with the same effect and then stopped as, with the third inrush of cold air to my open mouth I realized that there was a terrible pain growing in my jaw. As a man I have only ever been a silent witness to childbirth but there can't be many other pains that occur in an otherwise healthy body that get you quite like a toothache. It started pretty quickly with an ache as it spread like wildfire through the nerve in my jaw so that within the space of a few seconds I had acquired a pulsing sensation of hurt that made my eyes water .

Within those seconds I had forgotten about all other worries about mobility (or the lack of it) and numbness as my jaw erupted in throbbing pain. With precious little movement available to me, I tried to stuff my tongue over the area of greatest hurt. That was not easy however as every now and then a pulse of intense hurt burst somewhere else along the path of the nerve. Somehow, and I didn't give a damn how, I managed to regain control of my neck muscles and managed to move my head to the side, trying to find an area of warmth to bury my jaw. I found that I was lying on furs or something similar, but it did nothing to calm the agony that was picking at the tender ends of my teeth. Again I tried to cry out but this time only managed a deep moan that seemed to erupt from the very core of my being.

Yet it seemed to do the trick because I heard voices from somewhere above or behind my head and I felt, if not exactly saw, some form of movement somewhere up behind me. That was about as much attention as I could give however as another surge of agony swept through my lower jaw and spread itself around on the left side of my head, running back up into my ears like waves running up narrow cracks between rocks.

As tears were forced from my eyes, I saw the stars in the sky overhead blink out and a dark shape came down towards me fast. A warm hand was placed on my sweating forehead and another came up along the side of my face and jaw, fingers running down the stubbly skin in a kind of caress. More words were spoken but I could not make them out. I wasn't even sure if I could hear properly. Besides I don't think that they were addressed to me as the sound seemed to be directed behind me again where another, deeper voice grunted a few syllables as if in reply.

The fingers that had gently traced the side of my face suddenly gripped the underside of my jaw, forcing my mouth open, whilst the hand on my forehead moved into place to push some hard stick of some sort into my mouth and onto my teeth. I tried to struggle against this intrusion and bit down hard but the stick in my mouth just yielded a little as my teeth sunk into it. I felt a burning sensation on my gums and mouth but almost immediately the agony in my jaw switched off, leaving a dull ache in its place. There was a smell of cloves in my nose.

"Take it easy, you have not been well."

A face came into focus in the darkness above me as my eyes accustomed themselves to the low levels of light that shone onto the wagon.

I tried to speak, but I could not. My tongue now felt larger than it should and it seemed to loll about in my mouth as though it had a life of its own. I could feel saliva running down the side of my face, cooling rapidly as it went.

"We're heading north from Trellsheim towards the foothills of the Trellsgut." She said this as if in answer to one of the many questions that I could not ask.

"You've not been well. You were lucky we found you when we did. Another hour or so and we would have just passed your lifeless body by on the road and you, my friend, would have been food for the foxes."

Questions were racing in my head now but my mouth just simply refused to co-operate. I don't really like to think what I must have sounded like lying there moving my mouth like an imbecile with my tongue flopping about like some pink kind of fish in its death throws. She seemed very much to take it in her stride though as she settled herself down above my head and wiped by face and mouth as it dribbled profusely.

"Oil of Cloves," she said, *"it does the trick every time. Nothing better than Oil of Cloves for toothache, especially the kind brought on by Chicken Fever."*

The man in my head erupted at this. What with one assault after another on both my senses and my sense of well-being, pursuers in every shadow and strange women around every corner.

"Now what the hell was Chicken Fever?"

I wanted to ask but I had now recovered enough presence of mind to realize the futility of speech in the current circumstances and decided to lie quiet and listen to the information that the woman clearly intended to provide me with. I think the boy in my head was just lying there quietly, sucking at his thumb.

"Must have been up Above Town recently," she continued, *"there's been an outbreak of it up there this past week. Fourteen*

have died of it already, including a bunch of foreigners who were there on a trade visit from way down south. It was probably them as brought it, I reckon. I was up there myself."

I tried to nod in response but the words were coming so thick and fast that by the time I responded there would have been at least six or more questions that could have been answered with that very nod.

XVIII
Judith's Tale

"No, you take it easy," she went on, *"I guess you'll be wondering how you ended up on the roadside a couple of miles from the main town gate."* She laughed.

I must have had some pretty weird expression on my face as she said all this because as soon as she looked at me she just hooted with laughter.

"Well how am I supposed to know?" She seemed capable of an endless conversation with herself as she continued on.

"We've got your pack and day sack as well. They don't look as though they have been raided but we haven't touched them anyway. They are up at the front with Jeff along with a book that fell out of the day sack when we picked it up out of the snow. Perhaps when you can speak a bit you'll be able to tell us what happened to you, though that's not going to be for a day or two. Really can't see how you got so far. Even if someone had dumped you out of the town they're not likely to have carried you a couple of miles in the snow so perhaps you just walked it and collapsed as the Chicken Fever overcame you. Then again, from the look of you, I'd say that you have been poorly with it for a fair few days now so I don't really reckon that you could have walked it."

She paused as if to draws breath and, seeing an opportunity, I did likewise. I was pleasantly surprised that the cold air did not make the pain in my jaw start up again and that my tongue had started to respond to commands and was no longer trying to operate independently. I tried to speak but words still failed to come out but it gave the woman an opportunity to fire off another series of sentences.

"No, it's no good trying to talk right now. You won't have that function back for at least another day as I said. If it doesn't

kill you off, Chicken Fever sort of knocks out your system, switching off various attributes as it does so. If your body can fight it off, you start to recover the lost abilities some two to three days later."

She looked at my worried face before continuing.

"Oh you'll live. You'd be dead by now otherwise. You should be starting to get back movement anytime now."

I nodded quite deliberately at this to show her that I had heard and understood and to point out that I was starting to recover gross movement in my neck at least.

"That's good." She said, smiling warmly.

"I'm Judith. We're heading up to the Trellsgut for the Fair in a few days. It's a big do. People from all over: happens each year about this time. Looks like you'll be coming along with us this year as we can't turn back now and there is nowhere else up this way. You'll be better by then so perhaps you'll enjoy it."

She stopped for a few seconds and busied herself about adjusting the covers over me as the wagon squeaked its casual way northwards through the night.

This gave me the opportunity to have a look at my captor or savior. (I wasn't really decided on which yet and, after all, I only had her explanations to go on so far.) It was fairly dark and I still only had limited movement of my neck and head but I could see that Judith was about sort of mid-forties – I say this because I have always been useless at peoples ages and what I really mean is that she could have been anything from late twenties to early fifties- and she looked much like many of the women did in this part of the world. They all seemed to have dark hair tied up in a tight bun, large skirts and heavy jumpers that hid all but the general shape from view.

Judith's face was pretty and her eyes were lively and she had a slightly medicinal smell about her as she moved about trying to make me more comfortable. What really had me intrigued was the fact that she spoke my language and I assumed

218

that this must be native because as far as I could tell, she hadn't heard me speak yet.

As I was mulling this one over, Jeff leaned back and said something to her. His words were unintelligible to me and I wondered vaguely if this was part of the wagoners' secret language. This thought was supported when she replied to him in the same language, quietly but with a good amount of irritation in it.

Then, as though she had thought the better of it, she added a little more in a slightly kinder tone and obviously for my benefit.

"Not in front of the stranger! We need to be more careful than that. After all we don't know who he is, what he is or where he's from, love. Do we?"

Then she turned back to.

"Jeff says that there is a fork up ahead and we need to take the narrower way. It'll be rough going as it is little used and the road becomes a track about a mile further on. I think that you are going to find it a bit uncomfortable as your nerves start to regain their sense of feeling but I'll dig out some herbs to settle that for you. I think that it might be an idea if we strap you down. It should stop you from being thrown about when we hit the ruts and the potholes."

I didn't think that Jeff (if that was who he was) had actually said this to her. Indeed, I know no language that conveys so much information in the brevity of his simple speech. However, I didn't really have time to dwell on that or any other implications of what might or might not be going on. I wasn't over keen about being thrown about in the back of a wagon like some bag of flour but then again, I wasn't over excited about being tied down in the wagon.

Despite my keen sense of paranoia and setting aside all the comment from within in my head (both man and boy) I realized that from where I now lay, I didn't have much of a choice in the matter and so I just waited there, all calmness on the outside and struggling like mad within. It really didn't help that I kept coming back to the simple fact that whatever Jeff had said, it had not covered enough ground to deal with the things that she had said. Then another voice pointed out that such mundane matters surely didn't need the use of language that was obviously not meant to be spoken in front of strangers. The man in my head muttered something about hidden agendas that I was unable to disregard.

So, when Judith reached over to strap me down to the wagon I nodded frantically at her.

"You don't trust me?" she said. *"That's OK, I don't blame you but it's for your own good. You really are going to get flung about and without the use of your arms and legs you are going to get hurt."*

I continued to nod, making the movement more vigorous and trying to make use of expression in my eyes as this was the only other faculty that I had available to me right now. Judith watched me with something resembling pity in her own expression.

"Look, I could leave you to start with but the minute we get into the track I am going to have other things on the wagon that aren't also tied down that will need sorting too. I don't want to lose stuff to spillage or breakage just because I have to attend to you. I am sure that you understand that. Anyway let's face it: you'll be no less mobile than you are now and you are not going to have movement back most likely until after we get to the fair."

I sighed and closed my eyes. I wouldn't say that it was acceptance but it was at least resignation. The night seemed to have taken on a slightly sinister turn and all that I couldn't work out was whether it was for real or just in my head.

"That's it," she said, *"you'll see that it makes sense."*

She set to work with some worryingly professional looking straps and soon had me secured to the wagon by means of some fittings (at least on the side that I could turn towards) that looked almost to be set there for the purpose. Judith must have seen me watching her because she commented.

"We carry all sorts of things around and often we need to secure them. It's just part of the standard rig in the wagon. Nothing to worry about, you know, although I am sure that that doesn't really convince you."

She smiled.

"I'd try to get some sleep if you can. It will help pass the time until you can move again and you need to recover some strength as you will be weak after the illness."

She was right about the road and the risk of injury. After I had been secured I closed my eyes, not so much as to sleep but more in an attempt to switch off to what seemed to be happening to me. I think that I might have nodded off for a while but I was soon awake, eyes open and alert as the wagon started to rock and shake with the change in road surface. I could hear Jeff in the front shouting and cursing the oxen as they laboured and pulled against various obstructions. At one point we came to a halt and I heard, or rather felt, Jeff jump down from the wagon for a while.

I lay there looking up at the stars with nothing else to do and feeling very, very helpless. After a while, he was back grumbling about some new ridges that covered the track. Then he went off into a rapid exchange of words in that strange language again with Judith that I couldn't hear properly as they kept their voices low and couldn't understand anyway. I knew however that whatever was being said, I didn't like the tone that it was being said in.

Then he was off again and I don't remember anything else until I heard him curse once more and jump back down to wander around the wagon. I Felt rather than saw him take something off the wagon somewhere towards the back, down beyond my feet. It was presumably an axe, because I soon heard the sound of a tree being felled and after a while and a fair bit of noise, he was back this time under the wagon doing something that made the whole thing rock in a way that started to make me feel a bit nauseous.

He got back onto the wagon and cracked the whip over the oxen. The cart started up again and began once more to rock and sway, this time we seemed to be moving slightly to the side and I assumed that we were going around some form of obstruction.

We made really slow progress for the rest of the night and I watched the light creep into the sky and obscure the stars as the night sky rotated slowly overhead and on into the dawn. I heard far away to my right the early morning call of birds. Presumably in this part of the world, unlike my experiences at Champneys, the presence of men was relatively light and the risk of exposure and decimation of the songbird population was pretty much non-existent.

I had more or less been left alone in the back of the wagon as both Jeff and Judith were wrestling with the movement and various implements and other unknown items that occasionally broke free from their containers and crashed to the ground below. Sometimes, and to my severe alarm, the items would fall inwards towards me but whether by good luck or careful placement, nothing actually hit me. A couple of times during this part of the journey, Jeff had looked back over his shoulder but he scarcely gave me a glance. I think that he was just making sure that the wagon was alright. Judith looked back once also and grinned.

"See what I mean?" She said. *"I'll bet you're glad that we tied you in after all. Otherwise I think you might now be lying battered and bruised somewhere behind us on the track!"*

She paused and then added, *"Are you warm enough?"*

I nodded as best I could and she laughed and then turned away. I suspect that she was right about the binding though because I think that I would have struggled even with all sense of movement available to me. As it was I felt really sick and was surprised that I hadn't converted the sensation into an action.

As full daylight came upon us the track started to change and level out a bit. It gave me a chance to gather my somewhat shaken wits and to test for signs of response from my limbs. I also tried to look about a bit as best I could. Daylight revealed a grim looking morning full of dark menacing clouds and a strange kind of oppressive light. Snow looked pretty imminent.

Putting all this aside as beyond me under the present circumstances, I tried moving my hands and was moderately relieved to find that although they were stiff and uncertain, my fingers were responding and there was a growing sense of feeling in both hands and wrists. I still couldn't move my torso though and so my field of vision remained limited.

After a while, the track must have leveled out completely because we went back to the fairly steady and dreary pace that the oxen naturally set and the wagon just rocked around as normal. Not comfortable exactly but not as it had been. Overhead I could see trees starting to appear. These tall straight conifers reached up high above us and as we progressed they got thicker and thicker until eventually the grim clouds in the sky were gone and above was a brown and green canopy. It was as I watched these great plants passing by overhead that I feel asleep. I slept for a long time.

When I woke up it was dark again and there was a light covering of snow on the tarpaulin that had been placed over me. The straps that had been used to secure me were gone and I could see them rolled up expertly and neatly on the one side of the wagon that was visible to me. We were stationary.

Automatically I went to sit up and was hit by an incredible pain down one side of my body at about the same time that a numbing ache in my lower back rose sufficiently in intensity to make me gasp. However, the good news was that with a bit of a struggle and aided by my arms and some of the heavier items in the wagon, I was able to get to a sitting position. From here I could see that we were now in a large clearing in the trees which stood back a fair way from where we were camped (as I assumed we were). The oxen were hobbled and were working their way through some bales of straw that had been placed before them in the snow.

There were several fires burning nearby and alongside each of these there was at least one wagon or cart and occasionally some strange form of covered wagon that I guessed was some kind of sleeping quarters for families. I could certainly hear children somewhere nearby and now and then a dog would bark and someone would call out. From what I could see there were close to maybe a hundred wagons in the clearing and these were gathered together in small groups or enclaves of varying sizes that I guessed must represent families. We were in a group of seven but some were larger and a few were just made up of one or two wagons.

Across the clearing, which was probably large enough to be called a field, towards the centre, there was a large area where there were no wagons parked at all. Here there was a large pile of wood and other materials that I could not make out at the distance. The whole thing resembled the kind of bonfire that we used to have when I was a child and when we celebrated Gravenham's Night and I would stand as close to the heat as I was able (or allowed) in order to be able to toast the field mallow sticks that were symbolic of his infamy.

I could see a number of people working at what appeared to be the construction of some kind of field kitchen. This was set well back from the central bonfire and appeared to be made up of a number of roasting pits that had been dug out in the snow and were now having some kind of wooden structure built above them.

There was no sign of Jeff or Judith either near the wagon or anywhere else. The small fire that had been lit nearby was beginning to take and the snow hissed and steamed and the twigs and sticks crackled and spat. Near it were some large rolls of cut turf. It looked like peat or some other material, presumably to be put on the fire once it got up to strength. Although there were people working in the distance and I could hear the sounds of people (mostly children) nearby there seemed to be no one else anywhere close to me. The other enclaves looked just as deserted.

As I felt the circulation returning to my arms and hands I thought that I would make an attempt to stand. At least that way I would have a chance to go and look about the place. It proved to me every bit as much of a challenge as I had guessed it would. I managed to get from a sitting position onto my knees easily enough and in this position I was able to grab hold of one side of the wagon. This, I reckoned, was sturdy enough to take my full weight as I tried to stand. However, I had not allowed for the growing headache and dizziness that began as soon as I started to move out of the sitting position and which, by the time that I was kneeling had become so painful that I was obliged to let go of the wagon side to hold the sides of my head.

The dizziness and accompanying nausea was such that I began to fear that I would end up making an unpleasant mess in the wagon and I was pretty sure that no matter how friendly and helpful Judith had been, that would not go down too well. I sat back down and leaned my head back against my pack, which I had found was now strapped in place behind where I had been lying.

It looked much as I had seen it last other than it looked a little more stuffed and untidy. My day sack, which was next to it, seemed to be much the same as my left hand felt around it, leaving my right hand to feel my forehead and stroke my head as the headache (and also, mercifully, the nausea) continued to subside.

I did not appear to have been robbed, much as Judith had said, but I decided to check what was still there once the pain had subsided a little further. However, until that occurred I just sat there with my eyes closed, listening to the occasional sounds around me that told me that I was not entirely alone in this place.

XIX
Judith's Tale Continued

Once I had managed to get my day sack in front of me I was able to check it. Everything seemed to be in place and even Welcome's book was there. There were also a couple of things that I didn't expect to be in there. The first of these was a small fabric purse with a little over forty trupps in it. When I took it out, it had a slight perfume, unrecognizable but not unpleasant.

I had no idea what this was doing there until I opened the second of the unexpected items: a note written on very heavy paper in a neat if somewhat idiosyncratic hand. It was that style of handwriting that people produce by keeping a piece of paper or some other guard beneath the line so that the effect is one of letters clipped off on the page where the pen has overrun the guard but at least you get a straight line.

"We hope you made it ok through the Chicken Fever: you might be a faw'kin farner but you're alright! You have to understand that you, bein' ill and all, was a risk to us all here at the Sun and there was too many o' those weird folks sniffin' about after you as well. That kind of stuff ain't much good for business, you see."

There was a bit more that basically went on to justify why the good folk at the Sun had decided that I was a risk to life, limb and, god forbid, business. Then there was some more to explain that they had packed me some extra clothes (new, they were at pains to point out) and provisions for when I finally woke up, if indeed I managed it. Of course, they hoped that I hadn't died in the meantime. They explained more than once although I suppose that it need not be said that, had this been the case I surely wouldn't have read the letter.

Then they informed me that I was a couple of leagues outside the town and on a main wagon route north to the Trellsgut Mountains. The bit that they missed out, I had already started to realise, was that this was basically a road to nowhere. The did however mention that there was a gathering of folk heading up that way over the next few days so someone was bound to find me.

It was a comfort to know now, albeit retrospectively, that these folk were a good sort in the main, or so the folk at the Sun reliably informed me. On the basis of the Bo' sun's performance so far, I believed this about as much as I believed the fact that the world was flat. Apparently these good people would take me in, sick or no and look after me until I was better. They also hoped that I had a speedy recovery and looked forward to seeing me back at the Sun sometime soon.

Frankly, these people (or perhaps all people) were amazing. It didn't matter where I was in this part of the world: it didn't matter how polite or impolite the indigenes were; or how clean or dirty their lifestyle; or, how bright or stupid they were. Here (and I suspect everywhere) despite all the trappings and comforters of so-called civilization, life seemed to be nasty and brutish and had a fair to middling chance of being short. What really got to me was that it all seemed to be carried out in some kind of detached or perhaps even clinical manner – perhaps that is the wrong word. I think that I would rather had have had a more honest outcome, although as the old man in my head is quick to point out, that would probably mean that I would be lying in an alley with my head bashed in.

Now of course I was with these travelling folk. They had indeed saved me no doubt from hypothermia and they had cared for me like I was one of their own. How could I know that they would not, in all probability, eat my liver and feed everything else left behind to the dogs. If that were to be the case, I probably take comfort in the belief that it would no doubt be done in a very matter of fact manner: yes in fact clinical, if not surgical, is very much the right word.

With such thoughts wandering about in my head it was no wonder that I jumped when I heard Judith speak to me. It didn't help that I had not actually heard or seen her approach.

"We're a bit jumpy aren't we?" she observed.

"Not frightened to be alone in the dark are you?"

She laughed and gave me a gentle slap on the back of the head.

"Good to see that you're at least half up," she said, *"but watch out for the headaches and the nausea. It will soon pass but I don't really want you making a mess in the back here."*

She winked at me as though she had already seen my attempts to stand and had guessed my thoughts about the whole matter. I just looked back at her and tried to keep my expression level and the colour of my cheeks constant.

Other people had also appeared in our enclave and more seemed to be coming back out of the forest to the side of us. They were carrying bits of dead wood and also a number of other items, including what looked to be dead hares, some giant puffballs (though where they got these in the snow seemed a bit of a mystery to me). I also saw a couple of deer being carried on poles by a small group of rather hard looking young men. They didn't come back to the enclave but headed off straight for the centre and presumably the field kitchens. Judith saw me looking.

"Our young men - jubenes," she said.

"Avoid eye contact unless you want a fight; don't speak to them and keep out of their company. Never laugh near them unless you really want to have the last laugh, because it would be. They normally stay away from the family groups until sex separates them off and they come skulking back with their tails between their legs."

She winked at this.

"After a few years away on their own, even the most desperate looking of girls seems like a goddess to them. They make wonderful husbands."

She looked lovingly over at Jeff who was scratching parasites off the rump of one of the oxen with a look on his face that would have made a snarling dog seem pleasant.

"At least most of the time," she added with a laugh.

Soon the enclave was bustling and alive with people of varying ages. All were speaking my own language and this seemed very strange to me. After a while I took the opportunity to ask Judith about this. It was the first time that I had spoken to her and she seemed a little surprised when I did.

"Why you're one of us," she said, obviously pleased.

It occurred to me then that all the conversation that she had shared with me since I had woken up in the wagon would have been completely pointless, had I not spoken or at least understood the language. She obviously hadn't known before I spoke to her just a moment ago. I wonder whether she had considered that fact as well. Perhaps it didn't really matter.

"That's a lucky break," she said, *"Jeff hates strangers of any sort and I have had hell and all trouble trying to persuade him not to drop you over the side. In fact, I have had to work so hard on persuading him, I'm surprised that you haven't heard us on occasions."*

She grinned wickedly and added, *"Still, there's not a lot of scope for coyness or privacy in this life and it's amazing what you can get up to in the early hours when everyone else is pretending to be asleep!"*

I could feel my blushes growing again in my cheeks as the real implications of what she was saying started to dawn on me. However, it didn't seem to cause her any issue and she started almost at once on the vexed subject of families.

"We're all from Cornal in the Western Peninsular and we make up one family. We're not all directly related of course but

we have a broad view of family. You're one of us if you come from roughly the same place."

She paused either for breath or for me to assimilate the information. I think it more likely that it was the former.

"Jeff and I are one of the more senior couples in the family and one of our lads is out there amongst the other Jubenes with his testosterone and his spots. I miss him terribly but it was a relief to see him go. Jeff and the boy had started to go the rounds on a couple of occasions and it was only a carefully placed kick on my part one time and the promise of my serrated cooking knife and a slow emasculation on another that stopped them actually taking pieces off each other."

She produced a broad bladed knife about a large hand span long with a black wooden handle and a tang that went back well into the wood. It was serrated and looked awfully sharp. She made a couple of gestures involving a slow sawing action with the knife that left absolutely nothing to the imagination and then with a scarily primitive looking lick of the knife, thrust it back into the folds of her skirt from whence it came.

"Men," she said, "they're pathetic, all balls and no brains. Well, I know the cure for them."

I think that I was a little put out by the fact that she didn't appear to include me in the category of creature under discussion but I let it go for now as she was looking a little feral.

"Anyway," she continued, switching back to her everyday brightness in the same way that the sun came out of the clouds.

"We're all one family here and we keep ourselves to ourselves most of the time. It's the same with all the other families around: like them over there."

She pointed to the enclave with the strange sleeping wagons.

"Roma Vinca, they are. And those," she said pointing further south, "they're Ruadean. They prefer to face the east and to stay as far south of the home field as they can. Can't see why, as it's not any warmer for being a few hundred paces south is it now?"

She paused and this gave me a chance to squint around the area and indeed I could now see that there were people of different origins, colours and in some cases shapes settled in distinct camps around this "home field" as Judith had called it – though it was neither home nor indeed a field in my interpretation of things.

"So where are you to?" she asked, *"and come to think of it, what's your name. In all the excitement of the past few days,"* she giggled, *"I have quite forgotten to ask. I feel that I know you already."*

The look on her face and the way she said it made me feel distinctly uncomfortable and it began to occur to me that if I had been unconscious for a few days, there must have been a few bodily functions that had been taken care of and not by me. I could feel the colour returning once more to my face.

"Like I said," she laughed guessing the all too obvious cause of my discomfort, *"There are few secrets between families here. So where's your family to?"*

This question seemed far more important to her than my name, which I found a little odd but the only way, as it were, was forward and so I told her where they were.

"Well then!" she called back to Jeff.

"Did you hear where he's from? That's close enough to be family for sure."

For some reason she sounded relieved.

I decided that I wasn't going to explain that I had moved there as a child and that my family actually came from the midland capital. I don't really think it was that important a matter. However, it was important to Jeff, quite clearly, because he stopped his task on the filthy back end of the ox and came over to me with a look that struck me as being halfway between murderous intent and adoration.

He clapped me on the back with one large hand and then gripped and proceeded to squeeze one of my flaccid paws with the other, crushing the bones in my hand as he did so. (Did I also mention that this was the hand that he had been working with on the business end of the beast?)

"*That's good, brother,*" he growled as he continued to shake my arm.

"*It saves me a nasty job.*"

Jeff was obviously a man of few words but I think that in that brief sentence (of sorts) he managed to convey a page of information about what I think might have otherwise happened to me. I don't think that he meant that he would get me to clean the oxen, either. Like a better man once said, life really can be nasty, brutish and short. By good fortune, not to mention economy with the truth, at least on this occasion, that wasn't going to be the case.

As Jeff returned to his oxen, Judith explained some more about the families; how they were not all wagoners and that there were other kinds of travellers among them. The one thing in common is that they all led a peripatetic life. The gathering that was now nearly complete, was an annual festival held over the night of the winter equinox: the Festival of Light was what she called it.

It was a chance for the families to meet up, renew friendships and share experiences. It wasn't all of them, she said, as not everyone could make it each year. In fact, she guessed vaguely that it was less than a tenth of them (but it was obvious to me that she didn't really know). The one big question that had begun to grow in my normally untidy mind was simple. These people needed a label before they could be catalogued properly by me. So the big question was to establish who or what were they?

Judith hadn't really explained this yet and I wasn't sure if this was because she thought that I was one (and hence family) and therefore didn't need an explanation or whether she had simply forgotten to explain. I decided, based on the slight chill in the inferences from Jeff a few moments before, that it was better not to ask right now and so I let it pass for the time being.

"It helps us keep our culture alive," she said, as she threw one of the cut turves onto the roaring fire to dampen it down.

I watched it as it began to smoke with a rather pleasant smell that I couldn't place.

"The smell keeps off the insects around here," she explained.

I hadn't noticed any insects to be honest and was about to say so when she explained as though she had read my thoughts.

"You wait until daybreak. They are perishing little nuisances and there are swarms of them. That's why we tend to travel and forage at night."

She moved without pause back into her explanation of the festival.

"It's not easy for the diaspora to keep a sense of identity. It tends to make us distant from others and to keep ourselves apart from other cultures. Of course that makes for problems with the young folk: you know, sex, babies and all that stuff. That's another reason for the Festival of course, otherwise we would lose too many of our children to marriages outside."

She paused here and I saw that she had a rather sad, distant sort of look in her eyes.

"That's how I lost my daughter and my grandson."

She sighed then seemed to gather her thoughts back in the present and continued.

"It also gives some of our lost ones a chance to get back to us," she paused, then added brightly, *"Like you for instance. I had a feeling that you might be one of us when I first saw you: even before I saw the book in your bag."*

Pieces of puzzle were starting to slot into place now, although my biggest problem was that I still didn't know what

234

the finished article looked like. My mind was racing a bit but there were two books in my pack and the one Welcome had given me in my day sack. I thought that it was unlikely (there no rationale for this of course) that she had searched my pack, although it was possible and I hadn't yet had a chance to check it. It was very likely that she would have looked in the day sack as it would be an obvious thing to do to find out more about an unconscious old man lying in the snow by the side of a wagon road. She also said "book" and not "books".

My face must have given my thoughts away because she stopped talking and look at me for a while.

"It must sound a bit strange to you: all this."

She waved her arm around the clearing and the people moving around within it.

"And you're probably wondering whether you really are one of us or not, I'd imagine. I did when I first came into contact with them."

She paused and looked at me as if waiting for me to speak. I remained silent because quite frankly I wasn't really sure what to say. All that I kept thinking about was the ominous growling of Jeff.

"Well aren't you?" she said with a slightly agitated manner when I failed to reply.

"I guess I am," I said and added, *"but then the events of the past few days have been a total mystery to me anyway and I really don't know at this point where I am or how I have really got here. Never mind considering who I am, which I have to say, up until today I thought that I had under control."*

The words came out in a bit of a rush and I think that she must have heard, if not felt, the anxiety in my voice. I was also surprisingly tired for someone who had seemed to have slept (or been unconscious) for the past countless hours and I must have looked it.

"Perhaps you should be getting a bit of rest," she said, *"so that you'll be fit for the Festival tomorrow night. You ought to have full use of your legs by then and the headaches and nausea should stay away too. I was going to show you off to everyone here but I guess that it can wait a while. They can always come and have a look at you whilst you're asleep anyway."*

I wasn't sure that I really wanted to be put on display whilst I slept. Somehow that seemed a bit of a violation but I wasn't really in any state to argue the point. Instead I made myself comfortable in the back of the wagon and curled up as best I could.

I guess I must have been tired because I was asleep almost immediately. The last words that I heard drifting into my waking mind were those of Judith telling me to stay close to the fires during the daylight to keep off the midges. This last piece of advice turned out to be completely unnecessary however, as I slept through the remains of that night, the full length of the following day and on into the early hours of that next evening.

This meant that I missed a lot of the activity that took place to prepare the camp for the festival the following night. Much of it was completed before the light of the new dawn came up over the trees in the East. The tasks that remained were completed by the men during the early parts of the morning: the women and children having headed off to sleep the daylight hours away as was their habit in this part of the world. My lengthy sleep also meant that I didn't have to suffer the marauding swarms of insects that plagued the daylight hours. Fortunately for me, Judith had covered my head and arms in some form of light mesh so that the vicious little brutes couldn't get at me whilst I was at a disadvantage.

XX
The Fire Dancers' Tale

When I finally awoke, things had changed considerably in the camp. For a start it sounded as though it was a lot more crowded and it seemed likely that a large number of additional wagons and other vehicles had arrived during the previous night. As I lay in the wagon looking up at the stars that were now forming in the sky above, I could hear an underlying noise that either I hadn't noticed the night before or that had not been there.

If it wasn't obviously ridiculous, I would have thought that the sound was that of the sea. I sat up carefully, checking for sign of headache but nothing came. The scene in the home field was quite astounding. There were now hundreds if not a thousand or more wagons of different styles and descriptions set out in tight but distinct enclaves around the central area. In the centre was the fire and a broad swathe of snow covered grass that was otherwise empty of people despite the press and throng of bodies at the edges of it. On the eastern side of the camp were the great fire pits of the field kitchens and on the various spits and other devices I could see huge carcasses of meat roasting. I learned later that the fire pits had another purpose and that they were placed at the eastern side to accommodate the prevailing winds.

The central fire had been lit and was beginning to take as the flames leaped up amongst the timbers and the moss that was piled high. I could see a group of large men tending it. When I say large, here I do mean large. From where I sat they looked each to be over seven feet tall and powerfully built. If human then they were not a race that I had met before. Amongst the enclaves, including the one in which I was now apparently a family member, there were various lights and flames burning and now and again I caught the smells of various perfumes. At least I assumed they were perfumes as they were unlike any other plant or mineral smell that I had ever experienced.

The biggest change however was in the people. The family members in my enclave came and went past me busy about various tasks but they looked bright and lively and their clothes were strange. Gone were the broad plain skirts and baggy over clothes of the women, replaced now by a dazzling array lighter and brighter skirts, trousers and tops that seemed to accentuate the shape of the wearer and made their skins seemed to glow in the reflected light of the fire and the reds and greens and oranges, yellows and blues of the fabrics. Their skins seemed to be darker, richer somehow.

No longer did they wear the pale colours of people living a crespuscular existence in the cold and sunless north but rich, vibrant and warm like those of the peoples of the Mid-World Seas. The men were no less brightly dressed, and the faces and demeanour of them all spoke of eagerness and brightness and expectation. They were excited: like children. In contrast, I considered how different I looked, old and grey and shabbily dressed amongst them: very much an outsider.

I didn't see Judith some up alongside the wagon and when I did, it took me a while to recognize that it was in fact her. She looked utterly astounding. She had the body of a goddess and her hair, which she now wore down, was a rich chestnut colour that fell in luxurious waves down her shoulders and over her breasts which were just about covered by some colourful, if lightweight, blouse.

"Well, what do you think?" she asked as I stared like an idiot at her.

"It's all right," she said, *"if you look a little higher you'll find my face if you have managed to recover the use of your neck muscles."*

Embarrassed, I moved my focus up to her face where I saw her eyes smiling back at me, dark and girlish and inviting.

I realized then that this was the woman that I had seen outside the walls of Trellsheim all those nights ago (how many was it really?) and then again in the alley in the town after: the one who had handed me the strange newspaper. This realization crystallized further as I noticed as if for the first time, her eyes as they stared back at me shameless and inviting. Was there a pattern in all this, some kind of plan?

I was about to say something when she spoke.

"Do I scrub up well or not?"

She asked but it was kind of rhetorical because she laughed before I could even think of an answer.

"Don't worry; you'll get your voice back again before the end of the night and your eyes have paid me some kind compliments already."

As she was talking, a man stepped up behind her. He was good looking and well built. He wore a green shirt that also seemed to be too thin a fabric for this part of the world. I couldn't see his trousers as I was still sitting in the wagon and the sides obscured him. His face was painted and the colours and shapes brought out the prominence of his nose and accentuated the depth of his dark eyes. Only when he spoke, did I realize that this was Jeff. He looked completely different: he even seemed taller.

"You can't go like that," he said and his voice now was rich and strong and clear. There was a gaiety about him that seemed to radiate outwards and I could see Judith looking up at him with an unguarded look that showed both love and lust.

"Come on, we need to be quick. I've something you can wear, although it might be a little tight in parts and a bit baggy in others."

He winked and grinned boyishly at me.

"You need to clean up, too. Can you walk yet?"

I was about to explain that I wasn't sure as I hadn't tried but I wasn't given the chance. Jeff leaned into the wagon and grabbed hold of me.

"Please excuse," he said as he grunted under the weight of me, *"but time and the Festival wait for no man."*

With that he lifted me bodily out of the wagon and flung me over his shoulder like a slab of meat before making off towards one of the strange covered wagons that had now joined our enclave.

I expected people to laugh at me as I was carried along in such an ignominious fashion through the wagons. Yet no one did. As we passed by, men and women called out to me wishing me well on my recovery and greeting me. Even children, some of who were almost at eye level with me in the manner of my carriage, smiled and greeted me. There wasn't a single instance of ridicule.

When we got to the covered wagon, Jeff put me down carefully and stood back warily as I tottered on my two legs for the first time in a good number of days. I was relieved that there was no pain and that the nausea that I had feared was completely absent. Once he was satisfied that I wasn't about to keel over he leaned up into the wagon and called out.

"We need to get him ready. He's from the east of us so he needs the yellow and reds!"

He then turned to me with a wicked grin and said *"Two choices – you jump or I throw you in. What'll it be?"*

I didn't understand but I followed his eyes. He was looking at a large half barrel filled with water that was beside the wagon. It didn't look particularly warm – in fact it looked perishing.

"You can't be serious," I said weakly.

"No," he said, *"I try not to be but you are going in, one way or another. What'll it be?"*

Again he grinned and again there was no menace in it.

"And you'll need those dirty rags off first," he added.

My mouth must have dropped open because he suddenly laughed and looked around at the onlookers.

"God's man, there are no secrets between families here and besides the cold here makes us all look like boys. Come on or I'll fetch some of the older girls to help you out of them!"

I looked at him completely aghast for a moment or two but then something seemed to go off in my head. The man in there just shrugged and looked away but the boy in me yelled out with unbridled enthusiasm and I started to peel off my dirty clothes, reckless of the onlookers.

The water was icy and it made my bones ache and the breath catch in my chest. Jeff threw me some soap and I lathered up and then tried to wash it off.

"No," he said, *"not like that. Stand up!"*

I obeyed the command without thinking and he threw a large bucket of a light brown liquid at me. I gasped in anticipation of the chill but found that instead, as it hit me and washed over me, it gave a wonderfully warm sensation and tingling to my skin. I was doused in the smell that I had noticed earlier but could not place.

I felt that my skin was glowing in the same light as those of the bodies around me. Another bucket of the same stuff crashed over me from behind and I turned to find Judith there laughing at me and eying me up. Strangely, I no longer felt foolish or embarrassed and the only warmth to my cheeks was the glow of that fiery liquid.

"I'll tell you what my love," she said with a giggle to Jeff, *"he's got a lovely bum."*

"No you just settle down, my girl or I'll make you go and sit with all the other matrons as by rights you should."

Although he had replied sternly, he was laughing and again there was no seriousness in it.

As I stepped out of the tub a towel was handed to me from somewhere. I had no idea who gave it to me but I took it and started to dry myself off. I didn't understand why, but the cold no longer seemed to be a problem to me. I expected to be shivering uncontrollably and yet I wasn't. I expected to be acutely embarrassed naked as I was in front of all these strangers and yet I wasn't. All I could do was to look at all the faces looking in on me as I looked out at them.

"Come on, man, there's no time for dawdling!"

Jeff's voice broke through the reverie and called me from that other place.

"Into the wagon, brother, it's time to get dressed. They'll see to you in there. In you go now. It's too late to be shy."

I was ushered and partially bundled up the steps at the back of the wagon and then a door opened and, naked, I was pulled inside.

Nothing in my life could have prepared me for what came next. I don't know how long I spent in there and when I try to recall just exactly what happened I can never seem to remember what it was. All I know is that in some manner it was as though I had been broken down into my various parts and then piece by piece reassembled and with reassembly I was clothed in the yellow and reds of the East. After a time (and it could have been any amount of time) I was back outside, standing on the steps of that covered wagon feeling like a new being and looking down on all the upturned faces that cheered as I reappeared.

"Brother of the East," someone called out.

It could have been Jeff but it needn't have been. Soon the whole enclave took up the call.

"Brother of the East!"

Like the jubenes that were now amongst the crowd for the first time after years of isolation, I punched the air with my fist. The boy within me said that I was a hero. The man... well the man, strangely, was silent.

That's when I knew that I was a fool but I didn't really care. I looked around me at all those sublime faces and felt a great wash of emotion building up within me. Again I punched the air and without thought cried out. Oddly, the image of that newspaper handed to me in Trellsheim, popped into my head. Was that a lifetime ago or was it in another life?

"One life!"

In the faces before me I saw acceptance, recognition, acquiescence and a whole rainbow of emotions as, with their arms held high into the air and one voice they replied, *"One life!"*

What it meant, I mean its significance, I couldn't tell you. I knew that it came from within me and that it had significance for all those here tonight, not just this enclave. In every other family in the Home Field we could hear the same cry, time and time again. *"One life!"*

"Brother, take my arm"

This was Jeff's voice.

"And mine also."

Judith also stretched out her arm to help me climb down from the wagon.

"Walk with us," she said, *"for though the cleansing liquor will carry you far into the night, yet you are still weak."*

I reached out and took their hands, feeling the warmth and energy coming from them in a way that seemed unreal as it passed up through my arms and washed over my body and I was engulfed in a sense of warmth and well-being. Together we walked amongst the rest of our enclave towards the central bonfire which I could now see through the press of all the people as the flames leapt and danced high into the air.

I guess that I must have really been caught up in the general euphoria because as we approached I was sure that I could see, in the bright and vividly coloured flames, the shapes and forms of animals and birds: perhaps even people leaping there before us.

We crunched across snow that was white and crisp and icy and yet I was not cold, despite the lightness of the fabrics that I was wearing. Looking down, I realized that I was wearing bright boots of some hide that had been dyed a deep red colour, rich like the colour of blood. I didn't remember the boots but then again I didn't fully remember getting dressed.

Snippets of images kept going off in my head. Recollections of something past or so I thought but then could not recall them from my waking life. An old woman dressed completely in bright red: her hair, surely dyed, bright orange and green ribbons tied there. Bright green eyes, feral and piercing. A face looking deep into my own: not serious or severe though but bright and laughing. All was sheer joy and mirth and playfulness.

The noise around us was immense, again I thought of the sea and now it was as the sound of storms and the wind rising but on this night, I knew that the air around us was still and the sea was many leagues south near the land that I believed to be home.

It wasn't just the sound of people, though it was clear that their noise was great as they laughed and shouted and danced around as the madness of their joy grew upon them. It wasn't the roaring fire before us, fuelled with wood and turf and moss though it was loud and hot and intense.

There was something else, a something that I didn't really understand or that my senses were inadequate to focus upon. Strangely, I could hear the cry of wolves out in the forests. Their calls came in now and then above the other sounds and this was strange because it was deepest night and they should be silent. My heightened senses (though it was not my sight) told me of a great black wolf out there in the darkness of a story and of a sentinel watching out over them all: watching out over us all.

In the darkness of my waking mind dawn started to creep and with that the growing understanding that passed over me and through me with that same feeling of warmth that I had felt from Jeff and Judith some while ago and I looked up into the flames before and above me and I saw myself dancing there.

And then there was silence.

It came almost instantly and I was afraid of the change in sound as though a change in purpose and fearfully I looked around at the faces close to me. They were looking away, towards the great fire pits on the eastern side where I had thought the field kitchens to be.

They were not kitchens.

Above the fires the carcasses of the dead animals had long since burned away and merged the blackness of charred flesh and bone with the bronze and gold brightness of the fire pits.

In procession beyond the fires I could see the Jubenes walking slowly in small groups, bearing biers upon their shoulders. On these light wooden frames there were shrouded shapes and I knew that these were the dead.

All fell silent as they approached the pits and assembled to some pre-arranged order. There was the sound of a single symbol once in the night silence. It carried out across the home field, above and past the crackling fires and the sound of our breath. Even the wolves were silent now. No one moved. Even the thousand or more steaming breaths seemed to cease.

Then came the ring of a bell, a single tiny bell somewhere in the darkness beyond the fire pits and with that sound a great shout arose around us and I realized that I too was shouting and the words *"One life! One life!"* were reverberating through the air and in my mind.

As the bodies of the dead were placed with care (and no small amount of risk to the bearers) into the funeral fires the flames seemed to rise up in the shapes of men and women and of children. Then, as I gazed in awe at this, I saw young men running towards the fire pits and with great leaps rose up over them, their bright clothes igniting with flames as they caught the hands of the women who had leapt at the same time over the fires with them from the other side.

Together, with ribbons of red and yellow and blue fire they seemed to turn in the air and land to one side, rolling over and over on the wet ground as the fires were quenched and their bright and colourful robes turned black and brown and tattered. As each couple stood up there was a shout from the crowds as enclave after enclave greeted the newly married pair as they stood holding hands and looking foolish and childlike (as indeed really they were) and bedraggled where a few moments ago they had been resplendent in flame.

As one couple made the leap, I heard beside me the rich voice of Jeff and the strong proud voice of Judith cry out *"One life!"* as a hand of each of them blindly sought out the other to clasp in mirror image of the children before them.

XXI
The Coda

I can't really say how long all this went on for other than that it was over by the time night had started the slow walk back from the dawn and the light began to creep in once more over the trees from the East.

Somehow, and probably with help, I found my way back to Judith's wagon. Oddly, I don't remember much of the walk back but I don't think I was carried. Perhaps it was just that there was so much rushing around in my head and that in the maelstrom that was somehow in there I had become detached from the reality of a simple walk in the bitter cold across the icy fields.

What I did recall, as I started the painful climb up on the boards, was that I had turned to thank those who had walked back with me. Whereas moments before I was sure that I had felt a kindly hand helping me up against the gravity that weighed so heavily on my joints, I saw no one. I had looked through the cold, almost solid, air into the middle distance where the dark and smoldering remains of the fire pits were littered. I had seen the blackened ruins of the fire dance yet there was not a soul in sight.

Unbidden came the thought of that traveller's faltering words from a time before when we had sat in the shade of a tree against the heat of the southern sun and shared a makeshift meal. In the tiredness of my mind, old Markel's tale slipped into a space with its wolves and the fear and the mystery. I guess there was a general truth to what they had said but these tales, I knew, were poor counterfeits.

I gave a brief thought for my own story. I wondered how my own tale of the fire dancers would coalesce and take form when the excitement had finally passed to weariness. Slowly, I followed the path of weariness onward to contemplation and from thence into those words that both define and limit our comprehension.

It was cold, now. All sense of warmth and life had been erased and I was left alone with the bone aching cold of this cruel northern land. No, not cruel for that would infer intent and as far as the land was concerned there was no interest when it came to those creatures infesting it. In my mind I wandered reckless, my hand trailing in the ice-cold air.

Shivering uncontrollably, I found myself sitting once more with my head resting against my pack in the back of the wagon. I pulled the furs tighter around me, my breath coming in great steaming draughts. My body ached terribly and twinges of pain shot through my spine with each involuntary shudder.

Fortunately, it was still too early for the midges but I was expecting to sleep for some time so, after a while and as I could just about feel warmth returning to parts of my body, I hunted out the mesh that Judith had given me. All sense of lightness and euphoria was gone now and with it, though I had not really noticed it until now, the sense of youth and vitality. Now I was just plain tired and getting old, the fifty-two years of my life weighing heavily upon my aging frame.

Presently, though I have no measure of time but the growing feeling of warmth that was cautiously rising from my core, I began to hear the sounds of other folk. In the wagon-packed enclave I could hear parents settling young children and the voices of people talking. The noises must have been there all along but perhaps it was only as warmth diffused through my body, that I began to hear them. That was when I started to hear more noises but I chose to ignore those. The voyeurism of my story had, I guess, run its course. Judith was right: there were no secrets among these families.

Overhead, in the great expanse of colourful nothingness that was the early dawn, I could see the last lights of distant stars fading away. Vermillion and orange and purple tendrils spread out across the sky, chasing away darkness and drawing in behind the sun of the new day.

Within my head both man and boy were unusually silent and as images and ideas went off like dying stars. I wondered what all of this journey had really meant to me in the context of my own existence, in the context of my own journey through life. I would have liked to think that it was an epiphany; I would like to think that this was a life-changing experience but I knew that it was not.

There are many things that I would like to have taken from all that I had seen and done but how would I choose this story over any other tale already told or yet to come? Then I got hung up on a word. To take is not necessarily to be given. Was this experience just perhaps another acquisition? For that is what I had set out on this particular journey for.

Sometimes it is best not to think.

As I settled myself down and threw the mesh over my head, I heard the howl of a wolf and pictured the dark creature of my tale back in Champneys in a life that seemed a little distant now even though it was the passage of but a few days in time. In my head I heard the words of the tale as it came to its end.

"There were worse things than wolves out there in the darkness deep in the forest of Sumah. Much worse, yet the wolves did not fear them."

Then, oddly because there was no prescient thought, I was sure that I could hear my wife calling to me. Buried now in that cold wagon beneath the furs and the mesh against the flies, I closed my eyes and gave myself up to the animal warmth of sleep. It was a comfort. It could have been death. I could have been anywhere and perhaps I was indeed asleep in the upstairs room of my house. Who knows what really happens in those great ancestral arches of our mind as age and decay begin that purge of everything that we ever knew, or thought we knew or held dear?

She spoke again, and then I realised, as I turned to look into her wonderful face, that I had begun my journey home.

Printed in Great Britain
by Amazon